HUNTERS AND HERETICS

BOOK TWO OF THE LION'S DYNASTY

JOSHUA MCHENRY MILLER

BLUE INK
PRESS

ISBN: 9781948449076

Library of Congress Control Number: 2020943810

Cover by Greg Simanson simansondesign.com

Dedicated to my amazing wife, Erica

CHAPTER ONE

W<small>HITE FOAM DRIPPED FROM MY LIPS.</small>

It makes you question the choices you have made when that's how your story begins.

Squatting in the shadows of a side street, I snarled and lashed out a mud-covered arm at the unsuspecting mother and her two young children passing by. For added effect, I pulled the massive broadsword off my back and thrust it aggressively above my head.

The poor woman shrieked and bolted to the other side of the street, clinging to each child as they scurried away. I held a manic gaze on her until she was out of sight and then sighed, shaking my head in frustration. Another day of terrorizing the women and children. How the mighty had fallen.

There is an art to living among people who want to kill you. It'd been six months since I'd taken up residence in Gath, the capital of the Philistine people, who also happened to be the sworn enemies of my own nation, the Israelites. I had built a rather infamous name by besting them in battle on more than one occasion, but given that Israel's king had put a sizable bounty on my head, the decision to live among the Philistines had seemed like the least insane option out of a bunch of nasty choices.

Days like today, which was pretty much every day, I second-guessed that decision.

Unsurprisingly, the Philistines had chosen not to welcome me with open arms. Well, their arms were technically outstretched, but they did so while wielding pointy weapons, with all manner of ill intentions for the famous "Philistine Slayer."

During the first week of my stay, groups of men attempted daily to rid their city of its new visitor. Mind you, I had trained with some of the most elite fighters in the region, a covert group of soldiers called the Seraphim, so fighting these would-be saviors proved little challenge. The problem was that if I killed any of the men, my presence would change from public nuisance to public murderer, and whatever unknown reason the king of Gath had for *not* separating my head from its neck would disappear.

My opponents had no such limitations. They would undoubtedly be hailed as a conquering hero if they finally managed to kill me. So during each attempt on my life, I had to both beat them hard enough that they decided against trying again, while also letting them live. After a week of sleeping with one eye open, always one mistake away from being gutted by a random warrior, I realized this wasn't sustainable.

The solution had come in a maddening idea, literally. As long as my presence represented a hated, fully aware enemy in their midst, the attacks would never stop. However, if I was seen not as a belligerent foe residing in their city, but could convince them I was a man to be pitied, even if still dangerous, that would change the game. Thus began the last five months of my life, pretending to be a rabid madman who had lost his reason and mind to the ravages of war.

I checked the position of the sun and realized it was almost time for my nightly job to begin.

Standing up, I shuffled along with my head down, muttering

to myself. I made my way to the busy corner of the city's seedy side of town and settled down against the wall outside a dingy tavern. The tavern was located inside of a miniscule inn, the real name of which I did not truthfully know. I fondly referred to it as the Butcher's Backside, inspired by the burly butcher who worked there daily and did not seem to know any phrases that did not include swearing, often about his backside. The inn was often crowded, as it was one of the few places in the city that boasted a tavern that could feed its oft-traveling guests who passed through the town but also needed a place to stay.

As I walked toward the tavern, the falling sun cast long shadows over the establishment's regular patrons. Most disregarded me entirely, now familiar with my daily presence outside their drinking haven.

Pulling my old lyre from its sling, I briefly tweaked the tuning before my fingers began plucking the strings of the instrument, and I began singing the first verse of the "The Warrior's Mistake."

"His sword was large, his arms were strong
   And he never lost a battle
   Yet despite the warrior's mighty power
   Came the scent of pigs and cattle
   His servants washed him day and night
   To find the odor's source
   Yet despite their unrelenting work
   Their master smelled of horse
   Then one night his mistress called
   Saying a choice was his to make
   Remove the scent, or sleep alone
   For no more she could take
   Thus began our warrior's quest
   To discover why he reeked
   Of dung and vile, blood and guts
   And of crusty, moldy feet."

The entire song was as brash as the first refrain and it rarely failed to attract a glare from the more pious mothers on the street. Yet the patrons of the Butcher's Backside often hummed along with the brazen tune, helping the business of the tavern.

Rule number one to staying alive while living among sworn enemies; make yourself useful. You'd think staying out of sight was the obvious choice, but you can only hide for so long without drawing attention to yourself. The last thing you wanted was to give anyone a reason to suspect you of anything nefarious. Even in a city this size, it took less than a week before every man, woman, and child discovered that the infamous Giant Slayer receded in the city.

The trickier problem had come in figuring out how to eke out a living. While my presence in Gath was eventually tolerated, no upstanding Philistine would dare hire an Israelite, let alone one with such a poisoned reputation. I needed to find a trade not dependent on typical employment, which brought me to my current occupation as a street musician.

I had tried busking, the less patronizing term for an unemployed musician, in various parts of the city, but had come to an unspoken yet mutually beneficial relationship with the owner of the Butcher's Backside. The wire thin and graying innkeeper never spoke, preferring to communicate with the tavern's customers solely through a series of grunts and gestures. After the second day of playing near his establishment, he'd tossed out two loaves of day-old bread as he'd closed up for the night.

The food came with no explanation, but it made sense. My talent for song kept his customers drinking in the tavern far longer than they would have otherwise, a measurable benefit to his business. By throwing out the food, he didn't directly support me, but he also kept me coming back. It was a meager existence, but after surviving deep within enemy territory for over five months, I was still breathing. Sadly, that now qualified as a good day in the life of Niklas, son of Jesse.

I played though another dozen or so songs and then debated

4

whether or not to call it a night and head back to my home. Okay, calling it a home was a bit of a stretch, my shanty lean-to would be barely qualified as a hovel, but home is where the heart is, or at least where the rain only drips on your head during monsoon level storms. Since I already had a couple days' worth of food stored up, I decided to call it a night. Packing up the lyre, I pushed myself off the ground and onto my feet.

I froze when the screaming started.

My head whipped to the find the location of the shriek. A trio of shirtless men had cornered two young children, pressing uncomfortably in around them. The children, a small boy and girl, had all the markings of orphans; dirty faces, torn clothes, and emaciated bodies. They cowered in fear from the men towering over them.

"We told you both to collect enough barley to make at least one bundle," the largest and ugliest of the bunch shouted at them, grabbing the boy by the collarbone.

The boy yelped and drew back, too terrified to respond.

The few stragglers who passed by widened their distance from the conflict, no one wanting to get mixed up in the troubles of unclaimed children.

The smallest thug moved closer to the two kids. "We also told you the punishment if you failed to provide the toll for living in our city."

I bit my lip and shook my head as the scene played out in front of me. Rule number two of not getting yourself killed when living among your enemies: avoid fights that have nothing to do with you.

"We'll have to find a new way to get through your thick skulls," the first thug threatened.

Turning my back away from the altercation and moving away, I stopped again when the girl's fresh whimpers reached my ears.

My shoulders sank and I cracked my neck. Unfortunately,

there was one self-imposed rule that superseded all others: never, under any circumstance, tolerate bullies.

"Hey!" I announced loudly. "Dumb, Dumber, and Dumbest, it's past time you moved along."

The trio turned toward me. They each growled and muttered under their breaths before moving a couple of steps away from the children. I watched as they all placed their hands on the knives tucked into their belts.

"This doesn't concern you, Israelite rat," spat the youngest of the thugs as he unsheathed a sharp jagged dagger.

I shrugged my shoulders. "Probably not, but I've always been incapable of tolerating blowhards. Just ask Goliath." I narrowed my eyes. "Oh wait..."

Then I reached behind my neck and grabbed the golden inlaid handle of the sword slung over my back. In one swooping motion, I pulled the massive blade free with one hand, and five feet of razor-sharp metal gleamed in the air. The broadsword had been crafted for use by a literal giant and yet, by some unseen power, I was capable of wielding the almost fifty-pound blade as if it weighed no more than a weapon one-tenth its size.

Its appearance had the desired effect; the men took several steps back, swearing under their breaths. Bonus tip for living among your enemies: if you can manage it, carry around an all-but-mythical weapon and break it free during unwanted alter-cations.

Walking forward, I put myself between the orphans and the thugs. I twirled the broadsword in a swiping motion, its arc only inches from the men's throats. "So which one of you inbreeds want to lose a limb first?" I asked.

Shocker; none of them rose to the challenge.

"These three street rats aren't worth it," the largest of the bunch said through gritted teeth, and he motioned harshly for his friends to follow him.

I waited until they were out of sight before I turned my atten-tion back to the children still cowering against the wall of the alley. The girl was probably around eight. She had the most orange hair I had ever seen, although it was streaked with black lines of soot. The boy, a year or two younger, had long brown hair that covered his face nearly down to his nose and half his neck as well.

"Are you two alright?" I asked.

Neither responded. Instead, they pressed themselves further against the earthen wall. Their eyes, the shape of globes, were fixated in the air. I followed their gaze to my broadsword.

"Oh," I said apologetically and refastened the blade to its clasp on my back. The children didn't relax, but they did at least stop their attempts to mash themselves into the mud wall.

"Let's try this again," I said, crouching down to be at eye level with them and offering my hand. "I'm Niklas."

Silence.

I couldn't blame them. As bad as my current lot was, life as a street orphan was even worse. I could at least defend myself. Without parents or family to advocate for them, they had absolutely no rights or protections. They were at the bottom of a particularly vicious food chain.

"Well then," I said, pushing through the awkwardness and pocketing my still outstretched hand. "I'll leave you two alone." I stood back up but a strong sense of guilt gnawed at my stomach. They probably hadn't eaten a real meal in months. Grunting to myself, I pulled the loaf of bread from my pack and tossed it to them. The children waited a good five seconds, staring at the food in suspicion before the girl with orange hair suddenly snatched it, tucking it beneath her ragged clothes as she pulled her brother away. I watched them leave with my evening's earnings and sighed. I'd get another if I busked a few more hours. So much for turning in early for the night.

I shuffled back to my post and began my musical set anew. The evening turned into night, and after the last patron of the Butcher's Backside had shuffled out, another loaf of bread was ceremoniously tossed into the street. Now officially finished for

7

the evening, I collected my supplies and the loaf and began to head home. Halfway to my hovel, a wild scream bellowed from my right, and a sword swung out from a darkened alley, missing my nose by inches.

Had the Backwoods Trio returned for revenge?

Yet only one figure exited the side street. He was small and completely covered in dirt and what appeared to dry blood. The attacker dragged a bronze, three-foot, sickle-shaped blade across the ground.

I needed to understand the situation, so I unleashed my unparalleled wit to assess the assault, shouting, "What the what?!"

"My father is dead because of you," the unknown assailant said through clenched teeth, dragging the ugly blade forward. "I've come to avenge him."

CHAPTER TWO

Well that made more sense.

The sheer number of Philistine deaths I had, in one form or another, been responsible for made this an unfortunate side effect of living in a Philistine city. My people had literally written a song about it; "Niklas slays tens of thousands, giants and warriors alike." I'd thought better than to include that song into my regular busking set.

This also wasn't the first time a relative of a deceased warrior had sought me out. Men had frequently come to exact revenge for their family's honor, but never had they been *this* young. My attacker was a mere child, a boy by any definition.

Gabril, my former mentor turned traitor, had been adamant that sparing the lives of our enemies' children would only lead to them seeking vengeance once they got older. I had wrongly assumed there would be more time before that particular prophecy bit me in the butt.

"Look," I said holding my hands up and retreating backward. "I'm sorry about your father, I really am. But we were at war with the Philistines. Killing your people was never personal."

The boy cocked his to the side, confused, but then his eyes

went wide with rage. "I am not a Philistine!" he screamed and again lifted his weapon in the air to strike.

The attack was easy enough to dodge, but now I was thoroughly confused. Outside of the Philistines, there was only one other person I had killed.

"Are you Gabril's son?" I asked skeptically? He had never mentioned a family but, then again, he had never a mentioned a bunch of things, like his favorite kind of fish or the fact he was a bloody traitor to our nation. The question, though, seemed to invoke fresh anger through the boy, his eyes growing wide as he lunged forward again with the blade.

This time I unsheathed my dabar, a long knife I kept on my waist, and parried the attack. "So should I take that reaction as a yes or a no?"

He failed to appreciate my attempt at banter. The boy swung the sword again, but his attacks were getting sluggish. Soon he'd be more a danger to himself than me. It was time we ended this little dance.

I left myself open for another attack and the child whipped the sword in an arc at the opportunity. I moved into the strike, brushed aside the attack, and grabbed the handle of the blade. I placed one of my feet behind his ankle and pushed him back. He tripped and I pulled the sword from his hand, ensuring the child didn't impale himself on the fall.

"Look," I said, trying to keep my voice, "I realize telling someone enraged to 'calm down' is little better than trying to douse out a fire by throwing dry kindling on it, but I need you to explain what is going on here." I brought the tip of the blade to his throat. I had no intention of hurting the child, but he didn't know that, and maybe it'd scare him into talking.

The grime-covered boy glared at his own weapon being used against him and then looked back up at me from his now seated position on the ground. "My father is dead because of you."

"Yeah, we've already covered that," I said. "I'm going to need you to be a bit more specific. Who was your father?"

It took him a moment to answer; the pain of even saying the name was evident. "Matthias," he said quietly.

My world shattered.

Matthias, a priest from the neighboring village of Nob, was the living embodiment of good people. Years ago, I had encountered the merry monk at a time of particular distress and he had helped me navigate the way forward. We had only met twice, the latter when he gave me the massive sword across my back, yet I counted him as a confidant, mentor, and friend of the highest level, a short list at the moment. Now, it seemed, it had grown even shorter still. But who would want to kill him? Matthias lived in a sleepy town, welcomed any stranger, and took care of the local orphans.

I tossed the boy's sword to the ground and pocketed my dabar. "Tell me what happened."

Matthias' son seemed to shrink into himself and he avoided my gaze.

"It's Abiathar, right?" I asked, more softly, remembering Matthias' young son. "Tell me what happened, and I promise, if I really am responsible for killing your father, you won't have to kill me. I'll do it myself."

Hearing his name had an effect on the boy. The anger in his posture faded and he recounted the story.

"Three nights ago, a band of raiders attacked Nob. It was chaos. Smoke and the smell of blood were everywhere. My dad told me to hide among the tapestry cloths and wait for him to come back." He diverted his eyes. "He never came back."

The story stopped as the boy cried. I waited, not rushing him to recover.

"When I finally left my hiding spot, our town had been destroyed. Bodies were everywhere. His was among them." He nodded to the sword on the ground. "I found that in my father's corpse." He hung his head low, and he mumbled something under his breath.

"I'm sorry, what was that?"

"You were supposed to protect us!" he said with fresh fury in his voice. "Everyone told stories about you, the mighty Niklas, Giant Slayer, lion-slayer, savior to us all. But then you left and ran off to live with the Philistines, our enemies. And my father died."

I felt sick to my stomach. Abiathar's account of my activity was incomplete, but it was hardly inaccurate. King Erik would have killed me had I stayed in Israel, but it didn't change the fact that when a friend had needed me, I was nowhere to be found. Five years ago, I had been supernaturally chosen as Israel's protector, and since my self-imposed exile, I had been absent from my duties.

I got down on my knees until I was eye level with Abiathar. "I swear to you, I will avenge your father. With the last breath in my lungs–"

What I can assure you would have been a truly moving vow was unceremoniously cut short by an arrow slicing through the side of my stomach, leaving a deep red gash in my abdomen as it clattered to the cobbled street.

"You don't have many breaths left," said a cold voice from behind. "Your time has come, false savior. You will die here."

Of course I would. It had just been that kind of night.

CHAPTER THREE

SERIOUSLY, WAS THERE SOME KIND OF NATIONAL HOLIDAY DECLARING it open season on former Giant Slayers? I have a gift for making people want to kill me, but two separate assassination attempts in fifteen minutes was impressive even by my standards.

The searing pain of the arrow's attack pulsed through my side and cut short my musings, which were only magnified as I spun around to locate my attacker. I had expected to find one or more of the previously affronted Philistines, but instead discovered a lone opponent twenty feet in front of me. The bald, middle-aged man wore a set of dark robes and carried a short bow in his hands. Around his neck hung a familiar star surrounded by a golden circle.

"Doeg sends his greetings," my attacker sneered.

At the mention of the name Doeg, several puzzle pieces fell into place, and the rage I associated with it drove any thought of discomfort away from my wound. Doeg, an advisor to King Erik with a particularly creepy birth mark on his face, had made an attempt on my life six months ago, and when he failed, he and his group of religious fanatics had taken their rage out on my best friend Damon, leaving him bloody and on the edge of

He intercepted the strike using my bloody dabar, which he had unknowingly dislodged from his own body, and though there was a good fifty-pound difference between the two blades, he managed to divert my attack so that it only grazed his shoulder.

Just how strong was he?

I didn't want to give either of us a chance to find out, so I unleashed a fury of strikes against him with my sword. Strength alone is a poor substitute for skill, and though he blocked the first few attacks, he seemed to soon understand that he wouldn't win this fight.

This apparent realization led to desperation on his part, as he lunged forward. His blow never connected, but my parry did. Four feet of my broadsword went through him. The zealot still failed to show the effects of physical pain, but the attack at least drained his remaining strength out of him. Light immediately faded from my opponent's eyes, and his body went limp.

The adrenaline surging through my limbs slowed, and the deep gash across the side of my stomach from the arrow reminded me of its presence. Before any further investigation could take place, I needed to tend to the wound, or the lunatic's repetitive prophecy really would come true.

I placed my hand over it to slow the bleeding and looked down the back alley to find where Abiathar had hidden. My search was interrupted though when no less than twenty armed Philistine soldiers rushed into the street. All of our eyes glanced to the fresh corpse lying on the road, and then every soldier drew their weapon.

"Niklas," their commander said warily.

"I know," I answered the command before he could finish it, dropping the broadsword to the ground. "I'm under arrest." I held my hands out, readying myself to be bound.

The commander nodded. "The King requires your presence."

"'The King?" I asked confused and more than a little alarmed. "Why would he want to see me?"

The commander didn't answer my question. Instead, three men approached warily. Two of them grabbed hold of my arms as the third brought up the butt of his axe and slammed it into my nose.

My body fell forward, and the world went blank.

CHAPTER FOUR

THE SOUND OF METAL SMASHING AGAINST METAL JOLTED ME AWAKE.
I found two sets of chains, one binding my arms and the other
my legs. I was lying facedown in a darkened cell. The rotten
stench of what I hoped was a dead rodent and not a decaying
human corpse blasted my nostrils, while the bridge of my nose
pounded from...well...having taken a pounding.

Rolling to my side, I glanced around the square cell. The
windowless room had walls constructed from hardened earth,
and the iron chains were nailed to the wall, which strategically
kept the wooden door out of my reach. Outside, the rhythmic
clang of metal striking metal continued. The injury in my
abdomen had been tended to and bandaged. Maybe the
Philistines didn't want blood loss to finish me off before they got
around to it.

The night had gone south in a hurry.

Conflicting dark emotions battled for my attention. Guilt for
getting one of my mentors killed, concern for Abiathar, a traumatized child, now wandering the dangerous streets of the
Philistines alone, and powerlessness to do even the slightest
thing to help.

Abiathar had called me Israel's protector. At one time, he

would have been correct, but now I was little more than an incompetent, defenseless coward. Fleeing Israel had felt like my only play, yet it had meant abandoning those I had been charged to protect while the wolves still prowled.

However, wallowing in my failures wouldn't bring justice to Matthias. It was time to get back to work. What did we know? First, the entire village of Nob had been destroyed. Why? That Doeg would murder Matthias made sense from a vindictive standpoint, but unless Doeg assumed the entire village assisted me, it seemed like overkill to obliterate all of Nob. As unhinged as King Erik could be, even he wouldn't permit the destruction of an entire village.

I didn't have enough facts, which meant first I had to take a trip to Nob.

I jingled the chains around my wrists, acknowledging the small hiccup with that plan. Even if I could find a way out of the chains, get past the, undoubtedly, locked door, and elude the untold number of guards prowling the building, I still had no idea where I was even being held. So where did I stand?

Attempt an escape: dead.

Attempt to overpower my guards when they came to take me: dead.

Appeal to the Philistine king's mercy: laughably dead. I'm not even sure they had a word for mercy in their vocabulary.

So if flight, fight, and staying were all off the table, my options were pretty limited.

"Hey," I spoke to the ceiling, "any thoughts of what we should do next?" I waited. "You can notice I used the word 'we.'"

The last bit of advice Matthias had given me was to more regularly open the lines of communication between me and the Guy Upstairs. My people called Him Yahweh, and He had orchestrated me being chosen as Israel's protector in the first place. These types of unwinnable situations had been a regular occurrence over the past few years, and He had been kind enough to lend assistance more than once. Not always, mind you. He could be maddeningly selective of when and how His help would arrive, but it was always worth a shot. We'd been chatting more during my time in Philistia.

Okay, chatting was a misnomer, because it presumes a two-way conversation. I talked and assumed He was listening. I lived among people who wanted to see my skull mounted on a spike, so conversation with a more friendly party, incorporeal though He may be, had a strong appeal.

"At this point I'd even take a bit of that music you used to pester me with," I said, referring to the mysterious music He had used to direct my efforts in the past. Yet I hadn't heard it since I had left Israel.

The constant banging of metal was all that replied.

Shrugging my shoulders, I continued speaking to the air. "You know, I sometimes question your timing on things. I mean, really, shouldn't helping out a couple of orphans and putting down one of Doeg's lunatics have banked me a couple of bonus points in the grand scheme of things, as opposed to a time in lockup? Don't get me wrong, there's plenty of stuff you could justifiably smite me for, but it seems like a temporary hiccup in the universe's lot system."

Silence.

"Right then," I continued, only slightly disappointed. As long as breath still filled my lungs, He hadn't fully abandoned me yet. This might be one of those situations in which a supernatural assist wasn't required, so I continued processing out loud. "Why would King Achish want to see me now? Were he and Doeg conspiring together to rid themselves of a former Giant Slayer?"

Over the past six months, I had tried to gather a sense of King Achish, the current ruler of Gath, but the info had been spotty, at best. Supposedly not much older than myself, he had spent the first six years of his rule trying to conquer Israel.

Yet after a bold, brazen, yet classically handsome, young shepherd had repeatedly thwarted his attempts, the country had been marked by the longest season of peace in decades, exclusively focusing on expanding trade. The population as a whole had prospered from it, but the lack of regular war was the talk of many conversations at the Butcher's Backside.

It didn't add up. I had lived among Achish's people for almost half a year, and he could have killed me without anyone batting an eye. His people might have thrown a parade for his efforts. Taking my chances to live among the Philistines had been incredibly risky, the equivalent of a shot in the dark, blindfolded, hunting at a mosquito, while riding an irate camel. Any way you looked at it, the king didn't need to send Doeg to kill me. Which meant he probably still didn't intend on murdering me for the moment. I had time to figure out some way out of this mess.

Something slammed into the other side of the cell, cutting my musings short.

"Nap time's over," a disgruntled guard announced, opening up the door. He stood alongside five other men, all armed with enough weapons to fortify a small outpost.

"You guys don't mess around," I said, eyeing their weapons dubiously. "Are there another twenty prisoners in here, or am I just that intimidating?"

One of the younger guards stepped forward to put an end to my insolence, but the oldest one, a seasoned, scar-covered soldier, held him back. "King Achish said to bring him unharmed."

The young warrior growled but relented, and I smirked.

"Don't get too comfortable," Scarface said. "The last five men brought before King Achish for treason left without eyes, ears, or a tongue. He probably just wants you whole so he can take you apart himself."

And paired with that charming thought, they threw a black bag over my head and took me to meet the king of the Philistines.

CHAPTER FIVE

THEY KEPT THE CHAINS AROUND MY ARMS AND LEGS, MEANING OUR journey consisted of me shuffling along like my grandmother after a night of too much wine. Due to the musty sack covering my eyes, two guards needed to lead me from both sides, yet somehow they still managed to jam my knees into a dozen different corners and obstructions. Jerks.

We eventually stopped and for a good minute we waited, just standing around.

"I can come back tomorrow if now's not a good time," I suggested helpfully.

My suggestion was dismissed with an elbow to my kidney.

Eventually, I heard a door open in front of us as the men took off my head covering. The room within the doorway was massive, with the only light coming in from the hallway behind us. The guards pushed me forward, and about twenty-feet in, they stopped me, forced me to my knees, and attached my wrist chains to an iron loop grounded to the wooden floor. Patches of red stain surrounded my resting place in the oak floorboard. Blood. Apparently the guards weren't blowing smoke about the five men being executed before me.

Fun times.

After securing me, the escort left without a word, shutting the door behind them. Black nothingness enveloped the room as the light from the hallway faded with the closing of the door. Time passed and, other than my bladder threatening to leak all over the floor, nothing happened.

Unsurprisingly, as unrelenting banter was my go-to coping mechanism, I eventually broke the silence in the darkness. "Um, hello?"

The response took so long, I started to assume I was alone.

"The great Niklas," said a disembodied voice from somewhere ahead of me. "The slayer of giants, musician to kings, murderer of Philistines."

"King Achish?" I asked, a mixture of uncertainty and reverence in my voice. "It's my privilege to be granted an audience with you."

"Granted an audience?" the king replied with a hint of amusement. "An odd description of your current situation."

I shrugged uncomfortably. My time spent around the royalty of Israel had helped me realize nobles existed in a different world than the rest of us normal folk. Sure, they still did all the things we did—ate, pooped, slept—but they saw reality from an entirely different perspective. It created opportunities that otherwise wouldn't be possible with more down-to-earth individuals. On my journey here, I had decided it might be possible to leverage those royal oddities to my benefit.

I cleared my throat, trying to keep my voice from cracking with fear. "For six months, you've had every opportunity to kill or imprison me. Even on this night, you could have executed me, but instead you bandaged my wounds and granted me an opportunity to speak with you."

This was my first gamble, gaining favor with Achish. The Philistine king may indeed be in league with Doeg, but it seemed unlikely. Doeg worked for King Erik, an opposing ruler. So I was operating under the logic of 'the enemy of my enemy.' I just hoped he saw it the same way.

"Possibly," the king allowed, "but tonight my men found you standing over a dead body. Murder carries a rather severe penalty in my kingdom."

"Self-defense is not murder."

"True enough," Achish replied, "if that were the only reason you were here. National espionage, however, carries a very similar fate."

"Espionage?" I squawked, suddenly even more uncertain of the reason why I had been brought before the king. "For who?"

"Who else? Israel and King Erik," the Philistine ruler replied. "My counselors, generals, even my dear mother, all cautioned me against allowing the mighty Niklas to reside in our lands. They warned it was only a matter of time before you showed your true intentions and dealt a critical blow to our country."

"Your Highness," I pled, "I swear to you, not only do I not have a clue of what we're even talking about, I haven't talked to anyone in Israel since coming to Philistia. My name is mud back home."

"My agents tell me you talked to two separate Israelites this very evening."

Okay, technically that was true. "One of which was a ten-year-old boy whose hometown had been attacked, and the other tried to kill me; hardly the ideal partners in crime. Plus, it still doesn't explain the motive. Erik wants me dead more than most Philistines."

"Maybe you stole the plans to get back into the Mad King's good graces," he suggested.

"Plans for what?" I asked, frustrated by the absolute lack of information he was giving me.

Achish refused to answer my question. Instead, he directed his next response to another person in the dark room. "Are your men certain they kept tabs on him over the past three nights?"

"His every move has been watched since he showed up," answered a vaguely familiar voice. "Yet he still could have managed to conspire with someone else. The cleanest solution would be to execute him."

Well this conversation had turned uncomfortable quickly. I wanted to argue the point, but if I was honest, getting rid of an untrusted foreigner was the smart move.

The king took time with his response. "But would it be fair?"

The advisor grunted. "He's our enemy, Your Highness, directly responsible for the deaths of almost one thousand Philistines."

"But not your death," the king replied.

The same voice grunted.

Again the king waited. "Lights," he finally commanded.

A dozen different torches sprung to life.

We were in King Achish's throne room. Three counselors flanked the king on both his right and his left, but it was the man with the burned, marked face who stood behind Achish that made my eyes go wide. Zalmon, the owner of the familiar voice, watched me with calculating eyes.

Zalmon and I had only met twice. The first time was when he and several other Philistines infiltrated my hometown and murdered half a dozen guards. We had captured him, and after some supernatural prodding, I had offered him nominal aid to heal a nasty infection in his side. We wouldn't meet again until years later, when he returned the favor during my battle against Gabril. We certainly weren't friends, but we had left on good, if somewhat uneasy, terms.

At least I had thought so. His insistence for my execution certainly made me rethink our relationship.

King Achish sat atop a large, iron throne, blanketed in ornate pillows to recline on. His crown, too, was made of iron, which made sense, considering how skilled the Philistines were in metallurgy. He had short, blonde, spiky hair and was probably in his early twenties, only a handful of years older than myself. I was startled to see that a purple blindfold covered his eyes.

Achish was blind.

It was my turn to grunt. Doeg had his hand in this somehow. Still, I thought I'd found my opening.

"Let me help you."

The king turned his head. "And how do you propose to do that?"

I cleared my throat. "We share a common enemy. These Marauders killed my friend, as well as hundreds of my people. Gabril may have been a world-class tool, but he trained me well. I'll hunt down their base of operations and report its location back to you. Then you can rain down as much justice as you want."

"And you expect us to simply trust you?" the king asked, somewhat amused.

"I'm a lot of things," I replied. "A schemer, a loudmouth, and a dozen other equally insufferable annoyances, but I am not a liar. I swear to you, when I find them, you will be the first to know."

The king of the Philistines weighed my response, his face unreadable. Finally, he nodded. "Release him."

All of his counselors erupted with heated objections simultaneously. King Achish ignored them all and motioned for the guards to fulfill his command.

A soldier came up from behind and unlocked the metal bindings holding me to the ground. I stood up and glanced around the room. Overstaying my welcome seemed a poor life choice. I bowed to the king, but then grimaced when I realized he wouldn't be able to see the gesture. "Thank you for your graciousness, King Achish. I will find them or die trying."

"One last thing," the king said as I began to make my exit. "My soldiers tell me you've been carrying the sword I commissioned for our champion Goliath." His lips turned up in a sly smile. "Thank you for returning it to us."

Peachy. Not only had I sworn to locate a horde of bloodthirsty murderers, now I had to do it without the biggest and best weapon in my arsenal. This was already going well.

CHAPTER SIX

THE PHILISTINES RELEASED ME WITH ALL MY BELONGINGS INTACT, minus the broadsword. The sun was just coming over the horizon as I headed back to the location of my battle with Doeg's fanatic. Before gallivanting off after a murderous horde, I needed to find Abiathar. The streets of Gath were dangerous for even the hardiest of warriors, let alone a traumatized, foreign child.

People were already starting their morning routines, and a host of locals streamed in and out of their homes. Beyond the ominous blood stains on the compacted ground, there were no signs of the events that had transpired the night before at the place I had fought the would-be assassin.

I ducked down the alley Abiathar had hid in, but found nothing. I checked the next street over, and the street after that. With every failure, my search intensified, but again and again, I found no sign of the boy.

By midday, I was emotionally and physically exhausted and took a moment to catch my breath in the town's center. My mind started imagining all of the horrible things that could have happened to Abiathar; captured by slavers, killed by cutthroats. I shuddered thinking about the horrors he could be experiencing.

I rubbed my hands over my face for a good long while. My

fears transformed into disbelief when I finally looked up. Across the plaza, Abiathar sat playing with two other children, laughing in delight.

Bolting up, I sprinted to the trio and together they glanced up to me. I recognized the two other children; the street orphans I had rescued last night.

"You're okay!" I exclaimed to Abiathar, my voice carrying equal parts relief and confusion.

He nodded, taking a bite out of a loaf of bread. "When the guards grabbed you, I couldn't follow after you. I was scared, but then Tiger and Char found me," he said as he gestured to the other children. "They stayed with me through the night, and we've been hanging out here since morning." He took another bite and then set the rest of it down next to the curved sword that had killed his father. It seemed that Abiathar had retrieved it after I had been taken.

"Okay," I said, relieved and taking deep breaths. "Everything is okay."

"Yep," Abiathar replied, oblivious to the emotional terror I had just gone through. "So when are we going to start hunting my father's killers?"

The "we" in his statement caused my stomach to lurch.

"Abiathar," I said. "There may have been a miscommunication. I promised to avenge your father, and I will, but I'm going to do it alone. It'll be incredibly dangerous, and I'd never forgive myself if you got hurt, or worse. I owe your father more than that."

The boy's eyes narrowed and he reached out for the curved sword. "No," he said resolutely. "I'm going with you, and so are Tiger and Char. We decided earlier." He nodded firmly to his young compatriots. "Tiger," he said, pointing to the young girl, "doesn't speak and can't hear, but she can read lips and is super clever. And Char is good at getting into places unnoticed. He actually made it inside to watch you with the king. It's why I wasn't scared anymore. We knew you'd find me."

The boy named Char looked up through his long bangs at Niklas. "Thanks for helping us out yesterday. Sorry we were scared of you."

Blood and ashes, this just kept getting better. I needed to get Abiathar out of Gath, but the plan was to leave him with a family back in Israel. The last thing my already suicidal mission needed was a child getting dragged into the mess. And as if one orphan wasn't enough, now there were three of them. The fact that the other two were Philistine orphans only made things even more complicated.

This wasn't happening. "We can't take them with us," I said.

Abiathar continued to stare me down, but then shrank a little, letting go of the blade's hilt. "It's what my father would have done."

His comment might as well have been a sucker punch right to the gut. I never thought the great Niklas would be bested in a debate by a ten-year-old, but he was right. Taking care of all three children is exactly what Matthias would have done, and gallivanting after his killers at the expense of respecting his memory seemed like a poor tribute. I sighed.

"I will take all of you to Israel," I relented. "But when we get there, I'm finding you all a family to stay with."

Abiathar weighed my words, uncertain about the compromise. Tiger reached over, tugged on his shirt, and nodded.

"We'll stay with my family in Bethlehem, my father had two sisters there," Abiathar said. "As long as we first go to Nob. I want to bury my father."

His idea seemed reasonable. The village would be abandoned and safe, and he deserved the opportunity to put his father to rest. It was also less than a day's journey from Nob to Bethlehem, which meant that I could leave the children and begin my search in earnest. Plus, Bethlehem was also my hometown, meaning I'd get a chance to check in with my family.

"Fair enough," I agreed. "Are you three ready to travel?" Now that I had the trio of younglings under my protection, I preferred to spend as little time in Gath as possible. I doubted my agreement with King Achish had strengthened my standing in the city, and I didn't want the children to be caught in the crossfire of yet another attempt to kill the pesky Giant Slayer in their midst.

They nodded and rose from the ground. Abiathar struggled to pick up the curved sword.

"How about I carry that for the journey?" I offered.

He eyed my suggestion warily.

"I'll give it back once we reach Nob," I promised.

He consented, and then, with the strange weapon strapped to my hip, we began our journey to Nob.

It took two full days of travel, but the endurance of all three children surprised me. I'd seen soldiers travel half that distance with nonstop complaining, myself often taking part, yet the children never grumbled. Mind you, they weren't carrying much; the two orphans only owned two small cloaks. But still, it showed their strength.

Char kept the trip interesting. His time on the street had given him access to all kinds of hearsay, and he kept up a steady stream of questions and commentary about the Israelites and myself.

"Do the Israelites really murder their firstborn children?"

"No." I said.

"They say when you fought Goliath, you used witchcraft. Who taught you spells?"

"It didn't happen that way."

"Why do Israelites not eat pork? Bacon is awesome."

"Hmm." I paused. "I'm not entirely sure." I honestly just didn't want to go into it. On and on it went, though his more risqué questions were met by a whack on the back of his head by his sister Tiger.

Given the grim purpose for our travels, I endured the endless interrogation because it served as a good distraction for Abiathar from the loss of his father. The reprieve was broken when we finally reached Nob. The village's buildings now stood as empty shells, with the burnt and destroyed pieces of furniture, tools, and equipment scattered throughout the streets. The attackers had been thorough.

Abiathar had gone ghost white. "Where are the bodies?" He screamed and bolted forward, deeper into the town.

"Wait!" I yelled and sprinted after him. The village *should've* been deserted, but I didn't want to take any risks.

He finally stopped at the entrance to Matthias' orphanage and began frantically searching the area. "My father's body was right here. What happened to him?"

His question had merit. Had King Erik or some other Israelite come to put the bodies to rest? Our nation took burial incredibly seriously, so it made sense that someone would come. Yet there was no sign of our typical ceremonies. There was still too much blood everywhere, and any Israelite would have removed it in the process of cleansing the site.

A shadow moved inside the orphanage. My body tensed. Had the Marauders left men at the scene of the attack?

"Stay here," I said quietly to Abiathar and the siblings, pulling out my dabar.

The orphanage was large, and the multiple, windowless rooms limited my sight. By the time I reached the center of the building, only minimal light reached the sleeping area, yet nothing seemed out of place. That is until the unmistakable feel of a sword's blade was pressed against the base of my neck.

That was definitely out of place.

CHAPTER SEVEN

THE SHADOWED FIGURE SHIFTED BEHIND ME. "DON'T MO—"

Before he could finish the order, I lunged forward away from the blade's reach. Its sharp edge managed to slice a small cut across the back of my neck, but once out of the weapon's range, I spun to face my attacker.

He was a medium-sized man, but the darkness hid the rest of his features. This did not concern me, though, because I knew that once I bested him, I'd drag the culprit out into the light and get my answers.

Bolting toward him, my dabar flashed upward in an attempt to disarm him. In one deft motion, he parried my attack and immediately retaliated with a strike aimed at my chest. His sword gave him a good two feet reach on my own weapon, but it also required both hands. I used that advantage to lean into his attack, sidestep it, and counter it with my own. This time, I used my right hand to fake a strike with the dabar. When he moved to block the feint, I threw a left jab, but at the last moment he spun out of the way, and then lashed out again with his blade. This time, I had to retreat.

With each failed attack, the battle escalated in pace. I lost count of how many times his blade nearly ended my life, or how many near misses I had at ending his. My confidence in a fight was appropriately high. Outside of Gabril, I would take my chances against pretty much anyone, and my former mentor's corpse was rotting in a snake pit. Yet my opponent was matching me stride for stride. The challenge both frightened and energized me.

After what felt like hours, we both retreated to opposite corners of the room, panting. My mind raced to find the correct banter, but he beat me to it.

"The Lord seems to favor you today," said an all too familiar voice through winded breaths.

"Damon!?" I asked in astonishment.

The shadow-covered head cocked to one side, and as recognition seemed to dawn on him, a full laugh boomed from the prince of Israel, Erik's first-born son, and my best friend. "Niklas! I can't believe that I just tried to kill you!"

"I'll promise not to take it too personal if you return the favor, since I was trying to kill you too," I said and moved forward to hug my friend. "Let's get outside. I have children waiting for me."

"Children?" he asked in a mixture of amusement and confusion.

"It's a long story."

Outside, Abiathar, Tiger, and Char waited, sighing in apparent relief when we finally exited the orphanage together and unharmed.

Tiger pointed a finger first at Damon and then me, wonderment in her eyes. Char interpreted for her, explaining, "She wants to know what just happened and who the new guy is."

"This is Damon," I explained and threw my arm around my best friend, now easily recognizable in the sunlight. "The first prince of Israel and the second-best warrior in the land."

"Second best?" Damon asked. "I could have killed you in there."

"I recall the events differently," I replied. "And when I write a song about the epic battle, it will show that, though you fought valiantly, you were one step behind. It will be a soul moving ballad, remembered for time eternal."

"Cheater," Damon said, a smile on his lips. "Still, why are you and your new, tiny companions here?"

The moment of levity had passed. I recounted the bloody events that had brought us to Nob, the fanatic's attack, and my agreement with King Achish. "In short," I concluded, "Doeg must be connected to this somehow."

"Doubtful," Damon argued. "The Marauders have actually set his plans back more than anyone else's."

"His plans?"

Damon found a charred bench that was still structurally sound and settled down. "Doeg is attempting to unite the six major kingdoms in the region into one collective. He's been whispering to my father that Israel could be the first among equals, amassing enough power to rival the Egyptians and the Babylonians. He's sent acolytes to each kingdom in an attempt to spread his blended religion. He dreams of a time where every god and goddess in the region is worshipped under one roof. The Marauders' raids have set his plans back, because every nation thinks one of the others is using them as mercenaries. Doeg is a snake, but they've cost him more than anyone with their attacks."

The fact that Damon labeled the king's advisor a snake said a lot. The prince was in a class all his own when it came to integrity, kindness, and virtue. Yet six months ago, in an attempt to get to me, Doeg and his group—the blasphemers—had beaten my friend to the brink of death. The fact that King Erik had allowed such an action and still accepted his counsel only proved the extent of his madness.

The prince had spent more time at the royal court recently. I trusted his judgement, but the coincidence simply seemed too great. We needed more information.

"Hmm," I said, eager to look around. "So what brings *you* here?"

"Same thing as you," Damon answered. "Looking for answers. The attack shook the kingdom, and my father chose to close ranks, barricading every city. He refuses to allow anyone to investigate, and I'm one of the only people who could come without being executed for treason."

I grunted. "Daily fears of execution are on the list of things I don't miss about my time at court. As hard as being an exile has been, not living on the constant edge of being murdered by your father has been a nice change."

He chuckled, but then went ghost-white, and a look I had never seen on the prince's face appeared; guilt. "There's something else."

"What?"

"It's Michal," he said, uncomfortable with the conversation turning toward his sister whom I, during my time at the royal court, had a deep and passionate, albeit somewhat complicated relationship. "Father made her marry Carmi's son, Bartholomew."

"What!?" I shouted, instantly livid. "But we were engaged!"

Okay, technically Erik's announcement of our "engagement" had only been a ploy to lure me into a trap so her father could assassinate me, but still, we had been an item. "And General Carmi Combover's meathead of a son? He's dumber than the Philistines. If he's ever managed to formulate a sentence with more than eight words, I'd eat my sandal."

Damon refused to meet my eyes. "I know, and I told Father as much. He was just so upset after you escaped. He made some bad decisions."

"A bad decision is riding a horse bareback through a gravel pit. A bad decision is eating rare lamb that has been left out too long. This is unacceptable!" Part of me wanted to pause the investigation and march to the capital right then. Mind you, there were at least five hundred guards between King Erik and myself, but still, mad as I was, I'd take my chances.

"We need to focus," the prince cautioned in response to my outburst.

"Oh I'm focused," I countered. "I'm armed and ready to unleash all kinds of focus."

Forcing myself to take several measured breaths, I fought to calm down. As much as Erik had thrown my world for a loop, my immediate options were limited. Unless I wanted to go to war with all of Israel, I had to wait. I closed my eyes. "I'm fine, but this will be addressed."

"Agreed," Damon said, clearly relieved. Even our young trio seemed more at ease. I hadn't noticed, but during my outburst they had clumped closer together. "I only got here a few minutes before you arrived," the prince said, changing the discussion. "Let's see what we can find out."

With the children in tow, we began our investigation. Throughout the city, the remnants of a massacre were every-where, but there wasn't a corpse to be found. If Erik or someone else had ordered Israelites to stay out of the city, where had all the bodies gone?

Our answer awaited us at the city's center, in the Elders' Circle. The Elders' Circle was made of a dozen granite benches, and in the middle of it, a fifteen-foot pyre had been constructed. The charred bones of dozens of corpses lay at the bottom.

My blood began to surge throughout my body.

"What kind of monsters would do this to the dead?" the prince asked in disbelief.

One of the most sacred rites for our dead was the ability to be buried with their ancestors. Now it'd be impossible to distin-guish one body from another. It was one last unforgivable slight against our people, and it added another ember to the vengeance burning in my blood.

I turned to Abiathar. The mourning son moved toward the

pyre in a stupefied daze. "This is my fault. I should have buried him." He fell to his knees before the pile.

"No." I replied resolutely. "This is the fault of the Marauders. I will find them, and we will get justice for your father, and for everyone else."

Damon walked up to the child and knelt beside him. "Let's put your father and the rest of your neighbors to rest," he said, putting a comforting hand on Abiathar. He turned his head to the rest of us and motioned us over. "Come, together we will observe a burial rite."

"But we can't tell the bodies apart," Abiathar argued, as tears streamed down his face.

Damon gave him a reassuring smile. "The horrors of men do not impede the promises of our God. Your father was a priest, and these people were part of the flock. Yahweh knows each and every one of them, and He protects them now."

The assurance brought a look of comfort to Abiathar's face, and he nodded his agreement.

The prince's words were simple, elegant, and moving. He talked about the pain of death, the promise of new life, and the faithfulness of our God even in the darkest places. My red-hot desire for revenge fought against his message of peace, but eventually my smoldering rage began to subside.

When he finished, Damon placed an arm around the boy and stood up. Abiathar wiped the fresh tears from his cheek and stood up as well.

The prince placed a hand on his sword. "Justice will be had for your father, but for now, how about we go find anything you may have left at your home?"

Abiathar agreed, and together with Tiger and Char, they started back to his former home. Damon held my gaze and then glanced at the pyre. I followed his thought process. He'd lead the kids away so I could investigate the site. They left and I started the unenviable task of digging through the remains of the dead, looking for any clue as to who might have done this or where they had gone.

A ceramic cooking pot crashed to my left, splintering on the ground, and was immediately followed by someone cursing. The disturbance came from across the plaza, and as I looked to the source of the noise, I watched a figure dart away.

I shouted for Damon, but no one responded. I didn't want our first lead to get away, so I began the pursuit.

Whoever the individual was, he wasn't an Israelite. I knew this was the case because, per the Jewish traditions, the stranger would have come out in the open when he'd heard Damon's burial ceremony. This meant we were either dealing with a scavenger or one of the Marauders. Either could give us vital information on what had happened.

Our chase wove us through Nob, and as I gained on him, the stranger threw down every obstruction he could get his hands on to keep me from gaining ground; charred furniture, pots, anything. Eventually he ran out of the village and I grinned in triumph, as I knew he'd lose his advantage outside of town. It was only a matter of time until I made up the ground and caught him. However, he didn't head toward the open plains as I had expected, but instead ran straight into a long, rectangular building on the outskirts of town. Sprinting inside after him, I realized we had entered the village's wine press.

Wine presses were essentially open buildings with a stone pit for its foundation. Men and women would jump on the grapes and press the juice out into large containers. The criminal grabbed hold of one of the ropes that led to the bottom floor of the basin and slid down.

Where was he going? I tried to look ahead so I could better guess his plan. He was sprinting toward a hole that looked to have been built into the foundation's sidewall. Had the villagers built a passage he hoped to escape out of?

I reached for the rope and followed him down into the pit. The walls were straight and descended almost a dozen feet before touching the bottom of the press. Once I landed on the stone ground, I shot after him, expecting him to go for the hole I'd seen in the wall of the press, but quickly realized that the passage was actually only a small, closed off storage area. The man redirected and instead leapt to the edge of the press on the opposite side where a second rope was hanging down. He deftly climbed up the rope out of the press and then pulled the rope up after him.

Realizing his plan, I hurdled around to get back to the first rope I had used to climb down. The man whistled to an unseen accomplice and my last hope for escape was suddenly pulled up as well.

My head whipped around, searching for another way out of the press, but there was nothing.

I was trapped.

CHAPTER EIGHT

Since before I took my first steps, I have been ensnaring others in my schemes. Today was the first time in half a decade that the wool had been pulled so securely over my eyes. I felt conflicted at being on the receiving end of mischief. My feelings were mostly a mixture of humiliation and a bit of amusement. I'd give the culprits this; the plan had been deftly executed.

Again, I surveyed the other items in the basin, searching and failing miserably to discover an advantage I could use. Trying to scale the deep walls would be useless. Damon and the children were still out there somewhere, but it was highly unlikely they'd search for me outside of the village in a random building. In short, I was over a rather uncomfortable barrel with limited options.

The evening sun was descending in earnest, making it difficult to see much inside or outside of the pit.

As if on cue, fire ignited above me. What I thought at first to be a torch turned out to be a flaming arrow, and as the perpetrator reached the ledge, he pulled back his bow and unleashed the bolt. It landed inches from my left sandal, splintering as it smashed into the stone basin.

I let loose a squawk that sounded like a frightened bird,

which was a pretty apt description of my feelings. There was nothing in the pit I could use for cover, as the winepress had been ransacked like the rest of the village, which meant my situation was changing from over-a-barrel to shooting fish in a barrel.

The archer lit another bolt but this time he held it up long enough to give me a good look at his face. His skin was a deep brown, almost black, and his head was completely shaved. Tall and lean, he was probably only in his mid-teens.

The young man aimed his bow dead center with my chest. "I'm trying to scare you," he said flatly.

"Well then you're doing a great job," I admitted. "I'm about to wet my robes."

"I seek information on the Marauders," he continued. "If you tell me what I need to know, I'll let you out."

"And if I refuse?"

He unleashed another arrow, and this one passed within an inch of my cheek. "I kill you with my next shot." Someone behind him again lifted a torch and he lit another bolt.

"You watched me and my friends mourn the dead, so you know I'm not a Marauder," I reasoned. "We, too, seek information on them. You and I could work together."

"You got caught with a simple trap," he countered. "It's doubtful that you'd be smart enough to be much help."

Okay, ouch. "It's been a long week," I admitted. "I haven't exactly been at the top of my game. Still, we may be able to help each other."

"And why would I need your help?" my captor asked, skeptical.

"Because you're obviously not from the region, and if you're hunting the Marauders alone, I doubt you'll get very far."

The archer took a moment to weigh my words. "Your people are strange," he admitted. "Having a guide would be beneficial. Yet why should I pick you? Not to be repetitive, but you don't seem very intelligent."

It took a moment to stem the bleeding from the dagger he kept jabbing into my pride. "Because I have experience with these kinds of things. Let's say this Marauder situation isn't exactly new territory for me. I'm Niklas."

"*The* Niklas?" he asked, cocking his head to the side. "Rumors tell of a Niklas from Israel slaying a giant. We are in Israel and you are named Niklas. Are you the same one from the stories?"

"Rumors rarely tell the full story," I answered. "He was more giant blowhard than an actual mythical creature, but he was a formidable warrior."

"Did you kill a lion?" he asked, suspiciously.

"That one really did happen," I said and pulled out the lion's tooth that I kept as a trophy hanging around my neck. "The real question is why would I work with you? Why do you seek the Marauders?"

He waited before replying. "They stand in my way. You?"

"They killed a friend," I answered.

We stared at one another for a good ten seconds before he finally nodded. "I will work with you, Niklas, on your word you will not harm me or my companion."

I thought on his offer, but unless I wanted to chance him either shooting or leaving me, my options were limited. "Agreed, as long as you promise the same protection for me and mine."

"It is decided then," the man said. "I am Uri, and my companion is Pali." He motioned toward the pit, and his companion lowered the rope.

I grabbed hold and pulled myself out the pit. Reaching the surface, I discovered that Uri's "companion" was completely naked save for a yellow vest.

"You have a monkey." I stated in wonder.

"A chimpanzee," Uri corrected me, patting his thigh-high companion. "My father stumbled upon him years ago and gave him to me as a birthday present. We've been friends ever since."

Once my shock had returned to manageable levels, I reached out to my new compatriot. "It's nice to meet you…I think."

Uri grabbed my forearm. "And you as well."

"Let's get back to my friends. They'll be worrying about where I went."

Together we returned to the pyre and found Damon and the children eating in a circle as the prince told the children a funny story.

"Seriously?" I said. "I disappear without a word, and instead of searching passionately for your lost ally, I find you living it up and a having a bite to eat. Where's the concern for my well-being? I could've been in trouble. I did almost get shot."

Damon refused to show the least bit of concern, ignored me, and finished his story. "And then the bear fell on Niklas, literally bear-hugging him!" The children burst out in a fresh fit of laughter.

I shook my head in disbelief. "You're telling a story about me almost getting killed while I was, in fact, almost getting killed. Priorities!"

The children glanced beyond me. "Is that a monkey?!"

"A chimpanzee actually," Uri answered brightly. "His name is Pali, and he enjoys having his head scratched if you want to touch him."

The children squealed in delight and ran around me to interact with the monkey.

Damon also got to his feet and reached out his hand to the newcomer. "I'm Damon." No questions asked, no moment of suspicion.

"Uri," our new, dark-skinned ally replied and returned the handshake. He then turned to me. "He appears smarter than you. I'm more comfortable with our partnership now."

One of them was going to die. Slowly.

The prince motioned to a portion of bread and jerky atop his satchel. "I saved you some dinner."

The mention of food meant the accused received a temporary

stay of execution. I ate while Uri and Damon compared information on the Marauders. Unfortunately, Uri's information didn't tell us anything we didn't already know.

"You said they stood in your way," I said through a mouth full of bread. "What did they do?"

Uri nodded. "They have been terrorizing the trade routes of my fiancée's parents. Their setbacks mean they can't afford the dowry for us to marry, and my parents refuse to let the wedding take place without it. I need to stop the Marauders so that their business can recommence."

I raised an eyebrow. "That's a lot of hassle just to get married."

The young man grinned. "My fiancée is worth it."

"Fair enough," I admitted. "Still, it looks like we're not going to find anything else here. Let's bed down for the night and we'll figure out where to go next tomorrow."

Both men agreed. The night's air was pleasant, and given the blood splattered among the houses, we chose to make camp outside in the city's far west corner. It also gave us the best visibility of the surrounding terrain.

Damon offered to take the first watch, and as soon as my head hit my cloak, I passed out.

A hand jolted me awake.

It was still the dead of night. "Is it my turn for watch?" I asked groggily.

"Not quite," Damon replied. "We have company."

The possibilities flew from my mouth. "The Marauders? King Erik? Bandits?"

He shook his head. "I don't think so. They don't look like an army. They're just people."

"People?"

Uri sat up, the small commotion having woken him. "What is

happening?" Pali also woke up and quickly climbed up Uri's back.

"We're not sure," I said, "but stay and wait with the children. Damon and I will investigate.

Reaching the southern gate of the city, I saw what he meant. Now, only a hundred yards away, enough people to fill a village walked toward us. At least a hundred men held up torches. The light from the torches shone down on the group, and from that light I could see that there were even more men, women, and children surrounding the men with the torches. Some even had farm animals with them, as well.

"Who are they? I'm pretty sure we can't afford that many new enemies at the moment," I muttered, stunned by the size of the group.

Two people walked ahead of the group, a heavyset man and a petite woman. As they approached the city, my jaw dropped in recognition. Finally within talking distance, the woman held out her hand. It took me a good ten seconds of disbelief for me to take her hand in return.

"Long time no see, Niklas," said Deborah, the best black-smith in Israel. I shook her hand in silence, still shocked.

The pudgy man wrapped his arms around me. "It's good to see you," my brother Isaiah added.

CHAPTER NINE

THE ARRIVAL OF MY FAMILY BROUGHT WITH IT TOO MANY QUESTIONS to order and prioritize, so I condensed them into a single inquiry. "What the hell?" I asked, thoroughly confused.

Isaiah raised his eyebrows empathetically. "It's a long story," he admitted. "Father and the elders would do a better job explaining it."

"Dad's here?"

"Practically all of Bethlehem made the trip," Deborah explained. "But we've traveled a long way, and it'll be easier to explain in the morning. We plan to set up camp on the edge of the city."

I nodded, more in a stupor than out of any real agreement.

"The whole family's here," Isaiah said and invited me to follow him. "They're going to love seeing you."

I followed after him and, indeed, met my whole family. My father Jesse and my mother Samara greeted me with their individual oddities; my dad made a joke about how either I had grown again or he was finally shrinking, and my mother commented on how it didn't look like I had been eating enough, which to be fair was probably the truth.

Eliab, my eldest brother who had about fifty pounds of muscle on me, lifted me from the ground when he saw me. "Still getting into trouble I see." His wife Rachel hugged me and handed me my three-year-old niece, soundly asleep from the journey.

Abin, my second oldest brother, made a snide comment about my lack of hygiene.

"Why are you here?" I asked them, confused.

"We came searching for you," Eliab explained.

"Okay, but how'd you know I'd be here? *I* didn't even know I'd be here until two days ago." I said as Rachel silently took her daughter back from me and walked over to where tents were being pitched.

"That was Abin's idea actually," Isaiah said. "He told us, 'Let's head to the area with the most chaos, and then wait for Niklas show up.'"

Abin took a drink of his flask and flashed a bright smile.

I shook my head. "And you're looking for me because...?"

"We'll talk tomorrow," my father said, echoing Deborah's earlier suggestion, but he was noticeably more somber about the topic.

I helped prepare camp for what honestly seemed like the entire town of Bethlehem, and we moved the three orphan children out to sleep with the rest of our people.

Night turned to morning, and after breakfast, the village elders gathered to finally explain why they had left their homes. Damon and Uri joined us, but the elders shifted uneasily at their arrival.

"We're not comfortable with the King's son being present for this conversation," one of the younger men explained.

I shook my head. "Damon has saved my life more than enough times to deserve our trust. He was the one who sent us reinforcements in the Battle of Bethlehem six months ago. If you want to talk to me, he stays."

They still appeared uncomfortable, but nodded in agreement. The oldest elder lifted his head. "It's King Erik. Three days ago, he sent an emissary who accused our village of practicing heresy and claimed the king had revoked our rights as citizens of Israel. We could either repent and publicly disown you or face the full might of the King's wrath."

Eliab, upon seeing my expression, quickly added, "Almost everyone in the village balked at the order." I glanced around to check with the other elders; typically when the elders met, they were the only ones allowed to speak. However, no one seemed surprised that Eliab had spoken up. My brother had apparently been promoted to a village elder while I was away. Eliab continued, "The village leaders voted and only one of us thought bowing to Erik's blackmail made sense."

"Moses?" I asked, already knowing the answer. Moses was the elder who had offered to kill me for Erik on the eve of battle for our city. His default solution for every problem was, "Let's throw Niklas under the cart and hope that solves everything."

My brother nodded.

"A few other villagers chose to bow to the king's demands as well," the other older elder continued, "but the rest of us knew we were no longer safe in the city. So, we packed up what we could and decided to search for you."

"Why me?" I asked.

The white-haired elder smiled. "Because you're Niklas."

Awesome. This was yet another problem to be solved from the only dependable rule of my life; the law of unintended, Mesopotamia-sized consequences. This wasn't the first time my broken relationship with the king had brought misery to those I cared about, but the never-ending cycle was getting old. I was beyond weary of watching my family and friends' lives uprooted every time someone decided to make a run at my life.

Beyond that, the elder's statement made it clear they

expected me to have some kind of answer to their problems. They probably would've second-guessed their decision had they realized earlier this week I had been homeless, eking out a living singing bawdy songs to drunk Philistines.

"We have a proposition for you," one of the younger elders said. He paused, darkly eyeing the prince before continuing. "When the other clans in Judah find out what Erik has done, they will rally to our cause. Together, we could rebel against the king."

"You're proposing a coup?" I asked, shocked the elders would even entertain the suggestion.

"Against a mad, unfit ruler who terrorizes his own people," he replied, emboldened.

I rubbed a hand over my face. "The numbers don't even work. Judah is one tribe against twelve. I'm poor at math, but those seem like insurmountable odds to fight against."

To my surprise, it was my father who countered my argument. "Erik has mistreated other territories as well. Other tribes may join us."

"Plus," the younger elder added, "you've prevailed against those kinds of odds before. You're our champion, and while you're family refuses to confirm or deny it, there are rumors you were anointed, same as Erik."

The other elders in the group grunted their affirmations.

Anointings weren't a guarantee from the heavens you would win a fight. It mostly just ensured all kinds of hell rained down on your life. At least that had been my experience thus far. My whole family had been sworn to secrecy when it happened, but Erik, Israel's other 'anointed' had figured it out, which is why he was trying to kill me in the first place. He saw me as competition, and in his rage, information must have started leaking out. Yet this wasn't really about me; these men were eager to fight. Erik had never been the most liked king during the better parts of his reign, and those years had long since passed. Now, he had not only slighted Bethlehem, but he had also driven them from their homes.

This group felt betrayed and they wanted payback.

Humans are strange creatures. Individually, nine times out of ten, two people can find common ground no matter how far the gulf is between them. However, as individuals gather into groups, people become dumb. When the group shifts into a mob, they become rabid. These people were scared, betrayed by the man sworn to defend them. Civil war in Israel made sense to them, yet, even if we could convince enough people to join our cause, the conflict would decimate our country, leaving us vulnerable against any nation looking for weak prey.

I shook my head. "It would destroy our kingdom. I will not go to war against our rightful king." *Even if he truly has gone mad,* I left unsaid.

Turning to the prince for insight, his gaze was distant, unreadable.

War was out of the question, but so was having them return to Bethlehem. Ironically, we were currently stationed at an unoccupied city, but it was still within Israel's territory, meaning Erik could easily march on them. Not to mention the risk of another attack from the Marauders. They couldn't go home and they also couldn't stay here, which left only one option.

"Come with me," I said, more than a little surprised by my own reasoning.

"Come with you where?" my father asked.

"I don't exactly know," I answered honestly. "I'm hunting the Marauders."

Eliab's mouth dropped. "You want to take our families along as you hunt bloodthirsty raiders?"

"I'm not suggesting we send our people into battle," I argued, "but it will keep us on the move, which will make it harder for Erik to attack us."

Damon fingered the hilt of his blade. "It might work. My

father has his own trouble with the Marauders. He won't be able to spare the men to hunt you down."

The group was quiet, until the oldest elder started chuckling. "It's historically poetic really. Our people have lived as nomads several times in the past. We are probably due for another wandering. Unless someone has a better solution, I support the decision."

No one objected. Mind you, no one else seemed to be thrilled with the idea either.

"It's decided then," my father confirmed. "We'll go with Niklas. He will protect us from the Mad King and the raiders."

Yep, it sounded as unlikely aloud as it had in my head.

CHAPTER TEN

I HAD THOUGHT MY DAYS OF SHEEP SLOWING ME DOWN HAD BEEN behind me, but if my flocks of old had moseyed, traveling as an entire village crawled. On top of that, they had brought our livestock, so sheep were still an issue. Tiny, the unnaturally undersized ball of wool that had plagued my time as a shepherd, again scored the cushiest ride by traveling upon my shoulders.

Abiathar had been wrong about his distant relatives still residing in Bethlehem, but my mother was more than happy to care for him and the two Philistines. The one benefit of this arrangement was that I was no longer solely responsible for the well-being of the three orphans. Mind you, it came at the cost of being solely responsible for my entire village, but hey, one problem at a time.

Our first order of business had been figuring out where we should go. Nob didn't serve as a long-term solution to our problems, which had meant we'd needed to move. However, our foreign neighbors wouldn't exactly celebrate the arrival of several hundred refugees either; this had limited our options even further.

In the end, we had decided to head south to Mizpah, a particularly hilly region between Israel and our southern neighbor

Moab. The terrain would provide enough food for our livestock, and hopefully neither kingdom would consider our presence overly threatening. The trip would have taken less than two days by myself, but given our larger group, we had traveled almost a week and had only just reached the border.

My mother, Samara, had been walking next to me silently for about an hour, carrying Eliab's daughter. Having me as her youngest son, the magistrate of mischief himself, had caused her hair to gray early, but she wore it as a badge of honor. "Each gray hair is a measure of my wisdom," she had once told me, "and I'm going to need every bit of it if I'm to make sure you don't get yourself killed."

So far, anyway, her wisdom had paid off.

"You know you're part Moabite," she said suddenly, in an offhand manner.

My face contorted. "What?" International marriages weren't unheard of in Israel, but they certainly weren't the norm either. "Says who?"

"Says your father's genealogy," she responded, smiling. "Your great-grandfather Boaz married a Moabite woman named Ruth. The song 'Kinsmen' was inspired by it. A famine drove some of our people to Moab, and after a rash of unfortunate events, a widowed Moabite woman ended up in Bethlehem. Boaz fell in love with her, and the rest is, well, your family's actual history."

"How have I never heard about this?" I asked, shifting the small lamb's weight on my shoulders.

Mother shrugged. "It's not that your father is ashamed, but it's an interesting time in Israel. He thought it best that the village not know of his foreign ties."

"But I'm not the village," I said.

"No," she agreed, a sly smile on her face, "but you're not exactly known for subtlety, and you do enough to get yourself in trouble as is. We didn't think it prudent to give you another opportunity to sabotage yourself."

I opened my mouth to argue but then closed it. Point taken.

"Hungry?" Mom asked, pulling a small block of cheese from her knapsack.

One of my mom's spiritual gifts was that she always had food on her. I nodded and she passed me the cheese. I quickly began eating it. A diet of nothing but bread in Philistia made me wolf down any other option provided.

"Now then," Mom continued. "Maybe we can find you a nice girl in Moab, being as there's precedent and all."

The cheese went down the wrong tube of my throat and I doubled over coughing, nearly sending Tiny flying from my shoulders.

Once regular breathing became possible again, I shook my head. "We are not having this conversation."

"Sweetie," my mother said, undeterred, "it's about that time for you to marry. All your brothers have found someone."

"There is someone," I asserted.

"Isaiah told me about Michal," Mom answered. "And then your nice friend Damon told me she had married one of Erik's generals."

"I said we're not having this conversation," growing more indignant. "And he's the *son* of a general."

Mother ignored me again. "Even if she wasn't married, though, it wouldn't have worked, Niklas. She's Erik's daughter, and the relationship between you two more than likely won't get better. The tension would eventually poison your relationship with Michal."

"It hasn't with Damon," I countered.

"You have good friends," my mother agreed, "but friends and lovers are different things. Plus, I think you need a woman with a little more fire. I'm not going to be around forever to keep you in check."

"Are we done?" I asked.

She nodded. "Yes, just promise me you'll think on it. We only want the best for you."

I grunted something that could have been interpreted as either agreeing or simply passing gas.

"Thank you," she said and pulled more food from her shawl. "Here, have a honey cake."

I took it and looked around. We had ascended a rather large hill that would serve well as a place to make camp for the night. Plus, it would ensure I would no longer need to continue this conversation.

I called out to my father and he agreed with my assessment. After preparing dinner and setting shifts to keep watch, I climbed into the tent the elders had lent me. A level of solitude was one of the few perks of being the anointed I guess.

Someone moving within my tent woke me up. If it would have been one of my people, they would have called from the outside, meaning whoever was currently occupying it with me almost certainly didn't have my best interest at heart. The movement had come from behind me. My hand was on the dabar beneath my pillow, but given the skill it would take to infiltrate our camp and then get this close to me without anyone noticing showed a scary amount of training. I wasn't entirely sure I could pull the dabar out before they landed an attack.

My best bet was to use the element of surprise once they got closer. I just needed to wait.

The plan shattered when the shadow of a second person moved to the front of me. Two against one changed the math. I needed to act now.

The goal was simple; incapacitating both of the men was the ideal scenario, but even if I could only get my hands on one, I could use him as a hostage against the other. My dabar whipped out from beneath my pillow, and I rotated around and up in one fluid motion. A black mask covered my opponent's face in the shape of a half crescent moon. He carried a thin sword, and in one motion, he both blocked and parried my attack, aiming for my side.

I lunged back out of reach of the blade, knowing behind me

waited my opponent's accomplice. On cue, another crescent masked opponent, this one colored silver rather than black, jumped forward with both of his hands extended. At first he seemed to have no weapon, but then I noticed the glint of light extending from each hand; three blades extending like one foot claws. The silver-masked assassin let loose a series of jabs, and each pushed me further into the corner of the tent.

The first attacker struck again, and I had to suck in my stomach to avoid the strike. I needed more room, so I dove forward into a somersault to the other end of the tent. It gave me only a brief moment to analyze what was happening.

Both opponents were clearly well trained in combat. Against one, my odds of surviving were shaky. Against two, though, and we might as well start sizing me for burial clothes. I opened my mouth to call for help, but the choice was anticipated. The first one threw an empty bucket straight into my gut, knocking the wind out from me and effectively silencing me. Then they both advanced forward.

For the next five seconds, our arms attacked in a fury of motion. With the combined level of their skill, they should have made short work of me, but each seemed more interested in getting the fatal blow rather than working together to achieve victory. If I was correct in assessing their lack of teamwork, it might leave an opening. Gambling my very life on the assumption, I moved forward between the assailants and sagged my shoulders in faux exhaustion. They both saw their opportunity and attacked.

A single moment before the final blow, a hatchet sank into the edge of my sandal. "Stop!" whispered a man harshly.

My opponents froze in place, and I joined them. I turned my head toward the voice and found yet another masked man sitting cross-legged in my tent. His mask was almost a full sphere, save for the small circles cut out for his mouth and his eyes. He had a long gray beard that reached down to his stomach. He held up another hatchet in the air, ready to throw.

"That is enough," he stated. "You both fail."

"What?" yelled the silver-masked one with the blades protruding from his gloves. They turned to my other attacker angrily. "My katar's blades would be painted with his brain if you hadn't interfered."

"Incorrect," cried a female's voice. I actually had to turn to confirm it had come from my other opponent, because the idea that the assailant was a female had never even occurred to me. "My blade would have pierced his spleen, and he'd be bleeding out as we speak!"

The hatchet man shook his head. "Both of you were a moment away from killing each other. Look at your positioning."

My two opponents took inventory of where we stood, and both let out a simultaneous gasp when they saw it. The woman's blade would have missed me and entered her partner, while his strike would have avoided my skull and connected with hers. Had the elderly warrior not intervened, they'd both have been dead.

"Forgive my children's imprudence," the gray-haired man said, opening his hands. "They each seek to take over the family business, and they've been striving to prove their worth. Today they both came up disturbingly short."

"Mebi got in my way," the brother said.

"No, if Ahyim hadn't bumbled around in the first place–"

"I said enough," their father interrupted, and both of them halted their argument. "What is rule number three?"

Both assailants looked toward the ground and mumbled, "Admit when you are beaten."

Satisfied, their father continued. "My name is Shahar, and this is my son Ahyim and my daughter Mebi. You can all back away from each other now."

We were all still inches from each other, frozen and entangled in a fighting stance. The children backed off quickly, and I took up a defensive posture against the tent flap behind me.

"Why are you here?" I asked.

"We're bounty hunters," Shahar answered, stroking his long beard.

I growled. "Did Erik send you to kill me?"

The elder hunter laughed. "I doubt King Erik could afford us. No, we hunt much more dangerous prey. Our employer heard of movement along the Moab border, and we came to investigate if it had any connection to our assignment. When we realized the acclaimed Niklas had made the journey, our client wanted to meet you."

I eyed both of his children. "They just tried to kill me. Death would have made introductions a bit more difficult."

"My employer's exact words were, 'If he can't survive a hastily planned assassination attempt, what is the point in talking to him?'"

"Your boss sounds like a real charmer," I replied curtly.

"You have no idea," Shahar said, "but you will. When we infiltrated your camp, out of respect, we chose not to harm your men. Should you attempt to call for help, that dynamic will change."

"Are you planning on staying?"

He shrugged his shoulders. "I told you, we came because our employer desires to have a conversation. If that conversation goes poorly, I'll give my children another attempt at your life." He turned to the flap of the tent. "It's safe to come in."

"Safe?" asked another female voice from outside my tent. "Not for Niklas. It's definitely not safe for him."

CHAPTER ELEVEN

THE TENT FLAP OPENED, AND THE TALLEST WOMAN I HAD EVER SEEN entered. Seriously, she would tower over Eliab. She lit a torch as she entered, giving me a good look at her. Her neck stretched up like a stork. Straight black hair stretched past her shoulders, and she wore a dark orange tunic. Five bronze medallions hung around her neck, each engraved with a different resource symbol: cattle, wheat, lumber, armaments, and people.

"You're a merchant," I said.

"Oh," she smiled, "he's pretty *and* perceptive. I was warned we'd want to recruit him." She walked up to me and ran a long finger on my chest. "Almost correct," she said, responding to my assumption of who she was. "I am the trade ambassador to the god-king of Egypt himself, Pharaoh Osman. My name is Sethas."

"What do you want?" I asked, reluctant to try anything. Even if I got beyond my unease about using a woman as hostage, there was no guarantee the three warriors wouldn't kill me before I accomplished anything.

Sethas continued to play with the hem of the neckline of my robe as she spoke, saying, "The same as you; to put an end to the Marauders."

My face went blank. "How do you know what I'm after?"

She cackled and gently slapped me on the cheek. "Oh, sweet child, I am not from some backwoods country like Israel or Philistia. Very little happens in the East that we don't find out about. Take, for instance, your audience with King Achish. How is the blind ruler doing these days? I hear he finally cut the puppet strings from his generals. Or how about your friend Damon? Rumors say his relationship with his father is still strained."

I held my tongue, for the first time truly concerned about my safety. Sure, the three bounty hunters were dangerous, but against them, I could at least give myself a fighting chance. Knowledge, however, was a power far more dangerous. Leveraged properly, information was all but undefeatable, and Sethas was clearly flush with it.

The woman tapped my nose. "The Marauders have been disrupting trade for the last three months, inconveniencing His Highness. He sent me to clean up the mess." Her face brightened. "Your arrival with an army of refugees was unexpected though. You have no idea how rare a treat it is for me to be genuinely surprised."

"They're my family," I replied.

"Oh," she said, disappointed. "They're only fleeing from Doeg and his group of fanatics, then." Her absolute apathy for our people's plight was creepy. "That's much less interesting than you creating your own nation."

"My own nation?" I asked, now confused as to what she was even talking about. "What?"

She cackled again. "So naïve; I'll definitely have to collect him."

My voice hardened. "What do you want?" I asked again. "We're obviously not the Marauders, and this little-miss-psycho vibe you're giving off is getting old."

"Oh, I haven't even begun," she said and held my gaze, mad delight dancing in her eyes. She winked and turned away. "But we have time. For now, I need to figure out what to do with you."

Her eyes danced with what I could only assume were all equally disturbing ideas, and I realized that I had a choice to make. Sethas had obviously left the realm of sanity a long time ago, but she also could hold the first piece of actionable intel on the Marauders.

"You should help me," I stated, trying to keep my voice neutral.

"Should I now?" Sethas replied, slithering closer to me. "And why, my dear Giant Slayer, should I do that?"

I put my hand firmly on her shoulder and backed her off me. "Because of what I bring to the table. If your information is as good as you claim, then you must also know about how I was personally trained by Gabril, the leader of the Seraphim?" She nodded, seemingly delighted with my deductions thus far. I continued, "Well then, if your intelligence knows about the existence of the Seraphim and what they were, then you likely also know that while Gabril was a treacherous, heartless, sociopath, he also knew his craft well. You'd be hard pressed to enlist a better asset than someone trained directly by him."

"Doubtful," Ahyim mumbled, as he picked at the spikes on his gloves.

"You may be useful," Sethas agreed, but then shook her head, "but with your hands tied babysitting these refugees, I agree with the bounty hunter's assessment."

A sly smile split my lips. "That's what the Philistines thought at the Battle of Bethlehem. I can show you their corpses if you wish."

She cackled again and clapped her hands in delight. "That fire in in you is so much fun. Fine, I will help you, Niklas. Tomorrow I am set to have an audience with the queen of Moab about the pesky raiding situation. You can join me and we'll see how useful you turn out to be."

I fought against letting out a sigh of relief. The last thing I wanted to do was show fear in front of these four. That lasted for about one second, until Sethas moved to the center of the tent and lay down on my bedroll.

"I'm sorry, what are you doing?!" I asked.

She stretched out like a cat and glanced up at me. "It's dark and I don't wish to trek back to the city. Plus, late as it is, if your people noticed us leaving, it could get unnecessarily messy. Bloody fun, mind you, but messy."

"People would die," interpreted Shahar, still stroking his beard.

Sethas patted the ground. "You're welcome to join me."

My eyes went wide, and for a moment I stood there, stunned. I left without another word, hunting a new spot to sleep in my own bloody camp.

CHAPTER TWELVE

Damon gawked at me. "She spent last night in your tent?"

"I didn't join her," I sniped, grumpy from sleeping on an uneven patch of ground near a dying fire I'd come across in the camp. "Plus, there were three bounty hunters with her. At least I assume they're still around here somewhere."

"Wait," Uri said while his monkey Pali picked at the warrior's fingernails. "We had three trained killers slinking around our camp? The same three bounty hunters who eight hours ago tried to kill you?"

"Yes," I answered, "because we need them. If being around people who have tried to kill me concerns you, you may want to find a new group to travel with, because I'm pretty sure half the population of the region has tried to murder me at this point."

"It does happen a lot," Deborah agreed, and her husband, my brother Isaiah, nodded along. "You should really do something about that."

I refused to dignify her comment with a response. "She also agreed to having Damon attend the meeting with the Moabite queen."

Deborah nodded. "At least you'll have someone to watch your back."

"Exactly," I said. "And if everything goes well, I'll be able to work out an agreement with the queen to let us stay here indefinitely."

"Niklas," Isaiah said warily, "when has 'everything' *ever* gone well for you?"

"It's about odds," I countered. "Eventually something has to break our way."

"Really," cackled Sethas's shrill voice suddenly from behind me, "I've found the universal rule to be: if something can go wrong, it will."

Creepy crawlies made their way up my neck and I turned slowly to face her. "Are you ready?"

"Indeed," she replied, "I slept marvelously. Your scent was absolutely intoxicating." She evaluated our group and her eyes locked onto Damon. "Oh, the prince is a lovely treat indeed. This assignment just keeps getting better and better."

Damon bowed his head in respect. "It's an honor to meet a foreign dignitary." He said it with a straight face. Obviously he hadn't spent enough time with her yet.

"We must be off," Sethas said. "It'll take the better part of the morning to reach the capital, and Her Highness does not tolerate those who waste her time. I'd hate to lose two such treasures so early into our relationship."

The way she said "relationship" sent a fresh wave of the heebie-jeebies through my system, and I flicked my wrist for her to get going, if for no other reason than it stopped her from elaborating on the topic.

After leaving my father in charge of the camp, we left. About half a mile into our journey, Sethas's three bodyguards showed up. They must have been trailing us from a distance.

"Six," said Ahyim nonchalantly, as they fell in line with us.

"Eight," retorted Mebi.

"What?" I replied.

Their father Shahar smiled. "I asked my children to determine how many opportunities to kill you presented themselves before we left your site's perimeter. They're both wrong. Only once did you leave yourself open for a guaranteed kill."

Maybe Deborah had a point. I really did need to find alternative companions.

The rest of the trip was uneventful, save for Sethas's occasional attempt to make me or Damon feel uncomfortable. She had a high success rate.

The walls of Mizpah were easily twice the size of Bethlehem's. Light-brown limestone bricks rose thirty feet into the air. Guards stood atop the fortifications, glaring down at all who entered through the bustling gate.

We passed without incident and headed toward the center of the city. The largest building was the castle, which was topped by a single, dome-shaped parapet.

The street markets were similar to those in Israel, but they offered a much larger selection of goods. Israelites had a pretty restricting diet when it came to what animals we were permitted to eat. Here, though, every kind of meat save for tiger was available for purchase. One vendor even specialized in dog—ugh. The fashion sense was also noticeably different, with much more color in the apparel for both men and women.

The final section of the bazaar was downright depressing; the slave market. Men, women, and even children wore thick iron collars and lined up unevenly along the street. They came from every region, some with skin as white as snow and others as dark as obsidian. Slavers barked the advantages of their "wares" as empty eyes gazed out from the people in bonds. Slaves in Israel were uncommon, and if they existed, it was always as a temporary condition. Every seven years, all slaves, by law, were released and given back all their original property if they had any, so they were treated with a much higher level of respect. It was far from a perfect system, but it seemed outright civil in comparison to the way slaves were handled here.

"Today's offerings look rather poor," Sethas commented, unconcerned to their plight. "And old. Children are such under-valued commodities. They're much easier to mold." She tsked loudly. "In Egypt, vendors wouldn't have the gall to even bring some of these things to market. Look at him," she said, pointing to a large mound of a man, sitting ashen-faced against the wall. "He's the largest of the bunch, but he might as well be an invalid given his insolent posture. Who would ever purchase a slave with such disregard?"

I opened my mouth to tell her to hold her tongue, but as I looked at the man, my eyes grew wide. I knew him.

"Yash?" I said, confused.

Yashobeam had assisted me in rescuing two children years ago, and then showed up again during my brief stint as a general in Israel. He was an undeniable brute with a surprisingly soft heart. Incidentally, both other times I'd encountered him, he had been bound and in chains.

"What happened to you?" I asked.

His sunken eyes came alive as he recognized Damon and me, but when he checked the rest of our party, a low growl escaped his lips. "What is she doing here?" His gaze was fixed on Sethas.

"Brother!" she exclaimed in delight.

The statement didn't connect. "I'm sorry, what?"

Sethas bent down next to Yashobeam, bouncing merrily on her toes. "Sold yourself into slavery again, have you? Father had hoped you were beyond this."

Yashobeam kept growling. "Leave."

My head rotated back and forth between the two for a good ten seconds. "I have no idea what is happening here."

Sethas glanced up at me, rolling her eyes. "My dear half brother has been punishing himself for the better half of a decade. Something about his wife accidently being sold as a slave and then dying put him in an extended mood. We assumed

68

he just needed time to get it out of his system, but this has become a bit much."

"Leave," Yash repeated, his posture growing in aggression.

"I'm of half a mind to buy him myself," she replied, undeterred by his threats and standing back up.

Yashobeam also rose to his feet. "I won't let that happen."

Sethas snickered. "I think you've forgotten how slavery works, little brother. You don't have a choice in the matter."

Even chained, Yashobeam was dangerous. If he was provoked further, who knew what could happen, and right now I needed Sethas alive and well in order to meet with the Moabite queen.

"I'll buy him," I said, inserting myself between the two siblings and making my way to the slaver in charge of Yashobeam. "We don't have time for...whatever family baggage this is," I said shaking my head.

They eyed one another, Sethas amused and Yashobeam seemingly a moment away from launching forward in rage.

Sethas huffed. "Fine, he's your problem. Just don't come complaining to me when he sells himself off again."

The transaction went smoothly. My purse had been resupplied since reconnecting with my family, and I had no stomach for bargaining over the cost of a person. My clear disdain for slavery didn't seem to stop Sethas from commenting that I could have gotten him for half the price I had paid.

Yashobeam kept his eyes on his sister as if he was watching a deadly snake on the verge of striking. The moment he was free, he grabbed Damon and me by the shoulders and dragged us out of earshot from Sethas and the bounty hunters.

"We have to leave," he pleaded. "Now. My sister is one of the most treacherous, evil, conniving people you will ever come across. She has left more pain and havoc in her wake than anyone I have ever met."

"She's a grade-A sociopath," I agreed. "We know, but we need her."

"No, you have no idea what you're up against." Yashobeam said, shaking his head. I had seen Yashobeam literally run into battle against two hundred bloodthirsty Philistines with a smile on his face. Yet his sister left him terrified. "You weren't there when we were growing up. My father, a renowned war hero, refused to be in a room alone with her after she turned ten. She'll stab you in the back the moment she thinks it'd be fun, and she'll laugh in your ear as she plays with the bones of your spine. Nothing she says can be trusted."

The truly scary part was that I could actually picture that scene. Still, we didn't have a choice. I quickly explained to Yashobeam how we had ended up here and the threat the Marauders posed to everyone in the region.

"I don't trust her," I said, "but for now, our goals align. So unless you have some other lead, this is the only play."

"This is a bad idea," Yashobeam responded.

"Agreed," I said. "It just happens to be the best of the bad ideas available. At least now we have you to help watch our backs. That's a positive."

Yashobeam growled and turned to his sister.

She waved merrily back, and for a moment, I saw exactly what he was talking about. It felt like watching a predator eye its next meal.

This might end badly, very badly.

CHAPTER THIRTEEN

WE REACHED THE CASTLE, AND THE SHEER NUMBER OF GUARDS surrounding it gave me pause. In Erik's court, at least a dozen guards remained on duty at one time, but there had to be easily ten times that number stationed outside of the keep. They all tensed as we approached, but Sethas produced a scroll that allowed us to pass without incident.

Inside the castle, the atmosphere immediately changed. Instead of an obscene amount of military force, the palace opened up into an open-roofed garden, and there wasn't a soldier to be seen. In fact, there wasn't a man to be seen. Women of all ages, from toddlers to eighty-year-olds, reclined in the midday sun, reading, singing, or playing games.

A kindly stewardess approached and bowed low before Sethas. "Queen Phelia welcomes you and your guests to her home."

Sethas rolled her eyes. "I'm sure those were the old crone's words."

The servant rose and motioned toward a set of marble benches in the center of the garden. "Please make yourself comfortable. Queen Phelia is finishing an appointment with her husband and requires more time before receiving you."

Our group made our way over to the area and sat down. I did a quick count of our escort and realized we were missing one. "Where's Mebi?" I asked the absent bounty hunter's father.

Shahar's eyes crinkled as if he might have been smiling beneath his moon mask. "Working."

Realizing I wasn't going to learn anything else, I glanced around the garden. For as peaceful as the promenade was, something felt off. There had to be at least one hundred women around us, and while we weren't being shunned, all of them kept their attention elsewhere.

A small cohort of younger women sat twenty feet away from us. I caught one's attention and gave a brief wave.

The girl's face lost all color and she spun her head, pulling closer to her friends.

"This place is weird, right?" I said to Damon and Yashobeam.

The prince nodded slowly as Yashobeam grunted.

"Isn't it lovely?" Sethas asked, inserting herself into our conversation. "Queen Phelia has little patience or trust in men. They call her the Praying Mantis Queen."

"'Praying Mantis?'" Damon asked.

"Female mantises eat their partners after mating," the mad woman said, seemingly delighted by the thought. "Phelia has killed off her last four husbands. I wouldn't be surprised if she's killing off her fifth as we speak. It's a completely matriarchal society. A woman can kill virtually any man without trial."

I again surveyed the women around us. The atmosphere had gone from weird to downright eerie.

Ten minutes later, the servant returned and informed us that the queen was ready for us. The double doors to Phelia's hall were engraved with two huge insects; two of the aforementioned praying mantises, with long arms stretched out like scythes over the entrench. Unlike King Erik, who despised his reputation as the Mad King, the ruler of Moab had fully embraced hers. Owning her mania added a whole new level of terrifying to our host.

We entered the throne room and found Queen Phelia reclining on a raised chaise lounge at the far end of the chamber. She wore long, purple robes that hung to the floor, and her face was painted in makeup, which made it hard to guess her age. She was older, anywhere between fifty and seventy, and she had the longest fingernails I had ever seen. Each stretched out and curved like talons. Around her neck hung enough gold and silver jewelry to fill a small treasure chest.

Sethas led our group forward and then stopped about ten feet from the throne, prostrating herself on her knees. "It is a pleasure, Your Highness."

Phelia watched her for a moment and then burped loud enough that it echoed in the hall. "Oh get up, you conniving shrew. We've known each other too long to be impressed by such trivial actions. You'd as soon see me dead in a ditch as seated on this throne."

"Indeed," Yashobeam's sister answered without taking offense as she rose back to her feet. "But not today. Today we need each other."

"We shall see," Phelia replied. "And what of your tribute for bringing male retainers into my presence?"

Reaching into a cloth pouch at her side, Sethas pulled out an ornate golden necklace with a large morning sun hanging from it. "For my two guards, I offer this piece of jewelry from His Pharaoh's private vault. I took it during one of his dalliances with a young servant. I doubt he will ever know it's missing."

The gift brought a genuine smile to the queen's face. "You naughty girl. It is a fine tribute, indeed. Bring it here." Phelia inspected the golden bobble and hung it around her neck. "And for the rest of your entourage, what do you offer to bring three other males into my presence?"

"Oh, they are not with me," Sethas replied, her eyes growing bright and manic as she turned to me. "They are simply representatives from Israel whose mission aligned with my own. Their tribute is their own."

What-the-huh? A tribute had definitely not been part of the conversation when I had originally discussed the meeting with Sethas. The merchant kept her eyes on me, her gaze blazing with excitement. She knew exactly how far up the creek we were. I turned to Yashobeam who shook his head slowly. His gaze was easy to read though; *I told you so.*

Where in all heaven and earth were we supposed to find a suitable tribute? Judging by the gift Sethas had offered, I doubted the queen would be impressed by the meager money in my possession. If we pooled all the money in Bethlehem, we'd still likely never have enough to even match the value of what Sethas had brought as tribute. Damon had access to that kind wealth, but the prince lived like a hermit. Whatever money he had he gave to the poor. Still, I checked with him in desperate hope he may have something suitable to help, but he jerked his head once in the negative.

"Well," Phelia asked, her eyes narrowing, "what did you bring me?"

I swallowed hard, thinking quickly. If we had no appropriate offering, our options were fight or run. While we hadn't seen any guards, I didn't believe for a second the queen would leave herself undefended, which meant we'd be at the disadvantage of a surprise attack. Beyond that, Sethas would almost certainly unleash her bounty hunters on us. Yashobeam and Damon were both capable fighters, but the odds of survival were slim.

Which meant giving the queen something, *anything*, was our only option, but what? Judging by the amount of jewelry draped around her body, she obviously wasn't lacking in that department. Maybe there was another angle to approach this? Her reputation gave me an idea.

I took several steps forward and descended to my knees as Sethas had done. "Forgive my hesitation," I said, "but we were not made aware of the cost to meet with such esteemed royalty. Still, I can offer a tribute I believe worthy of your time."

Pulling off a simple hemp necklace from my own neck, I

offered it up. "While it pales in comparison to the financial value of the Pharaoh's necklace, it is far rarer. I ripped this tooth out from a living lion with my bare hands. Given your enjoyment of violence, it seems an appropriate gift."

The queen glared skeptically at the tribute, then pulled herself off the chaise and stepped down off the raised dais. Each stride came with a lurch, but when Phelia's outstretched talon-like nails finally grasped the lion's tooth, she grinned. "A rare gift, indeed. It pleases me."

Damon sighed loudly behind me, and from the corner of my eye, I saw Yashobeam's posture relax.

Sethas too sighed, but hers was clearly in disappointment. "So down to business then?" she suggested.

"Agreed," the queen replied, lurching back to her chaise. "What brings the Pharaoh's illustrious trade commander to our small country?"

"The Marauders," Sethas answered. "They have been a scourge across the region long enough. It's past time we took action."

"We?" Phelia asked. "Why should Moab help Egypt with anything? A strong case could be made that what hurts you favors us."

The merchant scoffed. "Our sources are well aware of the losses you've faced by the Marauders. Devastating would be too mild a description. Beyond that, the sheer number of guards outside your walls proves one undeniable fact; you're hiding under the hems of your palace walls like a scared little child."

The eyes of the queen narrowed. "Careful, Sethas. The protection of the Pharaoh only goes so far."

Sethas spread her arms wide. "Speaking the truth always holds certain dangers."

The two women stared down one another, both refusing to back down.

This was going poorly. The nations within our region had been at each other's throats for literally a millennium. Egypt was the powerhouse to the south, with Babylon amassing strength in the north. Countries such as Israel, Philistia, and Moab were not nearly as large, but our location along the major trade routes between them granted us access to stronger resources. We fought against one another regularly, constantly reconquering the border territories between our countries. That type of mistrust was ingrained deep, and it was easy to understand why the queen refused to see past it, even if it would benefit her kingdom.

Yet the only reason why the Marauders posed a threat in the first place was because none of the nations were cooperating. Our combined strength would crush them, but as long as we fought against each other, a crushing blow could never be forged.

Complicating matters, Sethas didn't exactly exude trust. It made sense that Phelia would have serious reservations about partnering with her. *I* had serious reservations, amplified by the fact that only moments ago, she had tried to kill me for the second time in less than twenty-four hours by not informing me that I would need a tribute for the queen.

Yet if someone didn't take the first step in sharing information, we weren't getting anywhere.

"We found a sword," I said, interrupting the standoff between the women.

"What?" Queen Phelia asked, skeptical.

I reached behind me and unsheathed the curved blade Abiathar had discovered. It was the only card I had to play in the discussion, and I had been careful to ensure Sethas didn't discover it until I wanted her to. "This was one of the weapons used by the Marauders. None of our people, including a very experienced blacksmith, have seen anything like it. However, if we can identify where it's from, we may have our first clue about the Marauders' origins."

Both Queen Phelia and Sethas showed interest in the strange blade, and each moved closer to inspect it.

"I've have never seen anything like it," the queen finally said.

"I have," Sethas answered with an unknown look upon her face.

"And?" the queen demanded.

"It's an Egyptian blade," the merchant said, taking a deep breath. For the first time since I'd met her, she actually seemed worried. "The shape of the weapon allows it to dismember a body, but it proved a poor match against longer, straighter blades. These have been out of use for generations."

"Hmph," the queen said. "It sounds like you're trying to escape the blame for a problem Egypt caused."

Sethas shook her head. "I can guarantee you, the Marauders are not Egyptians. We'd know if that many people went missing. Yet the presence of this sword is troubling."

Queen Phelia smiled, but there was no joy in it. "It's starting to look like you lost track of some inventory, Sethas. I wonder what the Pharaoh would think about that?"

Sethas tilted her head. It wasn't fear that covered the merchant's visage, but anger. When she spoke, her voice was hard. "I will discover where the weapons came from."

"And then you will tell us where they went," I finished.

Sethas turned and stared daggers at me. "You do not give me orders, Beggar Prince."

I refused to flinch. "That's how this has to work from now on, because we're not going to solve this problem independently. Unless we'd all rather lose alone, this is the only play we have. We have to work together."

Each woman appeared that they may choke on even entertaining my suggestion, but after a moment, both let out a huff as way of concession. For the first time today, I could finally see a way forward where we all didn't end up killing each other. The fleeting opportunity was broken though when someone started clapping from behind me. I craned my head around to find the source. My chest constricted when I realized who had entered the throne room.

Doeg, King Erik's fanatic counselor, stood clothed in a bright multi-colored tunic, flanked by two white-robed, bald acolytes. He continued clapping as he strode forward, nodding his head. "Niklas, I couldn't agree with you more. We need to work together."

CHAPTER FOURTEEN

HAVE YOU EVER MET SOMEONE AND, EVERY TIME YOU SAW THEIR face, you wanted nothing else but to walk up and punch them in the nose? Doeg had that effect on me, times one thousand.

He had a creepy birthmark covering the right side of his face, almost as if a broken mask had been grafted over his cheek. It went nicely with the creepy bronze, eight-sided star pendant hanging around his neck. He wore a costly, multi-colored robe, but I could only assume he had something equally as creepy underneath the clothes, maybe a tattoo of himself murdering puppies. In short, he was just creepy.

Originally he had served as an Israeli spy, living in the neighboring country of Edom. Yet in all my years at Erik's court, I had never even heard of him. My falling out with the king had a left a spot open in the court, and Doeg had quickly filled the gap.

"Queen Phelia," he began, strolling forward like he actually owned the palace. "It is with the sincerest gratitude that I bring King Erik's favor."

The queen's face contorted. "It takes a laughable level of impudence to arrive unannounced and uninvited in my court."

"Unless one brings the appropriate gifts," Doeg countered. "I believe you will find my token most pleasing."

Phelia looked skeptically at him. "Then where is it?"

Erik's counselor shook his head. "Unfortunately the gift would not fit within your throne room, expansive as it is. Elephants take up a bit too much space."

"An elephant?" the queen exclaimed, eyes wide.

"Indeed," Doeg said. "With a full carriage atop it for riding. I trust it will suffice as tribute."

Queen Phelia licked her lips in wonder. "You have done well. You may stay, though I was under the impression Israel had already sent its emissaries." She nodded toward Damon, Yashobeam, and me.

Doeg glanced at us. Instead of anger, he displayed a look of disregard. "An understandable misunderstanding. While the Prince may one day be the ruler of Israel, he has unfortunately been acting without his father's consent. It's past time for the wandering son to come to heel and return home."

Damon's face remained impassive as a statue at the implied threat, but his hand went to the hilt of his sword. This could get ugly, fast. My dabar was tucked in my belt; I shifted it discreetly to ensure I could unsheathe it at a moment's notice. Yashobeam was without a weapon, but that was less concerning. He most often just found the largest object in reach and swung it around until his enemies were broken and lying on the floor.

Sethas placed her hand gently on top of mine and shook her head. *Not now.*

"Still," Doeg continued, "errant as their party may be, there was truth in Niklas's words. The Marauders pose a threat the likes of which we have not faced in our generation. If we continue to squabble amongst ourselves, we all lose.

"Yet despite the challenges this presents, King Erik sees an opportunity to unite the region. For too long, our own petty conflicts have left us weak against nations who would keep us beneath their boot." The counselor looked directly at Sethas. "Yet if we were able to come beneath one banner of cultural and religious unity, we could create an unrivaled powerhouse.

Even the Egyptians would tremble before our combined might."

"One banner," the queen said, her eyes narrowing, "means one ruler. For fifty years, men have tried to steal my throne. Do you seriously believe I'd give it to some lunatic king and his rabid dogs?"

"We do not propose a single king or a queen," Doeg replied. "Each country will remain under independent rule. However, in dealing with matters of trade and military, a council made up from all six regional rulers would make the decisions."

The queen looked doubtful, but she didn't immediately dismiss the idea out of hand.

"Pretty words," Sethas said, "which will lead to one inevitable conclusion; Moab's subjugation."

"Oh come now," Doeg said, smiling at the merchant. "We all know you offer unreliable counsel at best. This proposal would create competition for Egypt's supremacy, so of course you'd argue to stop it."

Sethas opened her mouth to reply, but Phelia cut her off. "He speaks true, my dear. I don't trust you when our objectives align. When they're opposed, I suspect a dagger in my back."

This was one step away from becoming a complete manure show. Doeg was angling for a power grab far beyond anything I'd feared. He wasn't trying to usurp just one country, but the entire Mesopotamian region. If he succeeded, nowhere would be safe, for me or for the people of Bethlehem.

"Your Highness," I said, bowing low. "I completely understand your reluctance to trust Sethas. If she were the last living person on the continent, I'd move to an island. But I implore you, do not trust Doeg. He's an evil all his own."

Erik's counselor put a hand over his heart. "You flatter me, son of Jesse. I never knew you held me in such extraordinary regard. Still, my logic holds. If we cooperated, we would be a force without equal."

The merchant moved closer to the queen, her posture aggressive. "Do you believe the Pharaoh will allow a consolidation of power to occur without retaliation?"

The queen leaned forward. "Remember where you are, little Egyptian."

"I am twenty feet from your jugular," Sethas replied.

Phelia smiled at the threat. "It would be wisest to not trust any of you." She waved her hand. "Kill them all."

Four independent factions moved at the same time.

Shahar and Ahyim surrounded their merchant, their weapons at the ready.

Damon and Yashobeam moved nearer to me, their eyes I noticed were, like mine, sweeping across the throne room, seeking where the attack would come from.

Queen Phelia had taken cover behind her throne.

Doeg simply shook his head, disappointed. "Really?"

The sudden appearance of shadows above gave us only a momentary idea of where the attack would come from. I looked up to see six archers had been placed in the vaulted rafters of the room, meaning that there would have been an arrow for each of us had Doeg and his acolytes' arrival not screwed up the numbers; his unpredicted appearance had probably saved everyone's lives. The moving shadows, which had alerted me to their presence, had apparently been all of them nocking their arrows, which quickly began raining down on us all.

My group dispersed as two of the bolts descended on us, but both Sethas's and Doeg's crews held their ground. An arrow actually struck Ahyim in the face, or would have if his black mask hadn't deflected the bolt. What kind of material was it made of? His father parried another arrow with the flat side of his hatchet.

Doeg and his creepy gang didn't even attempt to block the attack on their group. Instead, his two goons stepped up, each taking a bolt to the shoulder. They didn't react to the injury, meaning whatever supernatural immunity I had faced against the acolyte in Gath wasn't a one-time incident. I logged that into the "Something I'll Have to Deal with Later" category and focused on the problem at hand.

The second volley of arrows was only a moment away. Yashobeam was the one who saved us. He dove toward a long food table. Instead of hiding beneath it for protection though, he threw it on top of his large back and used it as the world's largest shield. Damon and I hid under it as three more bolts slammed into the other side of the oak wood.

"So do you have a plan to get out of here?" Damon asked me, aiding Yashobeam in holding up our barricade.

I wanted to scream that of course I didn't have a plan for the fighting against Doeg's supernatural maniacs, the entire army Moab, and most likely Sethas and her killers, but instead I shouted. "Working on it!"

Staying here wasn't an option, because no matter how many arrows we deflected or guards we defeated, they could literally throw an entire army at us. Maybe if we could get our hands on the queen, we could use her as a hostage to barter our escape. I chanced a look out from the table. Besides the arrow that flew an inch from my head, I noticed Phelia being escorted out a back door in the throne room by ten armed guards. We could scrap the hostage idea.

Another arrow slammed into the table

Until the archers were dealt with, we weren't going anywhere. Yet the rafters were easily thirty feet up, and without long-range weapons, there was no way we could engage them. I scanned the rest of the ornate throne room but saw nothing we could use. It was just a bunch of stuff. Expensive stuff, mind you, patterned floor rugs and cedar furniture, but it might as well be kindling for the good it did us.

Oh.

"I have an idea," I said, huddling next to my friends, "but you're probably not going to like it."

They both looked at me expectantly.

"We set the throne room on fire."

Damon cocked his head to the side, but we all jolted when the head of an arrow actually made it through the thick oak. "Niklas, we're still *in* the throne room," the prince pointed out.

"To be fair, I did say you wouldn't like it," I argued hurriedly. "If we get a big enough fire going, the smoke will rise and make it near impossible for the archers to see us through the haze. It may give us enough time to figure a way out of here."

"While we're still in the throne room," Yashobeam repeated, more than a little skeptical.

"I'm open to other ideas if you have any?"

They both kept quiet, thinking, but the continued series of barbs blasting our increasingly weakened shield made them nod their head in agreement.

"We have to get one of the torches off the wall," I said, pointing to our right.

Together, we lifted the table and shuffled our way forward like some kind of oversized, six-legged bug skittering across the room. Our movement drew more attention though, and now it seemed like all six archers were focused on us, raining down a barrage of arrows on our splintered barricade.

Damon reached out and grabbed a torch off the wall, lighting the hems of the elaborate curtains before he pulled it back under the table to us. Fire engulfed the cloth as we shuffled onward, repeating the process with every flammable item within our reach.

The good news was that it was working. The bad news was that it was working really well. In less than a minute, flames had spread across the entirety of the room and now licked at our feet. Thick black smoke filled the room and soon the unrelenting series of arrows stopped.

"Now what!?" yelled Yashobeam over the roar of the fire.

This was a legitimate question. Doeg's men had engaged themselves with five guards who had entered the room from the front, each of his goons impersonating a life-size pincushion with arrows sticking out from them. I had no doubt more soldiers would soon reinforce the guards.

Sethas, Shahar, and Ahyim had built a barricade between the archers and the back entrance Phelia had escaped from. The door was shut and presumably locked, but maybe we could break through it.

I threw my head toward them. "Let's join up with them," I shouted.

We chanced not taking our makeshift shield to gain speed and made it to Sethas and her group unharmed.

"What are you doing?" I asked when we reached her. "You can't expect to capture Phelia?"

Sethas huffed. "Of course not, this was always our plan for escape."

"You planned on having to escape?" I said, squinting through the thick smoke that was now burning my eyes.

"I plan on everything," she replied. "A trait you would do well to acquire. We were entering into the den of one of the cruelest rulers in region, even by my standards. Of course I had a fallback plan in place on the off chance negotiations ended poorly."

"Whatever," I said, dismissing her chastisement. "Where do we go?"

"We wait," she answered.

"Wait?" I asked through a thick cough. "Time is kind of fighting against us."

"Indeed, especially since you set the room on fire," she replied, jingling the handle of another door to our left. "The door is locked," she said turning to Shahar.

"Any moment now," Shahar replied, rapping his knuckles on the wood three times.

A knock echoed back, and when the door flung open, Mebi and her silver mask awaited on the other side. "My apologies. Infiltration took two and a half minutes longer than anticipated. This way." She swept her arms down a long hallway.

We locked the door behind us and followed. The path she led us down winded back and forth. Along the way, we found the deceased bodies of five Moabite soldiers.

"What would you have done with their corpses had we not required an escape route?" Damon asked.

Sethas shrugged her shoulders. "I would've likely blamed you for their deaths. Plans within plans."

Of course she would have.

We exited the palace at the back near the stables and saw that Mebi had readied four horses for the escape. It meant riding two per horse, save for Sethas who received her own mount, but it would be faster than walking. We had made it out the west gate by the time the warning bells started ringing throughout the city.

The guards yelled for us to return, but we set off at a gallop. A few arrows sailed past us, one which grazed my calf, searing my leg, but we were free.

A dozen different emotions surged through my bloodstream; betrayal from Sethas, rage at seeing Doeg, and relief from escaping. My mind raced with the consequences of what had happened. Our actions guaranteed that Queen Phelia wouldn't allow the refugees of Bethlehem to remain on her border. We also were no closer to finding and stopping the Marauders, and our one piece of knowledge to trade with had been exhausted

Our options were now more limited than ever, but one choice seemed crystal clear.

We stopped to let the horses rest several miles outside of the city. I walked up to Sethas, and before any of the masked guards could respond, I grabbed her by the shoulder, pulled out my dabar, and brought the weapon to her throat.

"Is there any reason I shouldn't end your life for pulling that stunt?" I asked, heated and ready to end her.

"You still need me," she replied, insane delight once again dancing in her eyes despite my threat. She lowered her voice. "As an aside, I find this side of you most arousing."

My fingers tightened around the handle until they turned

white. I had never killed a woman before, but after betraying us twice, we couldn't afford to give her a chance to attempt a third time. Attacking her meant fighting Shahar and his children, but it was our only play. "This ends here."

"I know where the Marauders will be next," she said, a breath before I executed the deed.

"What?"

Yashobeam moved closer to me. "Do not trust her."

Sethas boldly met my gaze, unconcerned with my knife against her throat. "My brother is correct, of course, you really shouldn't trust me, but I do know where the Marauders will strike next, or at least where they will strike eventually."

I took several controlled breaths. "Explain. Quickly."

"What I didn't have the opportunity to tell Queen Phelia was we've noticed a pattern to their activities. The Marauders are attacking sites that hold select products; specifically metals and engineering plans."

I played through her logic. "No, that wouldn't explain why Nob was attacked. They were a farming community."

Her eyes narrowed. "A farming community that a caravan had been passing through."

Uri's caravan had been at Nob. At least we'd be able to corroborate if she was telling the truth. "And you think you know where they'll strike next?"

She nodded. "There's a merchant in Israel. He has something they will be interested in."

I pressed the blade deeper and broke skin, drips of red appeared on my blade. "What are they after?"

She touched the wound with her finger and then tasted the blood. She shuddered in ecstasy before answering. "No. I will not reveal trade secrets of His Holiness the Pharaoh, but I will tell you where to go. Assuming you remove your knife."

"And you expect me to trust you?" I asked, not even trying to hide my disbelief at her suggestion.

"No. I expect you to trust that I will do what is in the best interest of myself. I am in a perplexing situation. I can neither allow the Marauders to keep disrupting trade, nor can I allow the region to unite under one common banner. Sending you to stop the Marauders helps in both regards, so I'll aid you."

Every fiber in my body told me to finish the job and put an end to this deceitful shrew. It was only a matter of time until she succeeded in actually murdering me, and probably everyone else I loved. Yet she also had a point, and as disturbing as it may be, you can always trust a selfish person to do what's in their best interest.

She had what we needed, and we could serve her interests.

The moment I stepped back, the bounty hunters drew their weapons. Yashobeam and Damon immediately stood at the ready, and we all watched each other, waiting for someone else to make the first move.

"Stand down," Sethas told her people. "Niklas just needed to relieve a bit of frustration after his failure to anticipate my treachery. It was adorable, really."

I disregarded the insult, something I had been doing a lot recently, and glared at her. "So where do we go?"

She pulled out her flask and took a deep drink of wine. When she finished, she bared her red soaked teeth. "His name is Nabal, but fair warning…" Her smile grew. "He's not going to like you very much."

CHAPTER FIFTEEN

"Okay," I said to the group, "this is officially boring."

Night had long settled over the town below us, and I could make out the silhouette of every human head that nodded their agreement around me. Deborah, Uri, Pali the chimpanzee, and Yashobeam had all joined me on this particular reconnaissance mission. Damon had decided to return to the capital in search of new clues. The vast majority of our warriors had stayed with the Bethlehem refugees for protection. For the moment, we camped at the very edge of Israel's empire, hoping Erik's Marauder problem kept his attention elsewhere, but we had very little margin for error.

We had kept a close eye on Carmel, the location Sethas had predicted as the next location the Marauders would launch their attack. Yet two weeks had already gone by, and so far, we hadn't seen even a disgruntled grandmother lash out, let alone any kind of merciless attack. For all we knew, they could be pillaging the lands all around us, while we were stuck here, twiddling our thumbs.

Deborah shifted her weight and tightened her hands on her blacksmith handle. "And you're sure she didn't know exactly when the assault would come?"

"I'm sure Sethas knew all kinds of things," I answered, "but she shared very little with us."

"This is almost certainly a trap set up by my sister," Yashobeam said. "We're probably all going to die."

My head bobbed in frustrated agreement. "Considering the number of times she tried to kill me within our first twenty-four hours of meeting, I'd have to agree, but it's literally the only card we have to play."

Uri arched his black eyebrows. "So you're saying if the only option available is execution, you might as well stick your neck out and make it easier? You realize if we waited, the Marauders would eventually move again, and we could search for clues then?"

"And by 'move again,'" I clarified, "you mean kill countless more innocent bystanders before we could continue our investigation?"

Uri's head bobbled back and forth, weighing my words. "So we wait," he concluded.

"Yep," I sat cross-legged on the ground. "More boring wait—"

"Did you see that?" Deborah asked, pointing to a large circular building at the outskirts of Carmel. Four hooded figures ran toward the back of the building, and they all watched as one of them forced their way in through the back door.

"They're looting the granary," Uri said.

Yashobeam sat down, shaking his shaggy head. "This isn't our fight. From what we've heard about the Marauders, they wouldn't sneak in, they'd simply kill everyone and take what they wanted."

"His logic is sound," Uri said, joining the big man on the ground and taking out a rag and polishing his bow. "They are not the Marauders."

The two men were correct, but it was clearly a group of looters.

"Shady people often hang out with shady people," I reasoned, pulling out my dabar. "They may know something."

Deborah chuckled. "You're just bored."

I shrugged my shoulders. "And I'm bored."

We began descending the hill. Grain was precious even in the best of times, and the last thing families needed was losing their well-earned food to looters.

A smile crept up my face. For the first time in what felt like ages, I could actually start, and finish, something good.

The rest of my party fell in step behind me and we stalked toward the rear entrance of the granary.

"Yash," I said without looking back, "stand just outside of the back door. You'll ensure none of them slip out past us."

He grunted in agreement.

"The rest of you, stay close," I continued. "There won't be much light inside, and the last thing we want is to be picked off one by one."

We reached the side of the back door without anyone inside being alerted. The only light available came from the rear door, which limited our sight, but peeking in, the four hooded figures were spread out along one side, each filling their sacks with grain from large pots on the ground.

We could account for all of them, and we'd be taking them completely by surprise. Easy as stealing. Well, not as easy as stealing for *them*, but whatever. I counted down on my fingers and silently mouthed the words, "Three. Two. One."

Weapons drawn, we rushed inside the circular building. The bandits froze only for a moment before flanking to their right and left, mirroring our own position. They were all indistinguishable, save for the center one, who had silver hair escaping their cloak.

"Good evening, gentlemen," I said, showing a touch of bravado. "It's a bit late for shopping, wouldn't you agree?"

Our counterparts didn't respond. They tilted their heads toward the one with silver hair, who nodded. The concerning part wasn't that he'd nodded, but *where* he'd nodded—not at his compatriots, but behind us.

The realization came a moment too late. The rear door slammed shut, extinguishing all light in the granary. Yashobeam's voice could be heard shouting on the other side, crashing into the door to force it open, but they had must have managed to drop the brace shut.

Where had the fifth bandit come from? We'd had clear sight of four of them entering the building.

Still, that question would have to be answered later, and we could only hope they didn't have anyone else hiding in their party.

"Around me!" I yelled. Deborah and Uri both moved close, creating a three-person circle, each of us facing out.

"Quick math check," Deborah said under her breath. "Without Yash, we're almost outnumbered two-to-one."

"And my arrows are all but useless without visibility," Uri stated.

"But," I countered, "none of them were showing weapons, so there's that."

"Maybe they were hiding them because they knew the lights were about to go out," Deborah replied. "You know, like they had actually thought this through."

Ouch. "Let's stay focused on productive comments. If we get through this, there will be plenty of time to throw me under the cart."

I listened for movement, but the granary had gone silent. My time with the Seraphim had given me substantial lessons in the art of stealth, but our adversaries had clearly received similar training.

Someone whistled a dozen paces ahead of me. My stance shifted sideways in preparation for a frontal attack, but the assault came from behind. A dull thud resounded behind me, and Deborah let out a yelp.

A guttural clicking sound emanated from our right. Again, each of us braced ourselves for the assault, but this time the attack came from the front. A reinforced object struck my side, dropping me to one knee...but not before I managed to get my fingers on the source of the blow. My grip tightened around a surprisingly thin wrist, yet when I went to pull the attacker back, I felt the arm twist unnaturally, and I lost my grip. The assailant was gone. I struggled to piece together what type of weapons they were using.

"This is bad," said Deborah. "How are they managing to strike so accurately?"

"Quiet," said Uri. "Every time we talk, their job becomes easier."

"So you suggest we just wait?" I asked, unconvinced. "We need a plan."

"No," Uri said, a hint of amusement in his voice. "We need an ally who can see in the dark."

What was he talking about? Yashobeam was stuck outside, and there were only three of us here. Plus, none of us could see in the dark.

A woman's voice shrieked in a foreign language to our left. "Aiyo!"

Two breaths later, another female voice erupted from behind us. "Ta yao wo!"

Soon, woman's calls were frantically echoing all around us. A final woman cursed, although this time in a language that I recognized, and the silver-haired looter finally lit a torch in the center of the granary.

Surrounding us, the four other bandits sat crouched, each holding tightly to bloody ankles. Behind one of them, Pali stood in his little yellow vest atop a grain jar. The furry little creature was practically smirking. Each of the bandits had lost their hoods during their struggle with Pali, giving us interesting details about our foes.

First, all five were female and around the same age as myself. Second, the four warriors who had been attacking us in the dark were all identical; quadruplets. Their skin was a shade I had never seen before, a touch lighter tan and smoother than those in our surrounding region, almost yellow. Their silky black hair stretched down to their sides, but it was the way their eyes narrowed that set them apart. They watched our party warily.

The final member of their group, Silver Hair, was nothing short of beautiful. Two elaborate strands of braids framed her dark brown face, with the rest of it stretching down her back. Green, sharp eyes watched us, and she held an iron dagger in her hands.

"They're looters," Silver Hair said, before issuing the order, "Incapacitate them."

"Looters?" I started.

Her companions never let me finish my confusion. All four sisters lunged forward. Each wore a similar set of leather gloves, with exaggerated knuckles. That's what they had been attacking us with. The gloves were sewn with hardened padding on the knuckles, adding substantial attack force to their blows.

Beyond that, I had never been comfortable fighting against women. I had lost all stomach for using my knife against them. Two of them approached me, and the only solution I could think of was to lock one of them into an arm hold, with the idea I'd bluff that I would kill her to get friends to stand down.

The plan lasted for a good half a second after they closed their range. I reached out to grab the one on my right, but she arched back below the strike. In the same fluid motion, she slapped my hand further up, leaving my torso even more exposed. Her partner exploited the opening. I managed to recoil before the blow struck, but she had already unleashed another hit at my chest that did connect. I heard bone splinter at the connection, never a healthy sign, and before I could even retaliate, both sisters danced away.

Their fighting style was unlike anything I'd ever encountered before.

Deborah and Uri weren't faring any better. Deborah had taken a nasty blow to her forehead, and Uri was holding a hand over his thigh.

Outnumbered against an unknown type of enemy left us few choices. If we fought to kill, we might be able to turn the battle around, but there was a dangerous emphasis on *might* in that scenario. This whole encounter felt off, and battle seemed like the poorest option for everyone. The sisters had regrouped and were preparing for their next assault.

"Wait!" I shouted, holding out both of my hands.

The quadruplets didn't heed my request and dashed forward. I raised my blade in defense, still uneasy about using it, but knowing if I didn't fight back at full strength, I might not survive to second-guess myself.

"HOLD!" cried Silver Hair.

This time, all four of the sisters stopped short of engaging us and backed up several paces.

"Why are you here?" their leader asked.

I lowered my hands slowly. "We saw you sneaking into the granary and assumed you were bandits. We were trying to protect the town."

Silver Hair tilted her head. "And why were you watching the granary?"

This answer was a bit trickier, but a shortened version of the truth should serve well enough. "My group is trying to protect Israel from a gang of bandits called the Marauders, and we have information they may attack this region next. My name is Niklas, from Bethlehem, and these are my compatriots, Deborah and Uri."

Uri coughed and motioned toward the monkey.

"And that's Pali," I added.

"We know of the Marauders," Silver Haired replied. "And I know of you, Niklas of Bethlehem, the Philistine Slayer."

In my life it's rare, but occasionally notoriety has its perks. "The one and the same," I said, bowing low. "I've killed thousands of Philistines. These bandits should be easy work."

"All five of us are half Philistine," Silver Hair answered, shooting daggers of disdain from her eyes.

It took a few seconds to get the foot dislodged from my mouth.

Deborah saved me. "He meant no disrespect. We are after only the Marauders." She shook her head disappointedly at me. "This was an unfortunate, or rather, unnecessary mix-up, nothing more."

Silver Hair opened her mouth to respond, but the front of the granary flew open. In its entrance, five men were forcibly restraining Yashobeam.

Another of the townsfolk, one far older and still in his bed wear, rushed in, glancing around until he locked eyes with Silver Hair. "Mistress Abigail, what is happening? We found this brute trying to tear open the front door. Are these bandits?"

Abigail's eyes danced between our group and the men at the front. Finally, a smile covered her face. "There is no danger, Elder Thomas, we simply had a small misunderstanding with these travelers. Our paths crossed in the night, and we each mistook the other for looters."

"But why are you in the granary?" the elder asked, his eyes downcast. He was clearly both unconvinced by her answer but also uneasy about questioning her. His voice dropped quieter. "After three consecutive months of misplaced grain, you know the master's edict about unauthorized entry."

The silver-haired woman nodded once. "I am aware of my husband's order. As I stated, this was only an unfortunate misunderstanding."

The elder shuffled his feet. "Master Nabal's orders state clearly that if anyone is caught in the granary, they be brought to the manor posthaste. Even members of his own family."

Abigail's eyes softened. "Do what you must, Elder Thomas."

The old man bobbed his head uncomfortably. "And what of this brute?" he asked, motioning to Yashobeam, who was still being restrained by the men.

Abigail glanced at me and I signaled he was with us. "An unfortunate misunderstanding," she repeated. "Let him go."

The men released Yashobeam, who pushed himself forward toward the rest of our group.

Mistress Abigail drew close to the four of us and held out her hand. "It seems we're off to meet my husband." Her voice dropped to a whisper as I grasped her hand in a firm shake. "And for that, you may have killed us all."

CHAPTER SIXTEEN

ELDER THOMAS WALKED A DOZEN PACES AHEAD OF ABIGAIL, Yashobeam, Deborah, Uri, with Pali riding on his back, and myself, leading us toward Nabal's manor. Abigail's guards had been given permission to leave since their mistress would speak for them.

Nabal was the merchant who ruled the city. Rumors of the Nabal's temperament were what had stopped us from approaching him directly when we had first arrived in Carmel. Specifics about his disposition were almost impossible to nail down, but everyone from Sethas to the local shepherds had advised us to keep our distance if at all possible. Now we were marching right into the heart of his power.

Abigail kept a confident face, but between her pronouncement that we all may be headed toward our deaths and the still unknown reasons she was trying to steal from her own husband's food stores, counting on her for any kind of protection seemed foolish.

I cleared my throat and kept my voice low. "So your husband has a rather disagreeable reputation."

A hard smile tugged at Abigail's lips. "I can imagine. Trust me when I say it's worse than you've been told."

Fun times. "Any suggestions on how best to approach him?"

"If at all possible," she replied, "avoid the need to."

"Any chance his beautiful wife can temper his anger?" The compliment wasn't any attempt at flirting. More than once, I had a seen a temperamental husband be tamed by an alluring spouse.

The mistress shook her head. "Oh he's not interested in any wife."

"A beautiful man then?" I asked, more than bit uncomfortable of where that answer might lead.

My question inspired genuine laughter from Abigail. "No. Nabal's interests remain firmly on himself. You'll understand soon enough."

"Then why would you two marry?"

Abigail pointed a finger at herself. "One of us did so out of necessity," she said and then pointed to the large domed manor in front of us. "And the other saw it as an opportunity."

Our discussion was cut short when we reached Nabal's home. While not nearly as expansive as Queen Phelia's palace, the manor's workmanship was first class. The square, two-story house was built from thick timber and was accented by decorative limestone. The top of the home was flat, and on it perched a beautiful promenade covered with a lush garden that could be seen from the ground.

Instead of leading us into the manor, Elder Thomas directed us to a set of stairs on the outside of the house. We headed up to the garden. Torches lit the promenade, and their light danced off flowers of every color. In the center of the garden was a gazebo, and in the center of the gazebo reclined Nabal. His chair was not quite a throne, but the lush loveseat came incredibly close. He wore nothing save for a silken, turquoise robe. His tan skin was spotless, unnaturally so, and his hair fell in locks around his shoulders.

Within the gazebo resided two silver rectangular structures, mirrors I realized, and in its ceiling, I caught another image of the reflection of Carmel's master. I audibly gawked at the set up. The man had positioned not one, not two, but three mirrors through which to look upon himself.

The elder led us forward and bowed low before his lord. "Master, you ordered us to bring forth any unauthorized intrud–" he stopped, correcting himself. "Any unauthorized *personnel* within the granary. We discovered Mistress Abigail, her four handmaidens, and these four travelers inside earlier tonight."

Nabal gazed into the left mirror for so long that I began to doubt whether he had heard his servant's report. Finally, Abigail's husband sighed and tore his eyes from the reflection over to us.

"Understood, Thomas," Nabal said. "You may leave. These long nights do not suit you. You look absolutely ghastly, and you know how I abhor the presence of unsightly individuals."

"As you wish," the elder replied, and though he had just been insulted, he clearly appreciated the dismissal, taking his leave in hastened steps.

"As for this incident," Nabal continued, "I'm honestly disappointed, my dearest wife. It's been obvious for months that you've been stealing from my grain stores, but I thought my latest order would have given you pause. Or at the very least, make you slyer about your efforts. Yet here you are, two days later, already caught in the act. It's worse than betrayal. It's predictably boring."

It took obvious effort for Abigail to control her next words. "Husband," she started, almost choking on the word. "You know why we do this. The children–"

"Who bore me worse than your insolence," Nabal said, brushing aside her argument. "We have an agreement. I allow you to indulge in your little hobby farm as long as you refrain from straining any of my resources. And who are these bottom dwellers my men caught with you? I'm certain you can't afford more mouths to feed."

With that rousing assessment, I stepped forward. "Master Nabal, please allow me to introduce myself. My name is Niklas, son of Jesse."

Nabal's attention flared at my name, and he gave a closer inspection. "The Giant Slayer then. I honestly thought you'd be more impressive."

"I get that a lot," I answered, ignoring the insult. We had larger concerns than my ego. "My comrades and I have come because we have intelligence that says Carmel may soon come under attack. A band of bandits called the–"

"The Marauders," Nabal again interrupted. "Yes, yes, I am well aware of their recent activities. Yet I have agreements with every country in the region, which means whatever nation is behind their 'work' will leave me alone."

"What?" I asked.

"Oh come now," Nabal said. "Don't tell me you think these raids are random. Whether they are the work of King Erik, Phelia, Achish, or even the Pharaoh himself, someone clearly has been pulling the strings. Yet as long as whatever side is bankrolling them benefits from my wellbeing, Carmel is more than secure. And I assure you, everyone benefits from my work."

What type of leverage or resource could Nabal have to ensure such protection? "Nabal, if you could tell me–"

"I'm not telling you anything, oh Hero of Bethlehem," the master of Carmel said definitively. "You're lucky I don't string you up for trespassing. The only thing saving you from that fate is I've found dealing with self-appointed heroes often more trouble than they're worth. Leave now, before I reconsider that opinion."

Nabal and I locked eyes and it was clear he was daring me to challenge his rule. Yet this was a battle I couldn't win with my fists. He obviously held disproportionate influence in Carmel, and we had no leverage to get him to come to terms. Sure, we could attempt to forcibly remove him from power, but on what authority? Outside of being a next level jerk, he'd done nothing wrong.

I bowed low. "As you say, Master Nabal."

Clearly finished with us, he waved his hand. "Leave, all of you." The five of us turned to retreat, when he spoke one last time. "And my dearest Abigail, let me make this clear, because apparently our unspoken agreement has not been fully understood. If you pillage my food stores again, I will cull every single child. Do I make myself clear?"

Abigail's shoulder's tensed at the threat. "Yes, my lord," she said softly.

"Now leave," Nabal repeated. I didn't even have to turn around to know he had returned to admiring himself in the mirror.

The moment we were out of earshot, I turned to Abigail. "What was that? What children?"

"It's nothing," Abigail answered, walking forward.

I stepped in front of her. "It's clearly not 'nothing.' What does he have on you?"

The hard gaze she leveled at me caused me to step back. "Leave Carmel now. You have already caused enough damage."

"But the Mar–"

"Now," she repeated. "Or I'll turn you in to the city guards myself." At the bottom of the stairs she turned on her heel and entered the manor.

I raised my hand call her back, but Deborah caught it. "Not now," she said softly.

Anger swelled in my chest as I recalled the encounter. Nabal was risking the ruin of the entire city, but why? And what did he have on her and these unknown children? I felt my hand reach down to my dabar. I could stomach all kinds of injustice, but children were off limits.

"We need answers before we do anything else," Uri reasoned.

I pushed through my rage and calmed my thoughts. He was

correct. Before we could act, we needed to figure out all the pieces on the board. And after meeting the insolent "Master of Carmel," I was even more determined to unveil them than before.

CHAPTER SEVENTEEN

DEEP SHADOWS COVERED THE ALLEY WHERE I SAT PERCHED ON A ledge, tapestries drying on a clothesline in front of me. Both Nabal and Abigail had made it quite clear that if they discovered our presence in Carmel again, we'd be treated as intruders. So the key became ensuring that they never discovered our presence. As luck would have it, we had a trained, former Seraphim assassin to handle such a task.

For the last week, I had been secretly infiltrating the city, and piece by piece, the lay of the land was becoming clear. On day one, I had discovered the mystery behind the children Nabal had threatened.

On the far side of town, Carmel had a complex that I had only witnessed one other time; an orphanage. Orphans were common enough in our region, but they were always either adopted by a close relative or bought into servitude by another family, or left to fend for themselves on the streets, like Tiger and Char. The idea of caring for orphans as one large group seemed like a nice idea, until you realized the type of resource engine needed to sustain it. Matthias had been the only other person I'd ever met with the compassion to maintain one.

Parents provided for their families through the land they

worked, the herds they raised, or the trades they plied. Abigail's orphanage had none of those things, and with over three dozen mouths to feed, it was no wonder she and her handmaidens had been stealing grain. With that many children, feeding them became a never-ending struggle.

Yet for all their need, the overall cheer of their collective impressed me. Most of the children were between the ages of a toddler and ten years old, though the few young teenagers of their group provided excellent care to their younger counterparts. They regularly played games of tag and hide-and-seek in the streets, and save for those directly serving Abigail's husband Nabal, the rest of the village treated them with gentle kindness.

Abigail's four servants helped run the day-to-day operations. The townspeople called them the Daughters of Ira as, ostensibly, they were children from a Philistine mother, Ira, and a merchant from the far, Far East. Apparently they were talking the end of the world "Far East." Their parents had both died on a trip through the Mesopotamian region, and Abigail had taken them in. None of them spoke our language very well, choosing to communicate to the children through gestures or the occasional well-placed, motherly swat to a head. After facing them in battle, calling them handmaidens still felt like a massive misrepresentation, but with the orphans they fit the role well enough.

However, the winner of the most transformed personality definitively went to Abigail. Every time she engaged a child, it was like watching a flower bloom. At the moment, she was crouched next to a crying young girl who had been made fun of by some of the other children. Abigail leaned down next to the girl and whispered something into her ear and then draped her braided silver hair over the child's head. The girl giggled with delight and untangled herself from the locks before running off to her rejoin her friends.

For a short moment, a soft smile played across Abigail's lips, but once she was alone, her eyes soon narrowed, and what I recognized as a familiar look of worry covered her face. It was a scene I'd seen replayed almost a hundred times over the last few days. With the orphans, she was a ray of warm sunlight, but left alone or in discussion with her maidens, her voice lost its music to the realities of their situation.

If it were only the funds of maintaining the orphanage that concerned her, that would be one thing, but the longer I watched her, the more I realized Nabal must have a much larger sword hanging over her. Five days of watching Abigail from the shadows made it clear that her husband and his men had no intention of leaving her and the children alone.

I know, I know, insert stalking joke here. Yes, I said I was watching her from the shadows, but stop it. It's not stalking. It's called…reconnaissance. I can't help it if this particular mission required me to keep tabs on an attractive woman. Anyway, there had to be some way to assist the children. We just needed to know what specific plan Nabal had for them.

Abigail shook her head and moved to the backside of the orphanage. I checked the sun for the time and realized that she intended to tackle her most frustrating part of the day—scaring off the rats from their food shed. It was a battle of wills I had witnessed every day. Most homes kept their kitchens inside their main buildings, but for what I could only assume were space limitations, the orphanage did their food preparation in a shed on the outside of the building. It worked as far as space, but since it resided outside, it was far more likely to be infiltrated by insects and rodents.

Before preparing every meal, Abigail ventured into the darkened room with a broom and her sheer force of will, extracting the vermin from the makeshift kitchen. I ducked out from my recon spot, not wanting to miss one of my favorite parts of the day. When we'd first met, the silver-haired mistress of Carmel had squared off against some of my best warriors without even batting an eye, but she shrieked something fierce whenever a rat jumped out at her. Every. Single. Time. It was the joke that only got funnier to me on every return visit.

Fine. I'm a horrible person.

Ducking between buildings, I made it to the far side of the town and crept a bit closer to their kitchen shed. I got there right as I saw Abigail taking a deep breath, fortifying herself against the oncoming onslaught of rodent-fueled terror. She moved into the shed and I was greeted by the ever-humorous shriek.

What was significantly less funny, though, were the two goons I saw walking toward her. I had seen these particular men around town, playing the role of Nabal's enforcers. They terrorized traders, village elders, and any number of peaceful citizens, all in Nabal's effort to keep Carmel under his thumb. And right now they were headed straight for Abigail. If they were approaching her in public, that would be one thing, but here they were seeking her when she was alone and there would be no witnesses.

Yeah, this wasn't happening. I left the shadows and stalked forward, not even attempting to sneak up on them. There was no need. I'd seen them operate. The fight would be short.

"Hey boys," I yelled, brazenly waving my hand. "What are you two ugly fellows up to this afternoon?"

Goon One, the smaller of the duo, looked to his larger counterpart for assistance. It had obviously been a long time since they had been openly challenged.

Goon Two's gaze hardened. "Who are you?"

"Oh, just a well-intentioned, albeit nosey, traveler," I replied, closing the distance between us. "Seems like it'd be best for you two to halt whatever ill-conceived havoc you were about to embark on."

This time both thugs traded confused glances. Maybe I'd used too large of words. "Let's try this," I said, the levity disappearing from my voice. "Leave or get hurt."

This time the threat was understood. Cruel smiles covered their faces, and in unison, they bum-rushed me.

"Silly boys," I said, quickly side-stepping out of the grasp of Goon Number One.

He slipped by me, but not before I kicked my ankle out, tripping him up and sending him tumbling to the ground. His partner roared in defiance and rushed at me again. This was too easy. This time, I ducked beneath his arms, and before he had even realized what had happened, the edge of my dabar was pressed firmly against his throat.

"Leave or get hurt," I repeated, locking eyes with him.

His pupils grew large as he raised his hands in defeat.

I pushed him away and playfully winked. "The next time I see you at the orphanage, I'll finish what I started."

Goon Number Two collected Goon Number One and together they retreated back to the city.

Turning around, I found Abigail standing in the doorframe of the shed. I grinned like a pleased little boy, surprised by how proud I was for playing hero in front of her. She tilted her head and walked up to me, stopping just in front of my chin. An unknown look danced in her eyes.

And then she slapped me.

There are different types of slaps. There's the kind you give on the back of a friend who accomplished something worthy of praise. There's the swat from a mother keeping your hand off the desserts. And then there's the type meant for equal amounts of pain and rebuke. Her assault was firmly in the last category, and I'm pretty sure every person within a one-hundred-yard radius had heard it. My cheek burned hot from the sting.

Abigail took a deep breath. "You incompetent, unimaginative, idiot! Do you have any idea what you just did?"

I brought my hand up to my still raw face, my eyes darting between her and the disappearing thugs. "I put two brain-challenged goons in their place, stopping them before they roughed you up."

"Is that what you think just happened?" she asked, anger blazing in her eyes. "Because what I just witnessed was an egotistical, wannabe hero provoking my husband's hired guards.

When they come back, and they will come back, it's going to be five times worse."

"Then I'll stop them again," I answered. "They have no right to treat you or the children like this."

She shook her head and rubbed her eyes. "I don't know if you're the naivest man I've ever met or if it's simply that you're *that* detached from reality. My husband has every right to do whatever he wants."

My nose scrunched up. "Then let me help. Kids shouldn't be treated like this."

My comment caused her to bark out a harsh laugh. "You? Care about the orphans? Ha!" Her eyes narrowed. "We do not need *your* help."

Now it was my turn to be taken aback. "What is your problem with me? I can appreciate your concern for the children, but whatever this is" —I flicked my finger between her and me —"it has nothing to do with the children."

Abigail bowed her head. "You *are* that naive, aren't you?" She looked up and pointed to the orphanage. "Where do you think the orphans came from?"

"What are you talking about?" She continued to shoot me a silencing glare, so I relented and asked the question. "Fine, where did they come from?"

Her voice began to steadily rise. "Elah. Ekron. Gath. Bethlehem"

The names all had one common theme. "I fought battles there."

She shook her head. "No, you *won* battles there. And you left a trail of bodies in your wake, bodies that were fathers, and more than a few who were single parents. What did you think happened to their children when they had nowhere else to go?"

"They're Philistines?" I asked.

"Most of them," Abigail answered. "Your wars killed a few Israelites too." She moved close, sneering. "That's the problem with you heroes. I don't care if you're named Goliath, Erik, or

Niklas; once you've achieved your glory on the battlefield, you disappear, never to be troubled by the chaos left in the aftermath." A hard smile appeared on her face. "This is your legacy, Niklas, oh Hero of Bethlehem. I hope you're proud." She turned on her heel and left me standing there.

My eyes found their way to the suffering orphanage, and it slammed into me. This was all my fault.

CHAPTER EIGHTEEN

"Obviously," said Deborah, slamming her hammer into the iron spear shaft. Red, hot sparks flew into the air before she used a pair of tongs to inspect her work.

"Agreed," said Yashobeam, leaning leisurely against a tree.

"*You* knew?" I asked, skeptically scrunching my face. Yashobeam had many strengths, but a high level of deduction was not one of them.

"It was obvious," Yashobeam answered, echoing Deborah. "*If* you were capable of looking beyond silver hair's pretty face and thinking it through. How many people have died in the battles you've taken part of? Hundreds? Thousands? It was inevitable some would leave children with nowhere else to go. They're fortunate your little crush took them in."

"She's not my crush," I muttered and sat down cross-legged on the ground, still coming to terms with my responsibility for the orphans. So much of my self-worth came from my victories in battle. I'd seen dead soldiers before, but I had separated the soldier from the civilians they were connected to. Abigail's revelation had torn that possibility from me, and I had finally come face to face with the costs of my glory.

Oddly, what tormented me the worst were the words of my

fallen mentor. The first time we'd met, he had been orchestrating a squadron of Seraphim to exterminate an entire Philistine village. I'd challenged him on the order, arguing that there was no need to kill the women and children, and he'd warned me that war orphans turned into monsters, growing up to despise those who'd killed their parents.

Half a mile away, there existed an entire compound of that exact category of orphan, all with equal reason to hate me. I glanced up at the sky. Actually, all with equal reason to hate us. I'd all but been divinely appointed to go to war. Didn't He care what happened to the children?

I rubbed tired hands over my face. I had long since come to terms with the injustices in the world—I had even come to expect them—but it was something entirely different realizing that I'd had a part in creating them. The real question was what should I do next?

Abigail had good reasons to want me gone. Not only had I helped create this mess, but my continued presence would only provoke Nabal to further action against the orphanage. If I left, all of her other problems would still be present, but at least I wouldn't be adding something new to the heap of crap she was dealing with.

Removing Nabal was all but impossible. Property laws were strict in our region and skewed heavily in favor of the husband. Anything Abigail owned technically belonged to Nabal, meaning short of storming the city and taking over by force, there was no recourse. Abigail had adopted the children. Now he could do whatever he wanted with them. He could starve them, ignore them, or even sell them.

Beyond all that fun, the Marauders still posed a real threat to the region. I had yet to discover what leverage Nabal had acquired to remain so confident in his protection, but Sethas wouldn't have sent me here had she shared his confidence. Fury like they couldn't imagine was swirling around the village, Abigail, and the orphanage.

If I truly did have a hand in creating the circumstances of these orphans, I refused to leave them unprotected. And that, of course, didn't even take into account the several hundred Bethlehem refugees currently camped outside of the city. So far, our herds were being sustained on roaming pasture, but we needed a more permanent solution, if for no other reason than keeping a defensible position when the Marauders launched their attack. Our people had no official standing to remain here, meaning technically we could be driven off at a moment's notice.

"We need to find some legal way to remain in the region," I said, mulling over the problem.

"Why not ask to celebrate the Feast of Booths with Carmel?" my mother's voice suggested from behind me. She walked up carrying a small tray of honeyed bread for our group. "If we invoked guest rites, they'd be obligated to let us stay."

My eyebrows arched. With everything else going on, I'd lost track of where we were on the calendar. The Feast of Booths was the yearly harvest festival in Israel. It lasted seven days, consisting of an oddly paired mixture of religious and agricultural rituals, and ended with a massive feast.

"You're suggesting we invite ourselves over for dinner?" I said.

My mom shrugged. "Why not? It's tradition for a village to permit traveling Israelites to participate during festivals. Typically we'd only be talking about a handful of sojourners, but there's no maximum cap on hospitality."

I opened and closed my mouth multiple times. Each time rejecting my own counter argument on why it was a bad idea. Our nation took these ceremonies incredibly seriously because we found them directly tied to our relationship with God. If we invoked a guest rite, even Nabal would be hard pressed to reject us. It wasn't a long-term solution, but it at least served as a significant stopgap.

I jumped up and kissed my mother as the idea blossomed in my mind. "Mom, you're absolutely brilliant."

"On occasion," my mother replied. "You'd do well to remember it."

Six days later, a smile the size of the crescent moon rested on my face. I reclined next to a large bonfire in the middle of the town, sipping on a large glass of wine. Rarely do my plans work out so marvelously. Maybe this one was turning out okay because it was originally my mom's idea, or maybe God decided to take a more active role in the story. Regardless, for the first time in months, I had slept in the same bed for more than two consecutive nights.

By far, the most rewarding part came when our elders arrived in Carmel, formally asking to celebrate the Festival of Booths. Nabal's perfect face went into a series of never-ending twitches, contorting into dozens of less than perfect grimaces as he realized he had no standing to remove us. Since the start of the celebration, every time our eyes met, the ugly series of looks resurfaced. He hated me, but he had no opportunity to follow through on it.

On top of that, we were as safe as we had been in months. While the city didn't have fortifications, it had amazing sight lines in every direction around it. We had posted sentries around the perimeter, meaning we had ample warning if the Marauders made an attempt on the city.

Even Abigail had started to warm up to me, or at least to our group. At the moment, she and Deborah were chatting on the other side of the fire.

"Niklas!" exclaimed a youthful voice from behind me.

Turning, I found Abiathar, Char, and Tiger walking up. With each passing day, the haunted look in Abithar's face lessened, and he had found purpose by taking the Philistine children under his wing.

"How goes the celebration?" I asked.

"Great," replied Char, a fresh layer of dirt on his cheeks. My mother washed his face at least five times a day, but every time, within ten minutes, a new coat of grime would already be painted on his cheeks. At one point, you just had to be impressed and consider it a lost battle.

"I have a question for you," the young Philistine boy said. "Abi keeps telling us that the Festival of Booths is about the harvest, but in Gath we learned that the Israelites eat their first-born during celebrations. Which is right?"

"Wow," I said, chuckling, suddenly remembering him asking something similar when we'd traveled from Gath to Nob. He must have been secretly afraid of the veracity of this rumor to ask about it twice. "Eating people. I hadn't heard that one during my time in Philistia. I'd trust Abiathar; his father used to run the festival in Nob."

At the mention of his deceased father, the Matthias son grimaced but then quickly shook his head, and when he looked up, he'd forced himself to smile. "This was Dad's favorite festival. He said it had the best food, but there were definitely no babies on the menu."

Tiger flicked her little brother's ear in playful admonishment.

"Have you tried our sugar bread?"

All four of us turned to locate the source of the voice and found Abigail holding a five-year-old girl in her arms. "We have some of the best sugar bread in the country," she said. The girl in her arms nodded her agreement enthusiastically as Abi, Char, and Tiger's eyes went wide at the thought.

"Cindi," Abigail said to the girl she carried, "would you take these three over to Myra to get them a loaf of the bread? Tell her I said it was fine and you can have a second helping too."

Cindi squealed at the idea, scrambling down to the ground. "This way," she shouted and ran off into the village, correctly assuming my trio would follow after her.

"Thank you for that," I said, rising to my feet. "None of them have had the easiest go of it."

Abigail nodded once. "Deborah told me of their story and how you've chosen to look after them. It's a kind thing."

I raised my eyebrows. "High praise for, how did you put it, an 'incompetent, unimaginative idiot.'"

Shrugging her shoulders, she kept her smile up. "I stand by my words, but even the most hopeless of brutes occasionally do something worthwhile."

"I'll take what I can get then," I said, glancing around the festival. "This is almost kind of fun."

"Agreed," Abigail echoed. "A temporary reprieve from a dark time."

Taking a deep drink from my wine cup, I let myself enjoy the moment, but soon lingering threats imposed on the levity. "The children are not safe here," I said somberly.

"They're orphans," Abigail replied. "They're not safe anywhere. The best we can hope for is minimizing the pain."

I sighed. "You haven't seen what the Marauders are capable of, the type of devastation they can unleash."

"My dear husband believes they don't pose a threat."

"He hasn't seen them either."

"True," Abigail admitted, "but while he is many things, he is not stupid. If he has reason to believe they won't attack, then they won't attack. He wouldn't allow any of his resources to be at risk."

"Which is how he looks at the orphans," I said, "as resources. He'll leverage them for profit the first chance he gets."

"Agreed," Abigail repeated. "But as I told you before, the best we can hope for is minimizing the pain. He won't sell them until they're older and he can get a better price. I can at least buy them time."

"Seems like there should be a better option," I mused. "Why did you marry him in the first place?"

"I told you that too," she said, her demeanor growing uncomfortable. "Necessity. When my father passed, as long as I remained unmarried, I had no legal right to our estate. Nabal had enough resources that he didn't need to marry me, but he gained my family's estate from the union. I agreed on the condition of a certain level of autonomy running the orphanage. It's not perfect, but it gets us through today."

"But what happens when tomorrow comes?" I asked, looking into my now empty cup. "What happens when a horde of bandits and killers descend or Nabal decides to sell off his 'investment?'"

She shrugged. "I don't know. All I can handle is today. Tomorrow's problems will be handled tomorrow—"

Her admission was cut off by a resounding horn toward the edge of town. A trio of loud blasts echoed through the air. It was one of the sentries, and three blasts meant an attack.

We might not see tomorrow. The Marauders had come today.

CHAPTER NINETEEN

MY MIND RACED AS I TRIED TO COLLECT AS MUCH DATA AS POSSIBLE. The early barrage of facts was discouraging.

First, the horn had been sounded from the edge of town, not in the countryside, meaning the Marauders had either found a way around our sentries or had killed them before they had been able to get a warning off. Either way, it meant we had seconds, not minutes, before the city deteriorated into the chaos of combat.

The people in the village were all reacting differently. The Bethlehem refugees had a plan ready of where to go if the Marauders attacked. Parents were already gathering their children, and previously celebrating guards rushed back to our makeshift camp for weapons. We had no permanent structures to protect us, but we were organized, which kept the panic to a minimum and made it possible to shore up a defensible position.

The villagers of Carmel, however, had descended into lackadaisical confusion. While we had worked to spread the knowledge of a potential Marauder attack, few had taken our warnings seriously. They understood the horn was cause for concern, but almost all of them remained out in the open, vulnerable, and more curious than scared.

"Your people are going to be slaughtered if they don't get inside," I shouted to Abigail.

Her eyes grew large. "The orphans are in danger," she said as she sprinted off toward the orphanage.

Part of me wanted to follow after her and help secure the children, but I pushed back against that idea and headed toward the source of the horn. If we could manage to stop the Marauders before they entered the city, she wouldn't need my help in the first place.

Yashobeam and Uri found me among the chaos. Both were armed, Uri with his bow and Yashobeam with the largest, bluntest object he could find. This time, he'd chosen a thick, wooden beam that looked like it belonged in a load-bearing wall.

Uri pulled out an arrow and nocked it. "Deborah, Isaiah, and your father are organizing the Bethlehem refugees. Half of the soldiers are defending your people. The other half is headed for the Marauders."

"Let's join them then," I said eagerly. After over a month of chasing them, I was more than ready to finally see who we were up against. Yashobeam grunted, and as usual, a huge grin covered his face as we headed for battle. The man lived for this stuff.

We reached the outskirts of the city, and I immediately began to rethink my desire to see the Marauders up close. At least five dozen bandits were charging at us, now only one hundred paces away. The number of bandits wasn't the terrifying part though, because even with only half the soldiers from the battle of Bethlehem, we more than matched their numbers. My caution also didn't stem from the fact that each of the warriors wore dark, bat-like masks.

No, the fact causing me to nearly wet myself came from the realization that the enemy soldiers were armored to the hilt, and I mean that literally. Even the handles of their weapons had cross guards. They wore no single uniform armor, but they each were equipped with some form of metal protection.

Armored combatants complicated matters exponentially. Complicated like, oh dear sweet merciful God, we're all going to die horribly. Fighting general run-of-the-mill bandits at worse would leave us at even odds of victory. Among the refugees, we had dozens of former warriors from my military time with the Woolen Warriors, and our teamwork alone would have given us a distinct advantage.

However, none of us had armor. In fact, in all my years of fighting, I'd only seen a fully armored soldier a handful of times. The advantage it gave a warrior could not be understated, but it was also incredibly costly. Only the wealthiest kings or generals could afford that level of ultimate protection. Fifty such men were moments from descending upon us. We were hopelessly, borderline hilariously, unprepared for this kind of fight.

This also explained how the Marauders were having such a devastating effect on the region. Regional leaders wouldn't be expecting to engage against such a powerfully equipped force. The Marauders could engage an enemy five times their size and still expect to win handily.

I idly wondered how they had managed to acquire such costly equipment, but given that the answer wouldn't save a single life at the moment, I filed that inquiry away for future Niklas to solve, assuming future Niklas's body wasn't torn into pieces and scattered across the battlefield over the next fifteen minutes.

Yashobeam summed up our situation aptly. "Yeah, we're screwed."

Uri's eyes were large globes and his mouth hung open. "We're going to die," he concluded softly.

He was probably right, but as much as I agreed with him, if we lost hope, it only guaranteed the outcome.

"Oh come on, now," I chided Uri. "Don't tell me you're giving up on your amazing fiancée just yet. I've faced a literal giant who was armored just like these thugs, and he died just like the rest of us."

The mention of his fiancée did the trick, and the archer's posture straightened. "Fair enough."

We ran to the front of our troops, all of which realized the overwhelming odds bearing down on them. The same terror filling Uri and I threatened to overwhelm them. They needed orders. Orders that didn't guarantee they'd all get killed.

"Fall back to the encampment and regroup with our other soldiers!" I shouted. "Fight them out in open, and use our number advantage to isolate them."

Our soldiers appreciated that my plan temporarily gave them a reprieve from fighting the enemy, but even with our forces combined, this fight was already a lost cause. We could only delay them a bit longer.

However, as the group of raiders reached the town, the odds broke our way. Their horde split up into two groups, one headed toward the center of Carmel, and the other to edge of the city. If their forces remained divided, we'd at least have a chance to even the playing field. The first group bore down on us, while the other was headed toward...I swallowed hard. The other group was heading straight to orphanage.

"Yash," I yelled. "Tell Isaiah to form the largest party he can from the Woolen Warriors and attack in smaller engagements. Use our numbers to isolate and pick them off one at a time." Yashobeam grunted his acknowledgement and trekked off.

The plan was solid, if only because it left our men with a fighting chance to survive. It also left the orphans completely at the mercy of the rest of the Marauders.

I looked up at the roofs of the town. "Uri, get up there and use your bow to assist our men."

The dark-skinned man shook his head. "Sorry, not happening."

"What? Why the hell not?!"

"Because you're about to run off to try and protect the orphanage against two dozen armored goons all by yourself. You're going to need help. Also, I left Pali playing with the children earlier, so at the very least, I need to try to get to him, and at the most – you need me."

I wanted to tell him it was a suicide mission and that I didn't need his blood on my hands, but the argument would waste precious time. His assistance would be of use, even if it ultimately would be futile. We rushed through the city, using the straight path to our destination to gain a few extra seconds on the horde as my mind struggled to figure out a plan that would stop the bandits from getting to the children.

Try as I might, no grand idea came to mind.

Reaching the orphanage, the quadruplets were herding the children into the building. The decision was a double-edged sword. Outrunning the horde was impossible, and the walls would give them a few extra moments of protection. It left them trapped though, and it would only be a matter of time before the bandits breached the door. Yet their idea was better than nothing, and maybe we could use the bottleneck at the door to limit their number advantage.

Abigail came sprinting up with the young girl Cindi in her arms. Abiathar, Tiger, and Char trailed in her wake.

"Get inside," she yelled, closing the distance between us.

"The doors won't hold off the attack," I replied, shaking my head. "If Uri and I wait–"

She harshly grabbed my shoulder and propelled me toward the orphanage. "Get inside!" she repeated. "We have a plan for this!"

"What!?" I protested, while letting myself be forced inside the building.

Abigail ducked in after Uri and I. "Put down the crossbeam to lock the door!"

We found the large wooden beam on the ground, lodged it in place, and looked around the orphanage. The building was designed as one large open space, almost like a barn. Three dozen children huddled together, all of them clearly terrified, but they were surrounded by the Daughters of Ira. Donning their padded battle gloves and wielding a number of craftsmen tools —a hammer, a saw, and the like—they stood at the ready for the oncoming battle. The second story of the building was an open loft, covered by an A-frame roof.

"What's the plan?" I asked, not seeing any kind of advantage besides an all too frail door separating us from the rampaging horde.

Lowering Cindi to the ground, Abigail moved to the center of the living space, first lifting up a worn out rug, and then removing a wide wooden plank. Beneath it was a tunnel.

She smiled faintly. "We built it in case my husband ever came intending to take the children. It leads to an opening a hundred paces outside of town." Abigail swallowed hard suddenly, having realized the same fact I had. The tunnel only worked if the Marauders could be stalled long enough for the children to gain some distance. Someone needed to stay behind.

One of the quadruplets moved up, placing her hands on Abigail's shoulder. "Go with children," she said through a broken accent. "We stay and hold off enemy."

"No," I said. "You wouldn't delay them near enough. We have to stop them from being able to follow."

"So what are you suggesting?" Abigail demanded. "Giving up?"

I looked up, a very bad idea forming in my head. "No. I'm just saying all of you should go. Now I have a plan."

A hard force slammed into the other side of the door, causing all of us to jump from fright. Immediately, subsequent forces struck the door. It wouldn't be long.

Abigail took a deep breath. "But–"

I held up my hand. "Please, trust me. Take Abiathar, Tiger, and Char with you and keep them safe."

Conflict raged in her eyes, but as the door clearly was on the brink of being smashed open, she relented. "Get them in the tunnel," she called to her handmaidens. "Now!"

The quadruplets leapt into action, one jumping in first with a torch, while the others lowered the children into the opening. Before the last one descended, I asked for her saw.

I turned to Uri and Pali, who was standing beside him. "Go with them," I advised.

He smiled, shaking his head. "Still not happening. You'll need all the help you can get."

"You don't even know my plan," I protested.

He shrugged. "I don't need to."

Arguing wasted what little time we had left, so together we helped the remaining children into the tunnel.

The only child left was Abiathar. "I'm not leaving," he stated, his lips twitching. "They killed my father. I'm going to kill them."

We didn't have time for this. I shook my head, grabbed him around the waist, and tossed him down the tunnel into the waiting arms of one of the quadruplets. He looked up at me with rage in his eyes for taking away his chance to confront the Marauders, but if he was still alive to hate me after this was over, I'd consider that a win. The final Daughter of Ira dragged him down deeper into the tunnel.

Only Abigail remained. "Thank you," she said softly.

My face flushed at finally getting her approval, but I winked to help bring the moment to a close. "You're welcome. Now go."

She paused but then jumped into the tunnel. The moment she did, I replaced the board covering the hole and threw the rug back on.

"So what's the plan?" Asked Uri.

I nodded to the second-floor loft. "We get to the second floor, you hold them off as long as you can with arrows while I attempt something incredibly stupid."

"So essentially you're going to do what you always do," he said.

"Exactly," I replied, rushing over to the ladder.

No sooner had we made it up to the second floor than the

door exploded open and twenty-five armed bandits rushed in to kill what they thought was a house full of orphans.

CHAPTER TWENTY

URI SCALED THE LAST RUNG OF THE LADDER, AND TOGETHER WE pulled it up and away from the grasp of a rampaging warrior. The horde filed into the orphanage, searching the building for the children.

I glanced at Uri, speaking in a hushed voice. "This is going to be tricky. We need them to keep their focus up here so they don't discover the tunnel that's beneath their feet. And I'm going to need you to do that alone while execute the plan."

"Not alone," the bald man said, the trace of a smile on his face.

It took me a moment to realize what he was talking about, but then it dawned on me. "Where's the monkey?"

"My *chimpanzee*," he corrected me, "is on the ground floor. He'll come out when I need him."

I gave him a thumbs-up and left him to it. I had enough complications to handle with my own assignment. I rushed to the edge of the loft, right beneath the far side, load-bearing beam of the roof. Then I began the work with the saw.

Below us, one of the Marauders, a man with a shrill voice, called up, "There's nowhere to run. Bring the children down, and we promise to let the adults live."

Uri took his time with his response. "You call yourselves the Marauders. Your name literally means you intend to kill everything. You will murder us at the first opportunity."

"Ha," replied a second male speaker. "Fine. We promise to make your deaths quick. You should know I find torture of all kinds to be enjoyable, so the offer means I'm sacrificing a fruitful opportunity."

"So you're the most skilled at torture?" Uri asked.

"Indeed."

The twang of a drawstring snapping broke the air, followed by an uproar below us. The warriors screamed their rage, as we waited above them. I glanced a quick peek and realized Uri had struck their leader right beneath his bat-like mask, an apparent gap in their armor. It was an impressive shot.

"I just took out the best one at torture," Uri said to me calmly. "I consider that a considerable victory. Our deaths will at least be less painful."

"Glad to hear it," I replied, almost finished with the first beam. The saw had cut through eighty percent of the wood. I moved quickly to the beam on the other side of the loft. "If you could stall our inevitable deaths another two minutes, we'll be good to go."

"Understood," Uri replied, and unleashed another arrow into the horde below us.

"Killian," a voice yelled from below. "He killed your brother!"

"My brother!" bellowed Killian, an apt named for a Marauder. "We will scatter your bowels across the continent in his name."

"That seems both unnecessary and unsanitary," Uri commented, drawing his bow and firing another bolt. A moment later he screamed, "Incoming!"

Three massive, flaming spears arched through the air and into the loft. One struck a foot away from me and stuck into the wall that I was leaning against. The other two landed among the children's bedding, which quickly lit aflame.

"If we can't take the children alive," cried Killian, "we'll leave you all burned to ash! My brother's death will be avenged."

Glorious, death by flame seemed less than enjoyable than death by a sword. The fire was already spreading, which meant I was racing against both the flames and the warriors.

I chanced a quick peek at the scene below and glimpsed Uri's new friend, Killian. The tall Marauder boldly stood in the open, daring Uri to try and hit him. He wore a similar bat mask like the rest of the raiders, though his was a blood red. The double-sided sword he was waving around was impressively large, and he had a gray, wiry beard that stretched all the way down to his waist. The Marauders seemed content to wait us out, knowing that if the flames didn't bring us down soon, the smoke would. Already, my eyes were watering.

However, I was done with the second beam, meaning there was only one left. I ran over to the central beam and put the saw to work. The smoke from the blaze burned my eyes and the fire was spreading all around me. All the while, Uri and the warriors below us continued to trade aerial assaults.

"It's only a matter of time before you're all dead," yelled Killian.

Uri paused, pondering the statement. "That is a factually true statement for all of us." He turned toward me. "Are we almost ready? I'm running out of arrows and this Killian seems quite eager to burn us alive."

The beam was almost finished. "Yes," I replied, coughing as a cloud of smoke filled my lungs. "The real trick will be keeping them all in here when it happens."

My accomplice inspected my work. He rubbed a hand over his dark, bald head and nodded when he understood the plan. "Pavi should be able to help with that." He pulled out one of his remaining arrows, one with a yellow ribbon tied to the end of it.

He quickly fired it into the wall right next to the still open entrance to the orphanage. A moment later, Pavi appeared out from behind a small cabinet and quickly pushed it to block the blasted open doorway, effectively putting it between the horde and any chance at escape. The plan was set.

Outnumbered as we were, surviving was never in the cards. This had been about buying Abigail and the children time. Reinforcements wouldn't be coming, and leaving the children to fend for themselves had never been an option. However, the bandits assumed the orphans were hiding on the second floor with us. The false assumption gave us one distinct advantage. They wouldn't expect us to do anything to risk the children's lives.

This assumption would cost them everything. You've heard the old phrase, "If you can't beat them, join them." Well today I preferred, "If you can't beat them, drop an entire building on them." As soon as I finished cutting this beam, the other load bearing components would falter, and the orphanage would crash down on all our heads.

Mind you, Uri's, Pali's, and my head were included in that counting, but sacrificing three lives to stop twenty-five murderers seemed like a decent trade.

As the blade of the saw made it through the final beam, it began to crack and the weight of the roof was transferred to the other beams. Already structurally weakened from the flames, within seconds the entire roof began to groan and crack. The men below us heard it as well, and Killian bellowed in frustration, screaming as he led the others, all running toward the blocked exit. I didn't get to see how their attempted exit fared as a slab of roof fell in front of me. I made it another two steps toward Uri when the rest of it toppled down between us, the wood engulfed in flames.

My world went black in a cloud of dust and chaos.

CHAPTER TWENTY-ONE

MY FIRST THOUGHT APTLY DESCRIBED THE SITUATION; THIS IS WHAT
Hell must be like. The sensation that greeted me when I woke
up was the feeling that someone was pressing a large, burning
coal deep into my forearm. The rest of my body was only
marginally better, with every bone and joint aching from the
slightest of movements. The cell I woke up in was pitch black,
save for a sliver of light coming in from the bottom of a heavy
door, and to top it all off, it smelled like feces. Considering I
didn't know how long I had been there though, it could have
been my feces.

My mind slowly pieced together my last memories and with
it the full recollection of bringing down a building upon my
enemies. I briefly entertained the idea that I had finally found a
way to get myself killed, but I honestly didn't seem to be lucky
enough to manage that accomplishment, mostly because I found
it unlikely that they needed to chain people up in the afterlife,
and currently shackles bound both my feet and my hands.

However poorly conceived the idea may have been, it had
worked. Meaning that Uri's and my actions had given the
orphans a legitimate chance at escape, as well as given the Bethlehem refugees at least even odds of driving the Marauders off.

Of course, if my people had survived, it left the troubling question of how I had ended up in chains.

Which begged another question; who had captured me? If the Marauders had gotten their hands on me, I'd be a corpse right now. The black, dank room left me few clues as to where I was being held.

"Hey!" I shouted toward the door. "Where the hell am I?"

No one responded, and a moment later, a shadow passed across the light of the door. Nothing followed, leaving me to deduce I'd been left alone. If there was ever a time to escape, this would be it. The shackles were attached to the walls, severely limiting my movements. I tried sliding out of the chains, but all I accomplished was reigniting the wounds on my arm. That plan was a no-go. Chains were quite effective at keeping a prisoner in a prison.

For the next ten minutes, I struggled against my bindings, with nothing to show for it but exhaustion and fresh marks around my wrists. This wasn't going to work, which meant that until a new variable was introduced to the problem, I was stuck.

I glanced up toward the ceiling of the cell. "We have to stop meeting like this."

Silence was all that responded.

"Any thoughts on getting out of here. It's not like I expect someone to simply open the door and let me out."

Not a breath later, someone appeared at the door, unlocking the cell.

"Seriously?" I said in bona fide shock. "After everything I've been through, that's all I had to do?"

"Who are you talking to and what are you talking about?" asked a woman's voice. A moment later, Abigail's silver braids appeared in the frame of the door.

I rested my head against the cold wall, chuckling. "Just an inside joke. I'm guessing by your presence, it was your husband who captured me."

She nodded gravely and entered the cell. Kneeling down, she

checked the wound on my arm. We both recoiled when the light displayed the extent of the burn, but she quickly pulled out a satchel and proceeded to pour a soothing ointment on my arm. "We don't have much time. The Marauders took something during their raid, as well as," she paused, "injuring Nabal. He's not taking it well."

I shifted, hesitant to ask the question on my mind. "What happened to my people?"

"They made out better than the rest of the city. Your brother Isaiah led a group against the Marauders and systematically drove them back. Apparently the older brother is more effective at battle than his younger brother. He didn't have to drop a building on himself to win a fight."

A wave of euphoria washed over me as she bandaged my arm. "He had a few more men to work with," I argued, "but when it comes to orchestrating military maneuvers, my brother's unmatched. And the orphans?"

"Thanks to you and Uri, we all made it out alive," Abigail said, turning her head. "Though after the Marauders had been driven off, what was left of Nabal's men found us and rounded up the children. He means to sell them as soon as he can."

"What?" I asked indignant, pushing myself further up. "No. That's not happening."

"You're not in a position to argue," Nabal's wife responded softly. "My husband ordered your people out of the city and promised that at the first sign that they attempt a rescue, he'd kill you. He gave them back Uri, though. He's shaken up and has a few more burns than you, but he should be okay. He finally allowed himself to rest once his monkey was found."

"Chimpanzee," I corrected her automatically, Uri's voice replaying in my head. Relief for Uri's safety battled with the fresh aggravation of Nabal's actions toward the children and me. "And why have I earned your husband's displeasure?" I asked, feeling the color rising in my cheeks. "If we hadn't been here, he wouldn't have a city to boss around anymore."

She finished wrapping my wound, tying the bandage tight. "I told you, he's not thinking clearly. He believes they wouldn't have attacked if you hadn't been here. He also considers you a way to recoup his losses."

"Outside of selling children, you mean."

She bit her lip. "Apparently both King Erik and Queen Phelia have placed a generous price on your head. He's sent messengers to both courts, negotiating a bidding war for which one gets to kill you."

Well that was a fun thought. Both the Mad King and the Praying Mantis Queen were willing to pay for the privilege to finish me off. One of the oh-so-many advantages of having a price on your head.

"It's not going to happen," Abigail said, her voice hardening. "I'm letting you escape."

"What?" I asked, excited about the prospect but terrified by the ramifications. "Nabal will have your head when he finds out. Or worse yet, he'll take it out on the orphans."

She shook her chin and pulled out a ring of heavy keys. "He'll leave the kids alone. He sees them as resources, and he wouldn't do anything to put their sale value at risk. As for me," she put her eyes down, "I'll figure something out."

"But why help me?"

"Because you risked your life for the children," she answered, a small smile piercing her dark thoughts. "You may still be a blowhard, but you're an honorable one with a good heart, and maybe not as incompetent as I first suspected. Once I let you out, my handmaidens will see you safely out of the city."

It took several controlled breaths before I could speak. None of this was right. "I refuse to accept that outcome," I said. "Neither you nor the children are going to suffer because your husband is an irrational, dark-hearted fool. I'll rally my people and we'll handle him ourselves."

She pulled back and stopped unchaining me. "No, you will swear on your life you will not, or I won't let you go. All that will end up happening is more people will die, which will create more orphans and more pain. Leave this to me. We'll figure something out."

One look told me she had made up her mind. I could always make the promise of leaving and then break it after I was free, but at what cost? The power system that allowed her husband to make these choices was all kinds of screwed up, but it was legal.

An insidious thought reminded me I had the means of assassinating Nabal. Tempting as it was, violence would only worsen this situation. If I had learned nothing else from my time with Abigail and her orphans, it was that using force only led to the most vulnerable being even more exposed. Sometimes violence was necessary as a defense, but it rarely solved the root issues of the struggle. Someone had to be the first to break the cycle. However, fleeing and letting her figure it out on her own was out of the question as well. Which left only one option.

"Then I'm staying," I decided, pulling myself back into the corner.

She shook her head slowly. "Then my husband will hand you over to either King Erik or Queen Phelia. You'll be killed. Horribly and painfully."

"A horrible death is a possibility that I've become oddly familiar with," I replied with a hint of levity in my voice. "But it won't happen before I have a chance to meet with your husband." I paused, steeling my resolve. "It's about time he and I had another chat."

CHAPTER TWENTY-TWO

GETTING AN AUDIENCE WITH NABAL WAS EASIER THAN EXPECTED. Once the regular guard had returned, I informed him that if I didn't get an opportunity to speak to Nabal by the end of day, my people had standing orders to come in and rescue me, regardless of the threat against my life. Sure, it was a bluff, and he probably knew it, but it was one Nabal couldn't afford to outright ignore.

An hour later, two guards collected me from my room, and for the second time in under a month, I was shuffled out of a cell with both my ankles and my forearms chained. They had been storing me in the basement of one of Nabal's storehouses, and when we entered the streets of Carmel, I got my first glimpse at the aftermath of the attack. The damage was worse than I had feared.

Burned-out homes littered the main street, and the stench of stale blood filled the air. Shopkeepers shifted through the remains of their broken street booths. Mothers and children huddled together in silence, and the men wandered around the devastated city as empty shells of themselves.

And this was the aftereffect of facing only half of the Marauders. How much worse would it have been if either I hadn't dropped a roof on the other thirty or if Isaiah and his men hadn't been able to drive off the other half? It was sad to admit, but these people were lucky. This was the first village to survive an attack by the Marauders, shattered as they may have been left.

The guards guided me toward Nabal's house. One look at his manor and I realized his home had suffered the worst of the attack. The beautiful cedar structure had been marred and plundered. The charred streaks meant someone had tried to burn it down, and judging by the damage, they had almost succeeded.

Like before, I was escorted up the stairs to the garden promenade on the roof. Or at least, what was left of the garden. Flowers had been ripped from their beds and every ornate planter had been crushed. The colored murals had all been vandalized and the pavilion at the center had been torn down. There was no strategic value in destroying the garden, which left only one rational explanation for why they did it; the Marauders had targeted Nabal.

The master of Carmel sat on a wooden chair where the pavilion had once stood. Three nervous servants knelt before him, cutting off most of my view of the man. His two full-length mirrors still stood in front of him, but they were each shattered and splintered.

"I said put on more foundation!" Nabal demanded to the servants, who recoiled at his words.

One of them, a young woman, placed her hand in a bowl and then brought it up to her master's face. She was applying something to Nabal's cheeks.

"Your Liege," said one of the other servants, an elderly gentleman. The yellow tassel hanging around his neck identified him as a town healer. "I would advise against applying too much more. If it gets into your blood, it could poison you. If we could simply wait until the wound finished healing—"

"No!" roared Nabal, this time flinging his arm out and

striking the aging man with the back of his hand. The healer fell to the ground, giving me a full view of the master of Carmel.

I stepped back. It wasn't simply that he was no longer pretty. His face looked like something straight out of a nightmare. Deep, blistered burn marks covered his right cheek, with a deep gash running through the center of it from his ear to his chin. Yet that wasn't the scary part. I had certainly seen worse wounds. The part turning my stomach was that he still wore the makeup. The purple eyeliner rose and fell on the blistered bumps, and the servants had been putting some kind of brown clay over the wounds. Instead of hiding the burn marks, it highlighted them.

Nabal's gaze narrowed as he watched my reaction, a new wave of hate burning in it. "The Pauper Prince," he said through gritted teeth.

I fortified my stomach and moved forward with as much dignity as the chains would allow. "We need to talk. This situation will get us all killed."

Abigail's husband moved up in his seat. "You brought this hell upon my house. Why should I listen to you?"

I shook my head. "I cautioned you of the Marauders' attack, and my people and I even protected you after you dismissed our warnings and insulted our village. You have no one to blame for this loss but yourself."

"*This loss?*" he responded, his vision turning to the fractured mirrors in front of him. His eyes grew large. "This loss? What do you know about my loss? They have taken everything from me, all because you were here!"

I moved closer and my guards inched nervously closer following me. "This had nothing to do with me," I said, dismissively. "They wanted the orphans."

He cackled, a dark sound that matched his face. "You think they came for a bunch of worthless brats? Your naivety of the situation would boggle my mind if I cared enough about your opinion to give it thought. No, they took something far more valuable and you led them right to it." He erupted in a new chorus of manic laughter.

My face scrunched up. "I have literally no idea what you're talking about."

His laughter subsided. "And one of the few joys I have left is knowing that you will die terribly, still having no idea what I'm talking about or of what is truly going on. I will wreak upon you pain you never imagined possible."

Abigail was right. He was unhinged. Reason was getting us nowhere, so it was time to try fear. "My people will tear you apart if you kill me," I threatened. "You've already seen what they can do, and if you harm me, they'll take what little you have left. But there's another way. Let the orphans, Abigail, and me go. Tell us what you know of the Marauders, and we will get revenge on them. We may even be able to return whatever it was they took from you."

"You still don't get it," he replied, shaking his head. He bent down to place his hand in the clay bowl and smeared fresh clay over his face, grimacing as he plastered it over the blisters.

"Sir," pleaded the healer. "Please, if it gets into your blood–"

Nabal grabbed hold of the bowl and shattered it over the man's head. The healer fell unconscious, and Nabal turned his attention back to me. "You claim you could return to me what was stolen." He gazed back in the mirror, loathing dancing in his eyes. "They deformed *me*! They took what was most precious and left it in ruins. I plan on returning the favor to the rest of the world."

A terrible and frightening idea blossomed in his gaze. "Bring my wife," he demanded to his guards.

Whatever demented action he had planned, I refused to allow it to happen, and despite my burning wounds, I lunged toward him. The guards stopped me before I could cover the distance. They threw me to the ground, each placing a knee on my back to hold me down.

"Hold him there, but keep him conscious. We don't want him to miss the show."

A handful of moments later, Abigail was dragged up to the pavilion. "What is the meaning of this?" she demanded, trying to pull herself away

"Dear, beautiful wife," her husband began, the words sounding like they were coming from a snake. "I was just informing our guest of my new plans. How I want those closest to me to understand the extent of my pain. How I wish to share a common bond with them."

"What?" she said, confused and seemed to grow afraid.

"Come now," Nabal said, pulling a small knife from his dinner plate and tracing it over the scar across his face. "Don't you think a wife should share the same brand as her husband?"

Abigail's eyes went wide.

"Hold her down," Nabal ordered another one of his guards. "And make sure Niklas can clearly watch it happen. I want him to get a front row seat, so he can understand what awaits him and everyone else that he cares for."

Abigail struggled against the guard, while I attempted to do the same with mine. Neither of us succeeded. The guards held her prostrate on the ground, her face less than two feet from mine. Terror threatened to overwhelm my senses. Nabal had always been evil, but before the attack he had been an evil with a level of common sense. With his face forever disfigured, he had become totally unhinged, focused on making everyone else's life as miserable and dark as his own.

The guards kept me pressed to the ground, and there was no way to protect Abigail. Which left only one way to stop this; redirect Nabal's rage upon myself.

"I don't know what you're so upset about," I shouted. "You were just as hideous before the attack as you are now."

The madman's face contorted and he drove his foot into my stomach, forcing the air from my lungs. "Silence!"

I wheezed but kept up the insults. "Seriously, this may actually be an improvement. Now at least the rest of the town won't be able to recognize you. Hell, you may even find a nice leper colony to retire to."

My words left him speechless. His eyes frantically returned to the mirrors, and he scraped his hands across the ground, digging out what remained of the clay from the broken bowl. He coated a fresh round of paste across his face, though this time it was mingled with dirt. "I don't care how much King Erik or Queen Phelia would pay me," he said softly, "I will take the pleasure of killing you myself."

His fingers went white as he grasped the knife handle and knelt down next to me. "It's time to die, little Giant Slayer."

The blade was an inch from my neck. My only hope was that after he killed me, his rage would subside, and he might spare Abigail. It was a fleeting hope, but the only option we had left. The blade touched my neck and jerked, cutting into my skin. At first, I thought Nabal meant it as a final blow, but suddenly his whole body jerked back, lurching away from me. The knife fell from his grasp, and he brought both hands up to his face. His whole body began to spasm. He fell to the ground, scratching at his face, but every time he did, he screamed louder.

No one knew what to do. The only healer lay unconscious on the ground.

For two hours, his screams rang loudly throughout the town. I could even hear them from my underground cell, to which I had been unceremoniously returned after the incident. Then suddenly, it was silent. Nabal, the Master of Carmel, had died of blood poisoning inflicted by his own hand.

CHAPTER TWENTY-THREE

"And you really didn't have a hand in killing him?" Isaiah asked skeptically, sitting cross-legged in my tent. After Nabal's death, Abigail, the temporary leader until the elders at Carmal could determine a new leader, had promptly ordered the guards to release me back to my people.

I pushed myself further up in the bedroll, laughing in spite of the dark accusation. "People die all the time with me having nothing to do with it."

"When it comes to your enemies dying," my brother replied, slowly unwrapping the bandages around my burned arm, "those times are the exception, not the rule."

I rolled my eyes. There was never any trust.

The flap to my tent opened and Uri ducked inside. Both of his arms were covered in bruises, and beneath his chin was a pink, large, oval-shaped burn, which contrasted brightly with his black skin. He, too, would have a lasting reminder of our latest adventure.

"That looks unpleasantly painful," I said, gesturing to his burn.

He shrugged. "It could have been worse. My fiancée is the attractive one in the relationship anyway."

"You're handling a face wound better than the last guy," I said, a sly smirk on my face. "It ended poorly for him."

He nodded and took a seat beside Isaiah. "So what do we do now?"

It was a valid question. "Our situation is a double-edged sword," I replied, reaching for my dabar. After waking up to Sethas and her goons in my tent, I had never let it out of my sight. "On the one hand, we survived our first encounter with the Marauders largely unscathed. We're the only group to have met them and even survived. However, now that they've attacked, we no longer know where they'll be next, meaning our leads of where to look next have dried up."

"So we do nothing?" Uri asked.

"Not quite," I said. "We do have at least some hard evidence to go off of. First, their armor proved them far beyond the typical rampage and pillage group of bandits. Someone is funding their efforts, and the list of who has that capacity is short. Like, you need to be introduced at parties as a king or pharaoh short. Second, we can now confirm their attacks are not only coordinated, but also that they're building toward something larger. As happy as I am to see the last of Nabal, he obviously knew more about their designs, and I would have loved to know why they attacked Carmel."

"And how does that information help us find the Marauders?" Isaiah asked.

"Right now," I said, "it doesn't, but we can start looking for patterns. If we can uncover what connects all the attacks, we can figure out what they'll do next."

"And how do you suggest we do that?" Isaiah asked. "Everyone who could possibly know is either dead, like Nabal, or has placed a bounty on your head, like Queen Phelia and King Erik."

"Then we go to the Philistines," I said.

Isaiah barked out a laugh. "You, Niklas the mighty Philistine Giant Slayer, want to trust the Philistines. I know you lived with them for a few months, but don't tell me you trust them now?"

"Trust would be a stretch, but their new king, Achish, seems remarkably reasonable compared to the folks we've dealt with lately. He's our best and, quite frankly, our only chance for information. They were attacked right before I left, meaning they'll want to end the Marauders' run as much as anyone. I've already talked to Eliab and father. We're waiting a couple more days so I can heal up and then we're heading out."

"I'd say it's your funeral," Isaiah replied softly, "but you realize you're taking all of us with you, right?"

"We'll be fine," I promised, but then I shrugged. "Probably. Now get out, I'm sick and I need to rest."

"You just want to take a nap," Isaiah jabbed.

He was right, but I'd earned it.

"I'd hate to intrude then," called a female voice from outside the tent. Abigail ducked her silver head in. "I can come back another time if that would be easier."

A fresh surge of energy ran through my blood and I could feel my face flush red. "No!" I replied a bit too eagerly. I settled my emotions. "You can come in." My brother eyed me slyly before he and Uri left us alone in the tent.

Abigail knelt down next to me, straightening out her dress. "I wanted to come and say thank you."

"I think you already did that," I reminded her. "Back in the cell."

"No, not for the orphanage. For not killing my husband."

I looked away. "When Nabal had the knife pointed at you, if those guards wouldn't have been holding me, I wouldn't have kept that promise."

"Maybe," she said. "But you could have simply waited until after I released you and gone back on your word. You tried to fulfill your promise. Few men do."

I smiled and felt my cheeks burn hot. "What happens to you now?"

She took a deep breath. "In many ways, I am back to where I started before Nabal and I wed. I do not deny being glad that he is gone, but we no longer have the legal protections he offered us, faint as they may have been. As a widow, I have no legal standing to his property, or the children. Technically I could marry one of his distant family members, but judging from those I've met, they wouldn't be much better than him, plus they'd have no obligation to take care of the children."

It hurt to realize how complicated, and quite frankly crappy, this situation was for her. As strong and wise as she was, in society's eyes, she could do nothing without the backing of a husband. She deserved better than that.

I looked up and the words stumbled out of my mouth before I understood what I was saying. "We could marry." My eyes turned into the size of globes when I realized what I had just suggested. The tent became uncomfortably silent for what I'm pretty sure was a full week.

For a moment, she seemed to entertain the idea, but then she let out a breath of air and shook her head. "No. Thank you, and I mean that, but I married for practicality once, and I almost lost everyone I cared about due to that decision. This time I will choose something different."

I weighed her words. "Then come with us," I suggested. "We can protect you, and if I tried any of that 'a woman can't make her own decisions' nonsense, about half the females in my family would leave my backside raw before I could finish the sentence. You'd be safe. You and the orphans."

She locked eyes with me, skeptical. "We'd be a drain on your resources."

I shrugged. "I'm sure we'll find a way to put you to good use."

She thought on my suggestion, playing with her silver braids. Finally, she nodded. "I accept your invitation."

"Good," I replied. "Deborah will love having another person to help keep me in check."

"A full-time job, I'm sure," Abigail replied, a broad grin on her face. It felt surprisingly good to make her smile.

The moment was interrupted by Yashobeam thrusting his shaggy head inside the tent. "We have a problem."

"What's wrong?" I asked, sitting up a little straighter.

He responded by handing me a sealed roll of parchment. "It's from my sister," Yashobeam replied, disgruntled. "Her three bounty hunters hand delivered it."

Breaking the seal, I unraveled the roll.

Niklas,

Your incompetence at Carmel has ramifications. The Marauders found what they needed and plan to attack the six peninsula kings and their advisors at a council meeting in two days at Maoza. Best we can tell, they intend to kill off the leaders of the entire region and plunge your continent into chaos. Watching you slaughter each other would be personally delightful, but it'd be an inconvenience for the Pharaoh, so I've dispatched my bounty hunters to assist you. Clean up your mess.

Love,
Sethas

P.S. Your boy Damon will be at the council. He will die as well. How marvelous.

I reread the message twice more before looking up. "Crap."

CHAPTER TWENTY-FOUR

OKAY, WE HAD A MINOR PROBLEM. FIVE THOUSAND SOLDIERS STOOD between the rulers we needed to warn and us.

Also, "minor" may have been a bit of an understatement.

Our company of fifty men had pushed hard over the last day and a half, covering the twenty-five plus miles between our camp and the seashore village of Maoza. Yashobeam, the bounty hunter Shahar, his children, and I now stood on a small hill overlooking the town of Garada. The marine town was built at the southeast corner of the Dead Sea. Yeah, someone actually named it the Dead freaking Sea, because where else would a terrible, horrible, region-shattering attack take place? The name actually came from the fact of the high salt water content, meaning no fish could live there. But in this circumstance, it seemed more like a dire warning.

Between the six rulers and our men were six armies. Each encamped within a quarter of a mile from one another, identified by their banners: Israel, Philistia, Moab, Edom, Ammon, and Aram. All the major players had gathered.

"Huh," grunted Yashobeam as he looked down. The guttural noise aptly summarized how each of us was feeling.

Shahar stood next to me, stroking his gray beard. His full

moon mask hid any emotions. "This proves to be rather problematic."

"Just a bit," I replied. Our fifty men would never be able to make it past that many soldiers, and the attempt would do little more than set off a full-scale war in the region. I took a deep breath. "Maybe this is a good thing. With that many soldiers, anything short of an army from the Egyptians or the Persians would be repelled. There's no way for the Marauders to successfully attack the council."

Shahar barked a harsh laugh and turned to his two children. "How often has Sethas's information ever been wrong?"

"Never," answered Mebi from behind us, and as she turned her head, a ray of sunlight reflected off her silver mask. "Her record is flawless."

"If I were the Marauders," her brother Ahyim said, picking at his black mask, "I'd consider this a perfect setup. Each army is already salivating at the idea of fighting each other. One wrong move will set them all at each other's throats, and then they can just ride in after and clean up the mess. Why waste your own troops when so many expendable ones are at your disposal?"

It was my turn to grunt my frustration. He was right. If they played their hand right, the Marauders could let the six armies destroy themselves and simply pick over their corpses. "And Sethas didn't give you any indication of what brought the rulers together?"

Shahar shook his head.

As things stood, there was no way we'd be able to make it down as a group. Yet if the rulers weren't warned soon, and the Marauders were successful in killing off the heads of the six kingdoms, the bandits would have the whole region at their mercy, and one thing they weren't known for was mercy.

If I could get to Damon, the prince could get a warning out, but he'll be with his father, surrounded by dozens, if not hundreds of soldiers with standing orders to put me down on the spot.

"I have to go down to the Philistine camp," I decided. "Our reasoning that they'd be the most likely to work with us is still solid, and Achish's men might not kill me on the spot. Plus, if I do it right, they won't realize I'm there until I'm confident that I'm talking to someone who will listen."

"Take me with you," Yashobeam said moving closer.

"No," I replied. "If I thought this could only be solved by physical means, we'd be dead in the water already. This is going to require stealth, which works better alone."

"I think we'll tag along," Shahar stated and he raised a hand when I started to protest. "I promise, you won't even know we're there."

The terrifying thing was, I had seen them move and he was probably correct.

"Plus," he concluded, "a handful of the Philistines know I work for the Egyptians. It may help our cause."

I nodded, uncomfortable with them joining me, but knowing there wasn't much I could do to stop them. At least this way I'd be able to keep tabs on the family of professional killers.

"Let's get his over with," I said, turning to Yashobeam. "Let the others know to stay here. Unless all hell breaks loose down there, do not engage the enemies. The last thing we need is you trying to rescue me and in the process start a regional war."

"And if a regional war does break out?" Yashobeam asked. "What should I do with my men?"

"*Then* you come and rescue me," I said in mock offense.

"And risk my men?" he said through a smile, but then nodded and left to bring the news back to the rest of our group.

King Achish's banners flew on the far west side of the encampments. My merry band of bounty hunters and I began our trek down. Shahar was correct, they knew their stealth, and we infiltrated the camp without any soldiers being the wiser.

The Philistine warriors were all understandably on edge, and even the ones off duty shared the same tense look upon their faces, keeping their weapons on hand at all times. Typically within a camp, you could only maintain that level of angst for a short time, but this showed no signs of letting up. Any spark would send them off to war, and in their minds, it was an expectation of when, not if, they would go to battle. The other armies were almost certainly in a similar boat. We were in trouble.

Darkness started to descend upon the valley, making our infiltration substantially easier. We agreed that the first place to check would be the king's command tent. If I could get straight to King Achish, no one would have to be hurt, and he could relay our warning to the other rulers.

We reached his pavilion but found it empty. We were about to move to his personal quarters when the guards outside the command center barked an order.

"Halt!" a man said. "No one enters until the king returns."

"I have orders from Zalmon," another man replied, "asking for documents to be brought to him."

The guards grumbled about protocols but allowed the man to enter the tent. A young page ducked inside and ran to the table in the center of the command center. He rolled up a couple of maps, tucked them under his arm and quickly left. I gestured to Shahar that we should follow the page, as reaching Zalmon would give us access to Achish. The elder bounty hunter nodded and off we went.

The page headed toward the coast of the sea, eventually stopping when he reached a small group of Philistine soldiers waiting on the beach. Similar groups from other nations were stationed on the coast as well. The group's torchlight revealed one to be the warrior Zalmon.

Mebi shifted uncomfortably. "We stand less chance of getting killed if we wait until he's alone. He may not react rationally to our unrequested appearance."

I weighed her idea for a moment and shook my head. "No. Time is not our ally here. The Marauders could strike at any moment."

Shahar bobbed his head. "Agreed. What's rule number two?"

Ahyim answered. "Always know when the reward is worth the risk, especially when someone else is taking the risk." He looked at me and smiled.

"Great," I muttered and stepped out of the shadows, my hands up high. "Zalmon," I shouted. "We need to talk."

A half dozen Philistines immediately drew their weapons and I pushed my hands further in the air, emphasizing my lack of aggression. "I'm here to save your king."

Zalmon eyed me warily, an ugly scowl growing on his face. He too drew his sword and stalked toward us. "You shouldn't be here," he replied. "Both King Erik and Queen Phelia have placed a price on your head. You'll start a bloody war!"

"I'm trying to avert one," I said. My eyes darted to Shahar. "*We're* trying to avert to one."

"He speaks true," Shahar said, his hands also up but clearly not as troubled by the Philistine's weapons as I was. "Zalmon, we met three winters ago in King Achish's court. I was escorting an Egyptian merchant. I am on a mission from the same woman, working in coordination with this young man."

Zalmon scratched the deep scars on his face. "Speak."

Not expecting a lot of wiggle room, I quickly recounted what we knew about the Marauders and Sethas's warning of an attack.

"You have to reach out to the other generals. The Marauders probably mean to ignite a war between the kingdoms and then clean up after you've all killed each other."

Zalmon shook his head. "Do you really think the rulers would have stationed their troops here had they not anticipated that possibility? The first nation to provoke a fight will be immediately attacked by the combined might of the other five. No one will act. It would be suicide."

"Then maybe the Marauders have someone stationed in an army's ranks to provoke an attack," I suggested.

"You're grasping," Zalmon responded.

I tightened my fists and shook from frustration. "Your king is in danger."

Zalmon chuckled. "The rulers are the safest ones here. Look out upon the water." He pointed past a long dock that led out to a massive barge upon the sea.

"The rulers are all convening on that boat," he continued. "This is a joint project within the region to extract asphalt for the Egyptians. No nation could do it alone without concern for the others attacking them, so we partnered to do it together. The only way onto the barge is through the dock, and between any Marauder and the landing are six full armies. They are safe."

The reasoning was sound. Yet something he said poked at the back of my mind. "What kind of 'joint project.'" I asked.

He shrugged. "It's a national secret," he said simply. "One I have no intention of sharing."

I locked eyes with him. "But your king does trust me. He sent me to find the Marauders, and now I come with information that they may be moments away from ramming a horde of death down your throats and you decide to send me away?" I moved closer to him. "Tell me what they stole."

Zalmon held my gaze. He blinked. "I can't give you the specifics, but it deals with how we pull asphalt up from the sea. Each nation had a part figuring it out."

I let that sink in. Each nation had a hand in developing the process, and each nation had been attacked by the Marauders. The pieces started falling into place, and the puzzle they displayed was terrifying.

"Zalmon," I said softly, "When you captured me and brought me before Achish, you accused me of stealing secrets. Did any of those secrets have to do with that barge?"

His lip trembled. "How did you..." his voice trailed off as he realized what I was getting at. "They know how to get on the barge."

I swallowed hard. "They may already be there."

CHAPTER TWENTY-FIVE

EVERYTHING SCREAMED INSIDE ME TO RUSH TOWARD THE BARGE, BUT I had only made it two steps before Zalmon grabbed me. "Stop. The landing is guarded by archers from each of the six countries, and if we go angrily sprinting toward them, we'll just end up as pin cushions for their arrows."

"So how do we get on the boat?" I asked.

"We play it by the rules," he responded. "If it's just the two of us, I should be able to get you on the barge, but your masked friends will have to stay on land. They'll also relieve us of our weapons, but it will get us where we need to go."

"Swell," I said. "So we get to walk straight into a Marauders' trap without any protection."

"You're welcome to stay here if you want," the Philistine leader responded.

I grunted. "Lead the way," I said through gritted teeth.

We lost precious minutes as Zalmon went through the protocol of getting us onboard the boat, and one of the Philistine guards took away my dabar, but eventually we were provided an escort onto the ship.

The barge was a good one hundred feet long, and the flat

deck was lit by dozens of tall torches. Excavation equipment was attached to the edges of the ship and in the center of the barge was a large square cabin. The six rulers were convening inside.

Our escort led us through the exterior vestibule of the cabin. Inside, the magistrates of all six kingdoms sat around a rectangular wooden table. Oddly missing was Damon. Sethas had said he was to take part in the council. Achish sat facing the door, the purple scarf covering his eyes. His head tilted as we entered. "Who approaches?"

The other rulers each turned to look. King Erik cursed loudly. He had lost so much weight. He was a tall man, and his skin stretched against his skeletal frame. His bald head was marred with sun spots and his eyes were sunken and shadowed. Yet fire ignited in his eyes when he saw me. He pointed a bony finger at me.

"You dare come here!" he roared.

Well that went about as expected.

Queen Phelia's voice cackled from across the table. "Oh dear," her fingers played with one of the five golden necklaces around her neck. "Never has one of the males I've targeted ever willingly presented himself to me. This is a rare treat."

One of the other rulers, a middle-aged man with tan skin shifted uncomfortably. "When Aram agreed to this parley, we were promised absolute adherence to the rules of attendance. These two men threaten to dissolve this whole council."

"True, true," nodded another one of the kings, an elderly fellow with bushy, white eyebrows. "The kingdom of Ammon concurs. This is unsettling, unsettling."

Zalmon bowed low. "We adhered to the code. We come only to bring news of the Marauders, the very purpose of this council. We have firm intelligence that suggest the Marauders intend to attack the barge."

"Intelligence," scoffed a male voice from behind us. I turned my head to find Doeg standing against the wall in his multi-colored tunic, his creepy pentagram necklace hanging around his neck. "Intelligence can be a dangerous thing if one does not have the wisdom to wield it."

I growled in response, baring my teeth.

"Oh come now, Niklas," Doeg said. "Let's keep the fangs to a minimum. I'd hate to have to muzzle you."

Part of me wanted him to try, but as personally satisfying as it would be to dismantle Erik's new rabid dog, it wouldn't help the current situation. "How are you even here?" I asked. "I thought protocol was that only the six rulers were invited."

"I orchestrated this parley in hopes of regional peace. This excavation project represents what we could gain by joining forces. We literally stand on the proof of how much we could benefit from working together."

My eyebrows furrowed in confusion. "Working together?"

"It must pain you so to be out of the loop," Doeg mocked.

"Patronizing Niklas doesn't serve us here," King Achish said, shaking his head. "This marine excavation is a partnership between the six countries. Egypt can't seem to buy enough asphalt, and beyond that, we recently discovered a rare mineral called potash, which set off a bidding war between the Pharaoh, the Assyrians, and even the Greeks. It's more lucrative than a gold mine."

"Quiet Achish!" King Erik demanded. "This man is a traitor who has been plotting for my throne for years. Before we proceed, he dies."

Queen Phelia pulled out a necklace, the same bloody lion's tooth I had given her. "I too am confused as to why we haven't killed him yet."

Well this was going amazingly. Between Erik and Phelia, I wouldn't have to worry about the Marauders killing me, those two would do it themselves soon enough.

"His presence is troubling," the Edomite king said, "but I fear we shouldn't dismiss his warning out of hand. If, indeed, the

Marauders are planning something, we cannot afford to take the risk. We should reconvene after new precautions are in place."

"Of course the Marauders are planning something," Doeg agreed, and my eyes nearly popped out of their sockets. "We've known that for some time. It's the main reason for summoning this council. We have to discover which nation has betrayed us."

"The main reason for this council?" squawked the Ammonite ruler, repeating Doeg's words. "Finding a traitor was not part of the terms of us coming here."

The high counselor bowed his head low. "I apologize for the ruse, but after the recent attacks, it became clear that someone was helping the Marauders. They knew exactly where to strike to most effectively hamper this project. Only the six rulers and myself knew the full extent of the plan, meaning the bandits had to be working with someone from this group."

"But the Marauders have attacked each of us," Phelia commented. "They have plagued every nation for over six months."

"Indeed," Doeg conceded. "Though it would have been beyond suspicious if only one nation was spared from their blight. The real question is whether we all have been attacked equally?"

"They wiped off three of my villages," cried out Erik.

"Two of mine," said the king of the Ammonites.

And then, as if fighting to prove who had been hurt more, each other ruler exclaimed their nation's losses. All, that was, except for Achish.

Doeg turned his head to the king of Philistia, and every ruler followed his gaze. "And what of the Philistine's losses?"

Achish's purple scarf concealed his gaze, but his brow furrowed, indicating that he had grown uncomfortable with where the conversation was leading. "They hit our blacksmiths and stole our marine equipment, along with a couple of homesteads," he said softly.

"What?!" again squawked the Ammonite ruler. "A couple of smiths as opposed to entire villages!"

"Preposterous!" cried the Ammonite ruler with the bushy eyebrows. "Preposterous!"

"And now," Doeg continued, shaking his head, "your advisor brings a known fugitive from two lands into our midst, claiming some secret knowledge."

"For the last year, I have sought nothing but peace!" Achish rebuffed.

King Erik scoffed. "Because you knew the Marauders were doing your dirty work for you. I knew we couldn't trust your country. Once a Philistine thug, always a Philistine thug."

The rulers all glared at King Achish, disdain evident in their eyes. Zalmon's body was rigid with tension. It seemed like he was only a moment away from jumping to his king's aid.

The high counselor approached the table, spreading his hands wide. "Let us think this through." He brought a hand over his face. "For over six months, Niklas has been banished from Israel, and for six months the Marauders have plagued our lands."

I threw my hands up in frustration. "I had been under constant surveillance in Philistia the entire time, just ask Zalmon."

"A perplexing mystery, your time there," Queen Phelia mused. "How did you manage to live among your sworn enemies for so long without them ripping you to shreds? Didn't they write a song about how many thousands of Philistines you killed? It makes no sense; unless of course you struck some kind of deal with them."

King Erik stood up, slamming his fists onto the table. "After all I've done for you, is there no end to your treachery?"

Blood and ashes, we were in so much trouble. King Achish was the only one who could vouch for my innocence, but his name was currently just as muddy as my own.

Doeg tapped the table solemnly. "Esteemed rulers, it was

with great regret I misled you about my true intentions for this meeting, but I believe we have caught the traitor in our midst." He bowed his head again, but then turned his back to the rest of the six, so that only Zalmon and I could see him from where we still stood in the doorway. His eyes were manic, and an overly bright smile split his face. "It's the very reason I brought you here."

In that moment, I knew with absolute certainty that Doeg was working with the Marauders. This was always his plan, and he had played it perfectly. Doeg had started a witch hunt, already knowing who he would put the blame on. It wouldn't give him more power, but it was more than enough to keep the rulers stuck here. Then, once the Marauders had killed the other six rulers, he could step into the void.

"We're wasting time," said King Erik. "We need to bind Achish and kill Niklas."

"It seems a prudent course of action," echoed the Edomite king, and soon every other ruler was echoing him excluding Achish.

My mind raced. Not only was dying not the preferred outcome, but also all this would do was leave the six rulers exposed and the region as a whole on the brink of utter chaos. These rulers were too confident that their armies could protect them. They considered themselves invulnerable, and right now they needed to be afraid. But how could any one man help them realize the danger they were in?

Then it hit me. I wasn't just any one man.

"ENOUGH!" I bellowed, and the room went quiet. "I am through with this," I said through gritted teeth, taking a step closer to the table. "Over the last six months, over half of the people in this room have tried to murder me. Not once have I retaliated, and in fact, I've gone out of my way to keep you and your people safe. Now, you *will* listen to me."

Queen Phelia snorted. "Who do you think you are, whelp, to order the six rulers of Mesopotamia?"

"Who am I?" I asked. Then I moved.

I lunged toward the queen, grabbing hold of the lion's tooth around her neck and snapping the cord and pulling it free. Armed with the fang, I slid the tooth across her neck. She shrieked, but before she could push me away, I had already moved on to the King of Edom. He lifted his hands in protection, but he too was far too slow. They were all too slow. Spinning and weaving, I darted across the room, every ruler crying out for their guards or pushing me away. None succeeded.

My circuit around the table complete, the door to the room opened, presumably an effort of the summoned guards, but I kicked it shut, and a loud *thud* echoed as the people fell down on the other side.

"Who am I?" I repeated, my teeth clenched. "I am Niklas, son of Jesse, the lion slayer, the Giant Slayer, and the man who kills by tens of thousands. I am a trained Seraphim operative, and if I wanted to, I could kill you all where you sit." I held up the bloody fang. "See."

Each ruler had a hand grasping or rubbing their injured throats. Small streams of blood trickled down each of their necks from where I had grazed them with the fang's sharp point.

"You dare threaten us," King Erik responded through jerky breaths.

I bowed my head. "I needed you to know that if I wanted you dead, you would be dead. But I *don't*, so whether you leave for fear of me or for fear of the Marauders, I don't care, but you *will* leave." I held the tooth out. "Now."

The king of Ammon swallowed hard, pulling a cloth to his neck. "Maybe it would be best to do as he says. Just until–"

A guard's deathly scream from the deck of the boat cut off his response. His howl was soon followed by another, and then another, and within seconds, the sound of metal ringing against metal echoed outside. Then the far wall to the cabin exploded, and a moment later, a foul odor and smoke started bellowing into the room.

A figure cut through the dark cloud and stood in the door-frame, blood dripping from the fangs of his horrid, snake-shaped mask. "I heard your little speech, Niklas, whelp of Jesse," he said, looking directly at me. "I've never drunk the blood of a Giant Slayer. I wonder what it tastes like?"

CHAPTER TWENTY-SIX

THREE YEARS AGO, I FACED OFF AGAINST A GIANT, WHO WAS THE closest thing I have ever encountered that could qualify as a mythical monster. Goliath was terrifying, an unending mass of muscle and armor. I bring it up because, in comparison to the nightmare in front of me, Goliath was a docile, cute kitten.

The smoke burned my lungs and I coughed as I tried to make sense of what my eyes were seeing. The massive Marauder was nearly as large as Goliath, but that was by far the least terrifying aspect of the warrior. The scales on his snake mask seemed to be alive, shifting across his face. His whole body was covered in spiked iron armor and most of the spikes seemed to be dripping with fresh blood.

"Illustriousss rulers of Mesopotamia," the snake thing said through a hissing voice as he stalked into the room. "I have longed to meet you."

Pushing past the fear, I grabbed Zalmon by the shoulder. "Get them out of here! I'll hold off Scaly, here."

I sprinted forward, diving inside his reach. Armed with only the lion's tooth against his extensive armor limited my options, but I could at least keep him occupied while Zalmon got the rulers out of this death-box. Through the hole in his mask, I saw Snake Face smile as he looked down at me.

"Hi there," he hissed and before I could land an attack, his arm snapped out, and with obvious ease, he struck my chin with an open hand.

A normal blow would have sent me tumbling to the side. His sent me soaring across the room and into the far wall at the speed of a horse at full gallop. I bounced off the wooden wall of the cabin and landed three feet in front of it. The blow knocked my skull, and while a hive of bees erupted inside my head, I idly realized that this wasn't simply your run-of-the-mill, crazy Marauder; I was dealing with the supernaturally strong variety.

Fighting against such an opponent was paramount to suicide-by-Marauder. The idea of curling up into a fetal ball and letting numbing sleep overtake me had considerably larger appeal. However, if the rulers had any chance of surviving the next five minutes, letting myself pass out wasn't an option. Pushing through the new bruises and the fog in my head, I forced myself back to my feet.

Queen Phelia scrambled out the door in a lurching gate, and the other rulers were quickly following her lead. Hopefully they wouldn't need much time, because I'm pretty sure one more blow like the one I had just received would take me out for the duration of the fight.

"Alright, big guy," I said, raising the fang and attempting to look as menacing as a still staggering former Giant Slayer could hope. "Are you ready for round two?"

Snake Face slithered forward, and I don't mean that figuratively—his body literally wiggled forward. "We are going to have sssuch fun together," he said, turning his face to the side. "The chaoss we will create."

"Yeah," I said, shaking my head but glad his attention was on me. At least as glad as I could be to have a monster's full attention. "Whatever you say."

I moved forward again, albeit with a considerably greater amount of caution. I didn't know how he was moving so fast, but I knew there would be no way I could match his speed or strength, meaning I had to win the battle of cunning. Smoke continued to bellow through the room. Maybe I could use it to–

Snake Face lunged forward and interrupted what I'm sure would have been a truly magnificent plan. His fists struck out again and again, and it was all I could do to keep my arms up to deflect the blows. I avoided a critical blow by the spikes on his armor, but at the cost of taking direct hits across my arms, the last of which connected with my freshly burned forearm. Every inch of my skin erupted in agony, and I fell to my knees, screaming in pain.

Snake Face shook his masked head. "Tssk, tssk. You aren't ready for this fight, hero of Bethlehem. Your time has not yet come." He kicked me in the stomach and punted me across the room and out of the open door.

Pain followed. Also a huge portion of humble pie, but mostly just pain. I lay doubled over, clutching my burned arm and wheezing. I tasted blood. That was never a good sign. The pain took up most of my attention, but a small sliver of my reason concluded that I was hopelessly outmatched.

Outside of the cabin, the deck of the ship was chaos, as the combined forces of the six rulers' guards squared off against a horde of Marauders. Soldiers fought for their lives, but were failing at their task, and screams of terror came from almost every warrior.

Snake Face stepped out from the cabin. "Niklas, together you and I will do wondrousss, horrible thingsss. I can't wait to sstart."

"I knew it!" cried a voice from within the cabin.

Both my opponent and I turned our heads to search out the source and found Doeg, the high counselor himself, holding out a ceremonial knife with both hands, trembling.

"Niklas, I knew you were working in concert with the Marauders," he said, fear and hate dancing in his eyes. "You won't survive this treachery. The six rulers you betrayed tonight will hunt you to the edge of the earth."

Was he serious? Did he not just witness the smack down the big bad Marauder had just laid on me? I was on the ground, literally choking on my own blood.

Snake Face turned around and looked down at the high counselor, peering down at the man like a serpent might look at a mouse daring to provoke it. "I have no usse for you."

Doeg's eyes went wide, and he lunged forward with the dagger. It struck the masked man's armor in the chest, but the iron protection easily deflected the blow. Amused, my opponent started chuckling. He then lifted the high counselor off the ground with one hand and threw him back into the cabin. Doeg slammed into the sidewall like a broken doll and bounced further inside, the ever-increasing smoke cutting off my view. Snake Face stalked back into the cabin.

Moments later, Doeg began screaming. "HELP!!!" he cried. "Get off–"

His cries were cut off by a series of bone-crunching thumps. The rhythmic smashing went on and on, as if some kind of demented drum session was happening inside. Finally, the noise stopped, and something flew out of the cabin. A body, no, more accurately a fresh corpse, fell three feet from me. The torso was dressed in a multi-colored robe with a starred necklace around its neck. All that was missing was Doeg's freaking head.

This was so bad. It took every ounce of strength from my body to push myself onto my stomach. The smoke burned my eyes, making it nearly impossible to find my opponent. Retreat was my only option. I just needed to make it to the edge of the boat. Not even having the strength to stand, I crawled, arm over arm, to the edge of the barge. I was a dozen paces away when a heavy boot slammed into my back, forcing the wind from my lungs. Worse yet, my shoulder cracked and shifted unnaturally forward, and a new type of pain erupted throughout my body.

"Don't leave yet," Snake Face chided. "Our fun has jussst begun."

CHAPTER TWENTY-SEVEN

I WRITHED IN AGONY. FIGHTING A SUPERNATURAL BEAST MAN HAD not been one of the eventualities I had planned for, and my lack of foresight was showing.

"You cannot essscape me, whelp?" Snake Face taunted. "I am avarice. I am war. I am chaosss!"

Great. I was dealing with the megalomaniac variety of supernatural mass murderer. "Does chaos have a name?" I mocked. If I could not win an outright battle, I'd settle for the consolation prize of dying while belittling him.

My opponent bent over, pressing his foot deeper into my back. "For centuries, I have been called Gungra."

"Centuries?" I coughed. "You've aged well. Still pretty limber and all that. Count me as impressed."

"You are feisssty," Gungra replied. "I like that. It will provide me joy watching that fire die in your eyesss. Soon, you will bow before my might."

I managed to roll one eye, the other was having trouble focusing. "If you're going to kill me," I said between labored breaths, "get it over with. Anything is better than listening to you prattle on like some kind of self-appointed priest of misery and murder."

"Priest?" Gungra echoed, laughing. "Not a priest, young brat. A godling."

"Godling. Priest. Blow hard. I don't really care," I said through gritted teeth. "Just kill me or shut up."

"You are in no position to make demandsss," Snake Face replied, pressing down on my dislocated shoulder and causing me to howl in a fresh round of agony. "Yet you may be right. My father alwaysss said I played with my food too much. But worry not; killing you is the furthessst thing from my mind. You and I are going to take a little trip."

Then, with one hand, he reached down and grabbed one of my legs. He hoisted me up like a caught fish and threw me over his shoulder. "The thingsss we will do," he mused merrily.

I tried to fight back, but my body was spent. Between his armor, my lack of weapons, and the fact that one of my arms dangled uselessly, there was no way for me to free myself. Gungra made it to the other side of the ship and held me up over the edge. Below us, I saw long wooden platforms floating on the water and tied to the barge with ropes. Already other Marauders were rappelling down the hull of the ship, back to their makeshift skiffs.

I'm pretty sure Snake Face intended to simply toss me down onto one, but he never got the chance. A streak of silver appeared to my right, roaring in defiance. The next moment, as Gungra cried out in a mixture of pain and surprise, he flung me back onto the deck of the barge. He raised a hand to his neck and pulled it back to find fresh blood.

Between the waves of mind-numbing throbbing from bouncing on the deck, I noted an important fact. If you can get behind his armor, apparently even godlings bleed.

My savior had come in the form of Mebi, Shahar's bounty hunter daughter. She continued her attack, her small blade lashing out again and again at the marauder. Her assault was enraged. When Mebi and I had fought before, her attacks had been measured, precise. Now she attacked almost by instinct, striking without thought for her own safety, cursing all the while.

"You will pay!" she repeated over and over.

No longer taken by surprise, Gungra parried the attacks with relative ease. "What do we have here?"

"You killed him!" Mebi roared.

Snake Face barked a laughed and backhanded the bounty hunter between strikes, sending her flying ten feet back where she landed near to where I still lay, watching the scene unfold. Snake Face laughed again. "I have killed many. I doubt I even remember who you're talking about."

Gungra's taunts struck true. When Mebi rose, her body trembled with raw anger. "You will die tonight," she said.

"You cannot kill a god," Snake Face said simply.

Mebi roared again and went to rush forward, but I grabbed her ankle a moment before she could. "No," I protested feebly. "You'll only get yourself killed."

The bounty hunter glanced down at me, her face curled up in ugly hate. "Let. Me. Go. They killed my father."

So that was it. Her father's death had sent her into a fit of rage.

"You will not avenge him tonight," I cautioned, panting. "As we are now, we can't win. We have to regroup. It's our only hope."

"He's right," Gungra mocked, boldly moving forward. "At leassst in part. However, you have no chance regardless how many times you regroup. Between godsss and demonsss, what hope do mere mortals possessss? Though fear not, you shall join your father very sssoon."

As the self-proclaimed godling stalked forward, my mind raced to come up with some kind of stopgap to keep him from tearing Mebi apart, but I had nothing. We were outmatched on every level. Then, with only five feet between Snake Face and us, the deck exploded. The blast sent both sides tumbling backward, and an inferno blazed to life in between us.

"We have to go," cried a man from our left. Ahyim appeared from the smoke, his black mask hiding him with the night.

"No!" Mebi said, pulling herself up. "They killed Father. I am not leaving until every last one of them is dead."

Ahyim grabbed his sister's shoulder. "Remember father's teachings. Rule number six: there is no profit in death."

Mebi growled harshly, but looked down. "This isn't over."

"Agreed," replied her brother, and then he turned to me. "Can you swim?"

I bobbed my head sideways. "Yes," but then I jiggled my limp shoulder. "But not with this."

Without asking, he grabbed hold of my shoulder and shoved it back into place. It hurt, a lot, which was pretty much the repeating theme of this latest escapade. The pressure slowly receded though, leaving me with all my other wounds to think about. But I could rotate my shoulder, meaning at least I wouldn't drown if we entered the water.

Across the burning and broken deck, Gungra watched us. The scaly mask still seemed to shift, and as the blaze licked at his legs without injuring him, he certainly did seem the part of either demon or god. He watched us as we shuffled to the opposite side of the deck. He actually smiled as we made it to the ledge, waving at us just before we dove into the ice-cold water below.

His message was clear; *I'll see you soon.*

CHAPTER TWENTY-EIGHT

WE DOVE INTO THE DEAD SEA BELOW, THE COOL SALT WATER managing to both burn my open wounds and soothe my deep bruises. The salt density in the water made us exceptionally buoyant as we started swimming away from the burning barge. Okay, swimming was a generous description of what I was doing. It appeared more like coordinated flailing than anything else, but eventually we made it to the shore. The entire beach was a chaotic mess, with troops from all six armies attempting to figure out what the hell was going on. The dock was also in flames, meaning there was no easy way for either the Marauders to attack the land, nor the soldiers on the land to get to the Marauders.

The chaos served our purposes well enough, as three more wounded and shocked soldiers weren't very conspicuous, and new warriors were constantly washing ashore. Ahyim seemed the most composed. He led the way through the various encampments. I shuffled after him because I had neither the strength nor passion to even attempt stealth.

My mind was a haze, making it difficult to figure out what emotions were rattling around inside of me. I was disappointed in myself that things had gone so poorly. Furious at the actions of the Marauders and the chaos they had stirred in our region, with a special level of hate reserved for the manic snake man Gungra. But more than anything else, I realized I was equal parts humiliated and hopeless. Snake Face had not simply gotten the upper hand in our battle; he had dismantled me on a fundamental level.

A hard smile crept up my lips. This was the first time I had failed so completely. My adventures had sent me against lions, bears, giants, slavers, and entire armies. In each case, I had been on the receiving end of a fair amount of pain, but I had always come out the other side victorious. There was no trace of victory tonight, only undeniable defeat.

The failure settled over me like a damp, soul-sucking blanket.

I didn't even realize the bounty hunter had stopped until my chest ran into his outstretched hand, calling our group to stop. Mebi must have been in her own little world as well, because she, the tail end of our line, then ran into me. Glancing around, I saw that Ahyim had taken us to the outskirts of the Philistine encampment.

He motioned to several large stones, and we each sat down around them. "So what did we learn?" he asked.

"That we have to kill the Marauders," Mebi snapped back.

"Think," he demanded. "You don't think I'm furious they killed father? I want to storm back to the beach and start ripping apart pretty much everyone right now. But it won't bring him back, and it won't get revenge. For that, we need to analyze what we learned from tonight's attack." He looked down, nervously fidgeting with his hands. "I'm not particularly good at this part. You're the smart one."

A crack in his sister's anger appeared on her face, and she took a deep breath. "The Marauders had inside information and probably help getting onto the boat. One of the six is the most obvious choice."

"Well I doubt it was the king of Ammon," Ahyim added. "I

watched one of the Marauder warriors run a sword right through him. The other rulers made it off the barge."

"I could have sworn it was Doeg," I said idly. "He was Erik's high priest. At least until our serpent friend pounded his fist through Doeg's face."

"So we have five suspects?" Mebi said, gazing forward.

"Four," I replied. "King Achish and his men got us onto the boat. If Doeg, Erik, and Phelia hadn't stopped him from defending me, this whole night could have been avoided."

"It could still be a long con," Ahyim said. "But I agree, it's unlikely."

"I appreciate the vote of confidence," announced someone from our left.

King Achish and Zalmon walked out from behind an outcropping of rocks. Zalmon led the king by the arm and carried a long, wrapped bundle slung around his back.

They reached us and the Achish bent his head. "Do you mind if we join you?"

Mebi and Ahyim traded a skeptical glance, but I nodded before they could interject. "Please sit, Your Highness."

Zalmon assisted the king in finding a spot on the rocks and then stood next to Achish, scowling. He clearly was not a fan of whatever reasons the king had for meeting us.

"Things have gotten messy," the ruler began, sighing.

"Messy?" Mebi snapped and launched herself to her feet. "Our father is dead."

Zalmon's hand went to the hatchet in his belt and Ahyim mirrored this motion with his daggers.

The king opened his palms and raised them into the air. "I apologize," he said. "I was not aware of your loss, and my words were inadequate." He pondered for a moment. "You two are the bounty hunter children of Shahar, are you not?"

Mebi nodded, but then realized the blind king couldn't see her. "Yes."

"My father spoke highly of him," the king replied. "He was a man of principles, who honored the bounties he took. I am sorry for your loss."

Ahyim lifted his hands from the hilts of his weapons. "Thank you. We all have suffered this day."

"Indeed," the king replied. "And the situation will soon spiral out of control. The attack has sent each nation back to recollect themselves, but soon they will turn their attention toward Philistia. Doeg had them believing I was the traitor in our ranks, and I doubt the assault did little to assuage their fears. Niklas is the only one who could confirm we're not the ones behind the assault, but they believe he's working with us."

"So what happens next?" I asked.

"If we don't discover the real culprit soon?" Achish asked. "Regional war."

Glorious. "So what can we do?"

King Achish placed his hands beneath his chin. "I need you to continue your investigation. Find evidence we can use, other-wise tonight simply becomes the precursor to something much worse."

I barked a harsh laugh. "I'm not sure if you've seen the success of my 'investigation' so far, but my track record has been a bit spotty with the Marauders. In fact, they just handed me my butt, toes, and head all in one fell swoop. I'm not the man for this job."

"If not for your efforts tonight," the king countered, "we all may have been killed. You're the only one who has had any luck in fighting against them."

If our hope rested on my shoulders, we were in a whole world of trouble, as the blanket of failure was wrapped tightly around my shoulders. "Again, I'm not the–"

"Niklas!" cried a familiar voice.

Yashobeam and Damon came running up. The prince rushed forward when he saw me. "Are you okay?"

I waved off his concern. "My ego is a bit tarnished," I looked down. "As well as my clothes and some of my limbs, but I'm fine."

Yashobeam walked into our little circle. "You look like something a drowned rat choked on."

"Thanks," I said, rolling my eyes. "How'd you two find me?"

"This is where we said we'd meet up," Yashobeam reminded me.

"Oh, right," I replied, so exhausted I had forgotten about our fallback plans, but was glad Ahyim had had the sense to remember. "Are our people safe?"

Yashobeam nodded. "I know you said to come riding in a blaze of glory if you were in trouble, but seeing as six armies were between us and the water, it seemed imprudent to attempt a rescue."

"You did good," I said to him, before turning to Damon. "Where were you? I was told you'd be at the parley?"

Damon's face crinkled in confusion. "I was never set to be a part of the talks," he stated.

I grimaced. Sethas must have lied in order to add extra motivation to get me here. Whatever, at least my friend was safe, though his presence now would not be a good sign. "And can I assume you're bringing some kind of horrible news?"

Damon's cheeks sank. "It's Father. He is marshalling his whole army to come after you. He's convinced you were behind the attack."

"Of course he is," I said, and my mind began working on some kind of plan. My brain was definitely working slower, but this seemed simple enough. "I'll just have to disappear for a little bit. It shouldn't be too hard to avoid his troops."

"He knows that," Damon answered softly. "So he isn't going to hunt you."

My eyes widened, already fearing the answer. "Who then?"

"Your family," Damon said. "He's aware they've been living as nomads along with the rest of Bethlehem and he has intel on where they're at. He also knows you won't let them die. You'll come to him."

Every time I thought this day couldn't suck any more, it found a way to surprise me. I ran the numbers in my head, already knowing that there was no way our people could withstand an attack by the combined might of the eleven other tribes in the Israelite army. We'd be slaughtered. Running wasn't a much better option. With as many elderly and children as we had in our camp, we'd never be able to outpace his men.

"Come to Philistia," King Achish interjected. All of us turned our heads to him. "If you can get your people within my borders, I can promise you sanctuary. Erik wouldn't attack my army and risk starting the regional war before we've all regrouped and prepared."

My head swung back and forth. "I'm not sure you comprehend how much Erik hates me." Still, I thought about his plan. It was our best option. I bit my lip, unsure. "Why would you help us?"

Achish smiled. "Because I believe you're the best chance we have at uncovering who is leaking our information to the Marauders, and you're not much use to me as a corpse. Beyond that, you saved my life tonight, it only seems fair."

"It'll be a foot race," I mused. "We should begin with a decent lead on his army, but once we meet up with our people and have women, children, and livestock to slow us down, they'll make it up quick. It's going to be very close."

"We better to get running then," Damon said.

"We?" I asked.

He smiled. "You didn't think I'd make you do this alone, did you? I've tried talking to my father, to reason with him. Now I'm going to try standing up to him."

The Philistine king stood up. "I do have one parting gift to aid you in your efforts." He motioned to Zalmon. The guard unfastened the large bundle on his back and handed it over to me. Even wrapped in sackcloth, I immediately recognized the grip of the hilt.

"Goliath's broadsword," I said, lifting it up over my head. It still felt supernaturally light.

Achish nodded. "Indeed. It should prove useful when you encounter the Marauders again."

"In the meantime," Mebi said, also returning to her feet, "my brother and I will return to Sethas and see if she has discovered any new leads."

Yashobeam grumbled something beneath his breath.

"She's helped us so far," I shot back, translating his warning. "And we're all aware she's crazy and dangerous. But right now the other team has recruited a freaking demon, so pretty much any type of dangerous aspect on our side might help even the playing field."

Damon's neck rocked back. "There was a demon?"

"I've got plenty of time to tell you about it on the trip," I answered, strapping the sword to my back and motioning him to follow after me. "We have a long run ahead of us."

CHAPTER TWENTY-NINE

"This may be my worst idea ever," I said as more of our people filed in behind the waterfall. "And that's saying something, given the history of my past ideas." As the refugees and orphans shuffled past me and into the deep cave hidden behind the waterfall, I reconsidered my plan for the hundredth time.

Isaiah shifted uncomfortably. "I remember some pretty bad schemes over the years. This one may work out." Despite his words, there wasn't much confidence in his voice.

The plan was a huge bait and switch. We had sent several men with a quarter of our combined flocks north, leaving a trail as if we intended to head to the heart of the tribe of Judah. Once they had traveled a dozen miles, they would abandon the flock and double back to our location. In the meantime, the rest of our herd and all of our people were packing into the caves of Ein Gedi—a massive mountain range on the west coast of the Sea of Galilee. Shepherds often used these enclaves as temporary sheep pens during storms.

It was a snug fit, but our combined group fit inside them. If our plan worked, they would serve as the perfect hiding place while King Erik and his men rode right on past. Once they were clear, we would have a straight shot to Philistia and to Achish's offer of sanctuary. If the plan failed, the caves would literally serve as our tombs.

At the center of the mountain range was a tall waterfall that poured into a beautiful spring. Behind the falls was the large cave, which also gave us access to a water source if we needed to hide for an extended period of time. The tan rock cliffs accented the crystal-clear blue water. In another situation, this would be a perfect spot for a nap.

"Do you have a moment to talk?" Abigail asked, walking out from the waterfall.

I shrugged and followed her back into the cave. Torches lit the way as we moved deeper inside. "Is everything going alright with the orphans? Eliab said they were integrating well with the rest of our people."

"They're doing fine," she replied, bobbing her head and pulling at her braids. "Your group has been beyond gracious. You have another problem I wanted to talk to you about though."

I smiled despite the circumstances. "Another problem? You mean beyond the fact King Erik has marshalled three thousand troops to hunt us down and murder us for treason?"

"Yes," she said, her tone very matter-of-fact. "Have you spent much time around the refugees lately?"

I stopped, looking at all the people around me. "What do you mean? They're all right here."

Abigail shook her head. "No. I mean have you talked to any of them?"

My head tilted to the side. "Deborah, Isaiah, Eliab, and my father have managed the day to day operations. I've had other things on my mind, like the aforementioned Mad King and the rampaging Marauders."

"That's my point," Abigail said, eager for me to see the connection. "Look around you."

I did. Refugees huddled together in small family units. Every man, woman, and child, each kept their heads down, refusing to even look up. Then I noticed it in their eyes, a feeling I had encountered a lot recently; hopelessness.

"Imagine what it's like for them," Abigail explained, her tone soft. "They've been driven from their homes by a mad king who has forsaken his oath to protect them. They seek out the one person who has ever managed to stand up to him, but where are you? Every other day you're running off to meet with this queen or that king, all the while leaving them alone." She paused. "They feel abandoned."

Ouch. Of all the crappy emotions I'd dealt with over the last few days, guilt hadn't been one of them, but it came roaring back with a vengeance. These families were hungry and scared. They had sought me out, believing the legendary Niklas could provide some level of safety and stability. Instead, they were met with a man who could never live up to his legend, who constantly placed them in danger, and who now had an entire army barreling down on them to destroy them.

Kudos to me.

"They need a place to call home," I decided.

"No," Abigail countered. "They need a leader. Actually, I take that back—they have a leader. They just need to know he sees them and that he has a plan."

I let her words sink in. She was right. I'd spent so much time rushing headfirst into solving the Marauder problem, I had removed myself from the people I fought for. It had made things simpler, but at what cost?

"You're kind of smart," I said, grinning. "Do you know that?"

Her eyes twinkled. "I'm glad you're catching on. Have you eaten yet?"

Her question gave me an idea.

An hour later, we had gathered our people together for a meal in the largest portion of the cave, and I stood over a cooking pot, ladling out stew to a long line of refugees. With every bowl distributed, you could see our people lightening up.

Prince Damon walked up next me. "An interesting use of your time," he said approvingly.

I offered him some stew. "I've heard it said a leader is measured by how he treats those under him. So I thought, 'What would Damon do?' and this is the best idea I could come up with."

"I'm honored," Damon said, a broad smile spreading across his face. "Food is the universal love language."

"Indeed," I agreed. "Plus, I have a speech lined up for our people. Bards will retell of its poetry and exhortation. It's equal parts humor and inspiration."

"I can't wait to hear it," the prince replied. "I'm sure it will–"

A piercing whistle echoed through the chamber, the designated alarm signal. Had Erik found us? I quickly put down the ladle. Sprinting back up the cavern, one by one, the torches were put out, making our trip up to the mouth of the cave all the more treacherous in the darkened shadows. The thundering of the waterfall pounded throughout the cavern, and as we reached its mouth, we found Eliab, Deborah, and Isaiah kneeling down and looking out into the spring.

"Has Erik found us?" I asked, terrified by the answer.

"Not quite," Eliab answered, clearly troubled. "But it's not that much better. Look."

Glancing down below, the evening sun sparkled over the spring. On its shore, no less than one hundred feet away, Erik's three-thousand-strong army was making camp for the night.

"This is an impressively large problem," I said.

"Do you think they know we're here?" Deborah asked.

Isaiah shook his head. "No, they're setting up camp. We just got unlucky on where they choose to do it."

Unlucky or stupid, I thought. We couldn't have known where his troops would rest, but it made sense they'd make use of the spring for the same reason we had; easy access to fresh water.

"If they discover the trail, or decide to peek around..." Eliab trailed off.

I finished his thought. "...then we're dead. Our only chance is to wait them out and hope they move on in the morning. Keep the people as far away from the cave's mouths as possible, and we'll set up sentries at every entrance. Make sure they do not engage the troops unless they're absolutely certain they've been discovered."

Isaiah nodded and went down to begin the preparations and set up a schedule for guard duty. I took the first watch without any incident. When my shift ended, I wanted to stay but knew exhaustion was counterproductive, even if the likelihood of sleeping with my sworn enemy so close seemed all but impossible.

I had turned over on my mat for about the three thousand and second time, when Uri came down to where I lay and shook my shoulder. "You have to see this," he said.

Following after him, we approached the entrance to the cave and he placed a finger to his lips. We crept up to where Yashobeam and Eliab, who had slept during the first watch, now waited. Thirty feet ahead of them, a torch burned on the ground and long shadows of a person flailed against the wall.

My brother Eliab's eyes were wide as I mouthed, "Who is there?" and he pointed emphatically toward the waterfall. I crept up a little further and discovered the Mad King himself standing in the mouth of the cave.

King Erik's hand lashed out. "I'll kill them all," he said and then took a long drink from a flask.

Great. At least he was being consistent in his objectives. No need to worry about what to do if he changed his mind on the whole killing me thing.

The king spun on his heel. "No!" he cried out, and turned to look further into the cave. I froze, but realized he couldn't see me in the shadows. "None of them deserve my trust. They're all plotting against me."

My eyes darted around the rest of the cave, fearful that if he had brought another ally, they might spot us. But I quickly realized Erik was alone.

"I know you told me," Erik continued to speak to the darkness, "but I can't kill off every general. Someone has to lead the army." He let out a piercing scream into the empty cavern, dropping his flask and placing both hands over his ears. "I need you to lower your voices and speak one at a time. I can't make out what you're saying if you all talk at once." He started breathing heavier and curled up into himself. He began softly crying.

I crawled backward to the rest of the group. "Get Damon," I said to Isaiah.

He nodded and went back down into the cavern, but Yashobeam's hand grabbed him by the shoulder, stopping him. "The king is alone," Yashobeam whispered, looking at me.

"Yes..." I answered, confused to what he was getting at.

"He has no troops to protect him," Yashobeam continued. "He's drunk. No one would suspect foul play if he were to have an accident."

I stared at him, finally understanding what he was insinuating.

"We have to at least consider it," Uri agreed. "*Before* we bring his son up here."

They were right. This opportunity was beyond fortunate. We were talking divine intervention level happenstance.

Eliab read my mind. "This could be bigger than us. Yahweh may be giving him into our hands. It's not like King Erik hasn't earned this."

I swallowed hard. I'd killed before. If I did it now, half of our problems simply disappeared. All I had to do was murder a man I had spent years living and eating with, whose son was my best friend, whose daughter I was once betrothed to, and who now lay sobbing, raving to himself on the floor of a cold cave. The decision tore me apart, but only one answer seemed clear.

"I need you to grab two things," I said. "The first is a knife."

CHAPTER THIRTY

THE MORNING SUN POURED INTO THE CAVERN AS ERIK WOKE HIMSELF with a jolt, still very much alive. Hungover mind you, but alive. Isaiah, Eliab, Damon, and I watched as the king picked himself up and stumbled out of the mouth of the cave.

Isaiah watched him duck behind the waterfall, white as linen. "This is now officially your worst idea ever."

"Noted," I replied.

Eliab stood next to me. "You do remember the last time you saved his life? He tried to kill you about a dozen different ways, right? What makes you think this time will be different?"

I had no good answer. "This is our only option."

"No," Eliab replied. "We could let him and his men leave and then proceed with the original plan of fleeing to Philistia."

"You saw him last night. He's not making rational decisions," I said. "Do you really believe he'll let us go once he realizes where we went? Or will he march his entire army against Achish, killing thousands of Israelites in the process?"

His silence spoke volumes.

"This has to end," I replied. "He will finally see reason, or he'll kill me. Either way, this comes to a conclusion today."

"Don't die," Isaiah pled. "Please."

"Noted," I repeated, turning to Damon. "Are you ready?"

He too was clearly uncomfortable with the plan, but he also hadn't been able to counter my arguments. Taking a deep breath, he placed a hand on my shoulder and bowed his head. "Almighty Father, protect our brother, Niklas." The simple prayer finished, he nodded. "I'll try not to get you killed."

I gave him a ten-pace head start before following after. The soldiers below had standing orders to kill me, and the last thing I wanted was an over eager warrior blowing up my whole plan before it started.

The prince ducked behind the waterfall, and I heard his voice address the troops. "Men of Israel, hear me! It is I, Prince Damon. I bid you a good morning. Behind me is a warrior who wishes to parley with my father. By order of your Prince, I command you not to fire upon or otherwise harm him until after your King hears him out."

That was my cue, though now I regretted leaving my broadsword in the cave. We didn't want to provoke a battle, but I felt naked and defenseless. Still, it was now or never, so I moved slowly out of from the thundering blast of the water.

The soldiers below collectively gasped, and an unpleasant amount of them drew their weapons. It made sense. For the better part of a year, I had been the most wanted man in the country, and now I stood available and vulnerable. A soldier may see an opportunity to impress his king. Here's to hoping that their love and respect for Damon kept them from acting on that opportunity.

No arrows sailed through the air, and I began my descent down the cliff. A messenger sprinted through the troops to alert Erik to my presence. Damon accompanied me, and we stopped ten feet from the mass of soldiers.

Erik stood a head taller than almost all of the men, so his approach was immediately apparent. The whole time he locked eyes with me, a deep, burning hatred dancing in them. His troops parted to let him pass, leaving a direct path between the two of us. He carried a long sword, his knuckles white from gripping it so tightly. His intention was clear; kill the Giant Slayer.

So everything was going as expected in the plan—this horrible, horrible plan.

He stalked toward us, but first turned his attention to his son. Without warning, King Erik slapped Damon across the face. "I could have you killed for siding with this usurper."

Damon didn't react, lifting his face to hold his father's gaze. "You will hear him out."

Every person who heard Damon's words, including myself, took a step back. The prince had given a direct order to the king. We were on a knife's edge here.

King Erik bared his teeth and growled, a sound far more feral than rational. He faced me. "You dare come into my presence? I should kill you and send one of your bones to each of the twelve tribes. It would be an adequate showing of what happens to traitors."

This was it. The moment of truth. Lifting my hand slowly, I opened my palm, revealing a tattered piece of linen. "I chose not to kill you," I replied.

His gray eyebrows arched, confused.

"Last night," I continued, "you slept in the mouth of the cave, defenseless and alone. I could have pushed you off the waterfall and no one would have been the wiser, but I didn't." I pointed to the bottom of his robe.

His eyes glanced down and noticed the torn corner of the cloth, the missing piece in my hands. He understood. His cheeks twitched and he began shaking. "I don't know what to do," he said softly. His gaze rose, and the longer it settled on me, the stronger it raged with hate. "You have to die. There cannot be two anointed! They say you have to die!"

"I know they do," I replied, dropping to one knee. "I place my life into your hands, my king. I only have two requests before you make your judgement. If you would kill me, first, promise to spare my family and those who travel with me. Second…" I paused to slowly reach behind my back and pulled free my lyre. "I ask that it be you who makes the choice and not the dark whispers in your head. Please allow me to drive away the demons one last time."

Bowing my head left me exposed and blind as I waited for his decision.

His response came as a bitter whisper, flicking his wrist. "Well musician, sing me a song."

CHAPTER THIRTY-ONE

I HAD THOUGHT THROUGH DOZENS OF SONGS BEFORE I SETTLED ON Forty Days to Forty Years. While there seemed very little commonality between Moses and Erik, I figured he might empathize with the leadership role.

I found a comfortable position to sit among the rocks. Erik followed suit, gesturing for the rest of his troops to take their seats as well. It appeared we would have a concert. Plucking the first five, I began the melody.

> "Drawn from a river into a palace
> Moses was doubly blessed
> No longer doomed a slave for life
> But given leisure and rest
>
> Yet day and night he watched his kin
> Be struck by rod and whip
> Fate offered chance to tear one brother
> From the oppressor's grip
>
> For to be called, you see
> Is an irresistible snare

And to be responsible
No room to forswear
Those entrusted to one's care

And for a single night it seemed
The rebellion would now commence
But once the pharaoh learned of the betrayal
Flight was Moses's only defense

Forty years in exile
Provided him a life
Yet the oppression of his people
Still haunted him, even far from strife

For to be called, you see
Is an irresistible snare
And to be responsible
No room to forswear
Those entrusted to one's care

Yahweh now became his answer
Send him against oppressors
This time armed with divine favor
Turned Egypt into the lessors

His people free, the time now came
For them to find a home
Of milk and honey, of land and peace
Where sheep and goat would roam

Yet one wrong word, and Moses lost
His right to join them hence
To only see it away from far
His only recompense."

The song usually finished with one last chorus, but given the circumstances, ending with the final verse seemed more fitting.

Throughout the song, I had intentionally avoided glancing at the king. I didn't want to seem patronizing, but I also feared I'd overcorrect if he didn't appear to be enjoying the song. Now though, I chanced a glance at him.

Tired eyes gazed back at me. I found no sympathy in them but saw that they also lacked the intense hate that had ignited them only minutes before. His hand was still on the hilt of the sword that rested across his legs. His fingers tightened around it, and he motioned for one of the soldiers to help him to his feet. The king walked up to me and rested the flat of its blade on my shoulder.

Every part of me wanted to close my eyes, or better yet, run away shrieking, but I locked gazes with him. If he planned to murder me, I refused to let it happen hiding as a coward. He moved the blade against my neck, its edge beginning to dig into my flesh. Damon shifted closer to his father.

"Walk with me," Erik said abruptly, removing the sword and turning on his heel. "Niklas and I need time alone. No one leave, and no one follow us. And keep special watch over my son. He has been acting like an impudent child as of late—treat him as such."

Again, the troops parted as he stalked forward, and I traded the briefest of terrified glances with Damon, but at least the king hadn't killed me outright, right? We still had a chance to salvage this mess. Walking through his troops, whispers of doubt and confusion moved like a wave through the soldiers.

"Aren't we here to kill him?"

"Did the musician cast a spell on our king?"

And the last, though spoken in a hushed whisper behind me, low enough that I doubted the king could hear, "What is King Erik thinking?"

All of a sudden, the paranoid whispers in Erik's head didn't seem so far-fetched.

We passed the edge of their camp, but Erik kept pushing further out. We walked the better part of a mile before he stopped our trek, glancing around a green meadow. "My flock used to feed here," he said, offering for me to sit with him.

I accepted his invitation and settled to the ground, surveying the land. "It's a great pasture." I agreed.

He was silent for a while. "Did you enjoy being a shepherd?"

Despite the direness of the situation, I laughed out loud. "I hated it something fierce. I considered it little better than babysitting crops that crap."

"A fitting, if not slightly jaded description," the king said, sharing a smile with me. "And what did you want to be?"

The answer came before I could realize what I was saying. "A hero."

It was the king's turn to chuckle. "It would seem you've gotten your wish, Giant Slayer." He took a deep breath and extended an arm out over the field. "This is what I wanted. It was peaceful, and I was good at it. This," he said, taking off the crown and flinging it to the ground, "was a burden I never asked for. Did I ever tell you why Alvaro even chose me?"

I had spent years in his court, but never had I heard that particular story. "I seem to remember the story of how he chose you, but not why, Your Highness."

"Alvaro told me the reason when he placed his curse on me. 'You were chosen,' he said, 'because you were the tallest Israelite in the country, and the people wanted someone who looked like a king. You weren't special,' he said, 'simply a few inches taller than the alternative.'"

"You've protected our country," I replied. "No one could ask for more."

"I've had help," he answered, raising his hand to stop me from speaking and nodding when he watched my eyebrows arch. "I know even now you work to protect Israel. Yes, I am aware you didn't have anything to do with the attack on the barge."

My neck rolled back in shock of his admission. "Then why do you pursue me now?"

The king bit his lip, and for a brief, terrible moment, something unsettling passed through his eyes. "Because you would steal from me." He took several measured breaths and shook his head, as if to fling the dark thought from his mind. "Do you enjoy being chosen? An anointed? A hero?"

I rubbed a hand across my face. "Enjoy is the wrong word. No one tells you about the terrifying reality of staring down rampaging armies, mythical monsters, and a seemingly endless list of enemies. I used to have to seek out mischief and trouble. Now it finds me." I paused. "I do find value in helping people though."

"Well said," the king agreed. "It's similar for me. Even after Alvaro sent this darkness upon me, the anointing remained. Since then, I've been pulled by two very different powers. The first, a deep longing to protect our people, and the second, a feral ferocity to protect that which belongs to me."

"The voices?"

He nodded. "They are strong. When they first came, I couldn't make them out. They were just background noise that sent me into fits of madness. Your music was my only salve, but then came news of your anointing, and I sent you away. When Doeg returned, he showed me how to listen to the voices. For a time, this served as an adequate replacement for the music that used to lead me.

"It didn't last though. Even before the Marauders killed Doeg, the voices were starting to lead me down a darker path. They nurtured the dark idea that only one man could be king, and that if I didn't root out those around me, my throne would be taken. That seed has bloomed, and its thorns are choking the life out of our nation."

"You're not alone," I replied. "Your son loves you, and he

would do anything to help you." I laughed. "And he's a hell of a lot better of a man than me and you. One day, your son will be the greatest king of Israel."

Erik leaned in, shaking his head slowly. "You don't know how the anointing works, do you?"

"What are you talking about? We protect Israel."

"Yes. We protect Israel, but as its king. You are the preordained ruler, and when I die, if you are still alive, you will be Israel's next king."

His words smashed down on me. It was like actually living through the expression "the weight of the world on your shoulders," but in real time. "No," I said, shaking my head as if having a seizure. "Damon will be the next king. He's literally perfect for it."

"I agree," Erik said. "It's why we have fought for the last year. Every time he's come to your aid, he's risked his birthright. Yet he never questioned it. He fully believes you should be the next ruler of Israel."

"I'll give him the throne then. If I offer it willingly to him, no one will question it."

The king glanced down. "Anointings don't work like that. Alvaro made sure of it."

"Then we'll bloody go find Alvaro and make him fix this mess," I demanded. "I'm not keen on usurping my best friend's throne. Alvaro pit us against each other, so he can figure out some sort of solution where none of us have to die."

The king's head tilted to the side. "Alvaro died two months ago."

My mouth hung open. The old codger had been an ornery, ancient fool, but for decades he served as Israel's judge, protecting our nation from countless numbers of horrors. When we first met, he told me he was to be our final judge, which meant there would be no new special savior coming to our rescue. We were alone to solve our problems.

"Without him..." I answered, not even able to complete the thought.

Erik spread out his hands. "Exactly. If Alvaro were still here, maybe he could figure something out, but as it is, if you stay, the voices will eventually win out." He paused. "I will kill you."

"I may have a solution," called a voice from the woods. The king drew his sword, and we both bolted to our feet. Uri walked out of the woods with his hands raised. "I apologize Niklas, but our people thought it best not to leave you unprotected, so I had Pavi follow you and lead me to where you went. However, as I said, I may have a solution if you need to speak to Alvaro."

"You missed the important part then," the king replied. "He's dead."

"I heard," Uri answered while approaching. "In my travels hunting the Marauders, I have come across many people with a number of," he paused, "let's call them gifts. One of these individuals was rumored to possess the ability to speak to the dead."

Erik tilted his head, unconvinced. "How would such a person exist within my kingdom without my knowledge?" He thought on the question for a moment, and then realized the answer. "Because they were afraid of me."

"Are you sure they're legitimate?" I asked, shaking my head. "Fortune tellers are common enough, but few possess any real power other than scaring a few coppers from the superstitious."

Uri shrugged his shoulders and readjusted the bow on his back. He left the cover of the trees, and his furry companion Pali leaped from the trees and landed on his shoulder. "The people from the surrounding towns certainly believed so." He paused. "There is one minor hurdle. She's said to have put a curse on her village.

"A curse?" I echoed. "Well that sounds like more than a minor hurdle. Who puts a curse on their own town?"

The archer raised his eyebrows. "You can go find out. They call her the Witch of Endor."

CHAPTER THIRTY-TWO

LESS THAN AN HOUR LATER, ERIK AND I BEGAN THE TEN-MILE TREK across the Jezreel Valley. Neither the king's nor my own elders were thrilled with the idea of the two of us leaving together. Deborah promised to say something kind at my funeral. Yet the double anointing situation was one the two of us needed to solve on our own.

Beyond that, Uri had cautioned us against scaring off the witch. It was said she had placed the curse on her village after a Marauders' attack, and then she had become a hermit. When Uri had ventured to her town, she wouldn't even come out to meet him, but spoke to him from the shadows of her home. If she saw three thousand plus troops approaching, she might bolt before we got a chance to talk to her.

So the Mad King of Israel and the traitorous Niklas set off on our own road trip. What could go wrong?

On a better note, the valley served as a major trade route between Israel and our southern neighbors, so our road was easily traveled.

"This witch poses a problem," Erik said, after an hour of walking silently.

"You mean besides the fact she may curse us as soon as we enter her city?"

"What if she deceives us?" he asked. "Uses our plight to her advantage?" One of his hands flew up into the air and the more he spoke, the more rabid the tone in his voice became. "We'll have no real way to discern if she's really speaking for Alvaro or if she's simply making it up as she goes. One woman could destroy everything."

We walked in silence for at least a quarter of a mile before I replied. The generals had convinced the king it was too dangerous to allow me to take Goliath's broadsword, but now I was kicking myself for not taking the lyre to calm his demons. They had just been pacified, but I hadn't expected them to return so soon. Finally, I said, "It must be hard."

The king arched his neck. "What must be?"

I shrugged. "Living without trust."

He shook his head. "You have no idea what it's like to know an entire country would as soon have you wrapped in a burial shroud as they would a crown."

It took concerted effort not to laugh. "You'd be surprised. It sounds a bit like having five individual kingdoms and a murderous gang of Marauders wanting my head mounted on a stick."

The king looked at me, and for a moment I wasn't sure if he would draw his sword. Then he shook his head. "How do you do it? Even before the voices, I dreaded the weight of our task."

I thought on his question. "I don't carry it alone. I have my family and friends to help me."

"But how do you trust them?" the king replied. "They could destroy you."

I shrugged my shoulders. "Trust is a choice. Each time you choose it, it gets easier."

I'm pretty sure the king and I were about to share a moment, but then the bolt of an arrow grazed my left calf.

"Blood and ashes!" I screamed, turning on my heel to determine where the attack had come from. Out from behind us, ten men wearing capes of black feathers approached us. One carried a bow, but the other nine brandished dabars, the same kind of knife I wielded.

"Your Highness," called the largest of the bunch, a man called Almon. "We have come to seek an audience with you concerning the wishes of our late master Gabril." He narrowed his eyes and his lips turned up into a harsh smile. "And then we'll kill you and your little pet."

Ten of the deadliest assassins that Israel has ever produced, the Seraphim, had come to murder us. Several coarse words ran through my head, all of which would have gotten my ears tweaked had my mother heard them aloud. The Seraphim constituted the most dangerous warriors in Israel. My training with them had turned me into an elite fighter. The ten warriors stalking toward us had the exact same training, and together a vast number more years to hone their skills.

Fighting one-on-one, I could hope to hold my own, but ten-to-one were long odds even for the most optimistic of outcomes. For a myriad of reasons, not least of all the fear that he'd literally stab me in the back, I couldn't depend on Erik helping me in the fight. Yet I knew these men, especially their leader. There was a small possibility of talking our way out of this before it escalated to battle.

I pulled out my knife, pointing it at Almon. "I let you live."

Almost a year ago, he, along with our master Gabril, had betrayed me in a larger plot to betray our country. Almon and I had fought, and after winning, I'd had the opportunity to kill him but had chosen instead to grant him mercy.

"A poor decision," my opponent replied. "You were next on our list to visit actually," he said. "After Gabril's defeat, we needed to figure out what to do, and we realized our training offered a unique opportunity. We'd try our hands as assassins for hire, and what better targets to make a name for ourselves than the Mad King and the famous Giant Slayer? We were determining how to get around Erik's guards when our two top targets left the protection of their men for a midday hike."

"Translation," I said. "You couldn't figure out how to get to the king and got lucky." I turned to the other nine seraphim. "You seriously chose him to lead you? He's the village idiot. If you need to lift an ox, he's your guy, but anything beyond showing you how to smash a bug with a rock is going to be beyond his mental capacities. We were trained to be the elite shadow force, not thugs for hire."

"Shut up," barked Almon. "These men chose me, not you, because Gabril chose me, not you. Our leader trusted me, while you destroyed everything we had worked for. Killing you will finally give us the respect we deserve."

The other Seraphim bobbed their heads in agreement, and their eyes told me they would not be swayed. The Seraphim had lived in Israel yet had remained separate from it; their own little enclave and family. Their organization had died the day I killed Gabril, and everything they had trained for had been ripped away from them. No matter how much I reasoned with them, they wouldn't hear me. Almon was offering them a way forward that still gave honor to their past.

Our options were worse than manure, because at least manure could be useful as fertilizer. My biggest concern though was that if Erik didn't make it back to his men, his army would slaughter my people, assuming I had been the one to betray him. "You're going to have to run," I whispered to the king out of the corner of my mouth. "I'll hold them off while you escape."

"No," he replied.

"If you die–" I began to plead, but he stopped me with a hand up.

"I do not plan to die today," he said, cracking his neck.

I gripped my blade tight. "The odds of us winning are nonexistent."

He drew his sword. "The odds of two anointed, fighting together, may exceed your expectations."

"You want to fight together?" I asked.

"You suggested I make a choice to trust someone," he said. "If not here and now, then when? Plus, don't you hear it?"

"Hear what?"

He laughed merrily. "The music," he yelled as he ran forward into ten, trained Seraphim assassins.

CHAPTER THIRTY-THREE

HUH.

It'd been almost a year since I had heard the music that used to guide me, the method the Guy Upstairs had chosen as His preferred form of communication when He had a task for me to accomplish. Erik, at one time, heard it as well, but when Alvaro cursed him, it had been replaced by the dark voices. The fact that he had just heard it seemed like a good sign. After all the bad blood between us, fighting alongside the king was never one of the options I had considered. Knowing we had divine favor on our side boosted my confidence, but these were still long odds.

Then again, rolling over and letting them poke us with their pointy knives seemed like a poor use of what little time we had left. I rushed forward. Our enemies were spread out in an open V-pattern and Erik correctly decided against attacking the center where they could more easily surround us. The king moved toward the furthest soldier on our right. The soldier parried, and immediately both of them began trading blows.

For a moment, our frontal assault took the rest of the group by surprise, but their training took over and they regrouped. However, not before I isolated the next two warriors on Erik's left.

Outnumbered as we were, we needed to remove as many Seraphim from the fight as possible in the shortest window, so I took a chance. I threw my dabar toward one of the soldier's legs, and he parried the attack. I was now without a weapon, but I had closed the distance between us. I grabbed the hand holding his weapon and pushed it down toward him, watching as the edge of his dabar cut deep into the meat of his thigh. He howled in agony as his other hand went to the wound, and I used my momentum to continue forward, tearing the weapon away from his grip and into mine.

I spun, and his closest compatriot was already upon me. He was an older warrior, his beard sprinkled with white, and he was much more tactical about his attacks. We circled each other like two lions, which suited his needs just fine. Every moment he kept my attention was a moment the other Seraphim could surround me. He made one miscalculation though, and as a sword slashed across his back, the mistake cost him his life. Erik had finished his opponent far faster than any of us would have given him credit for, freeing him up to come to my aid.

"Impressive," I admitted, panting while I did a quick check of the other Seraphim. "I had kind of assumed kings couldn't fight."

Our enemies had now managed to fully surround us. Even with three of their warriors out, they'd gained position on us, making our challenge significantly more difficult.

"Back to back," I suggested, turning my shoulders to Erik and scooping up the dabar I had thrown at my feet. I now wielded two dabars, one in each hand. Gabril had always been better at dual wielding than me, but hopefully I was a quick study. Like, boy genius, quick study.

"Now comes the hard part," I whispered to Erik. "This is basic tactics. Half of them will attack full on, while the other half wait, looking for an opening to strike. Be careful, if you see an opportunity that seems too good to be true, it's because it is."

Erik grunted an affirmation and then the next wave of

warriors were on us. Two Seraphim approached. A dabar's biggest weakness was its short reach, meaning they had to get close to connect their attacks. The warrior on my left went low while his partner attacked high, and both of my weapons managed to intercept their attacks, redirecting them off course. I positioned myself to lunge forward and counterattack, but stopped a moment short.

The decision saved my life. A second later, an arrow sailed through the air where my chest would have been had I lunged. My opponents gave me no chance to savor my decision and repositioned themselves for another assault. This time, they both went for my center torso. The position left me in an awkward stance. My arms had almost no leverage to fend off their attacks because I fought back-to-back with Erik and could not retreat to avoid the blades.

I leaned forward instead, and let gravity pull me to the ground, diving underneath their outstretched blades. I'd managed to avoid one of the blades, but the second nicked my side. It was not a life-threatening blow, but it would likely require stitches once this was all said and done, and for a moment my face split into a smile at the thought of Deborah tsking away as she patched me back up. Of course, enjoying that conversation required me to live through this fight.

I hit the ground and landed hard on my hands and knees. From this vantage point, I realized I was level with my opponents' ankles. I quickly lashed out with my dabars and managed to cut each of them. The wounds weren't serious, but it did force them to leap back.

I heard an unsettling twang and instinctively rolled to my side. An arrow pierced the ground where I had just been lying, and their archer was readying another shot.

Scrambling to my feet, I pushed back into Erik. "So you're still alive," I commented.

"Indeed," the king agreed. "But one of their blows cut my

wrist. As a result, I've been forced to fight with my off hand at the moment."

"That's a rather significant problem," I whispered. So far Erik had impressed me with his skills, but fighting with an untrained hand dropped one's ability by an order of magnitude.

"This could have gone easier," Almon said, walking up and scratching the scar on his cheek. "You realize the longer you draw this out, the longer I draw out your deaths. At this point, I'm going to make sure it takes hours to kill you."

King Erik's shoulders tensed behind us. "You will be the one dying today."

Almon began laughing. "We have you cornered and outnumbered. Niklas, explain the basics of battle to our soon-to-be-dead ruler."

Dumb as our opponent was, he was right. We'd done well enough holding them off as long as we had, but our luck was about to run out. "Erik," I whispered. "There's still a chance you can get away. If you–"

Erik ignored me. "I never knew the Seraphim were so bad at simple math. We are no longer outnumbered."

"Come again?" I asked quietly.

"Enough of this," shouted Almon. "Kill them."

"Yes," the king agreed. "Kill them, my pets."

One of the Seraphim behind me screamed. Every eye turned to see him crumble to the ground in a tangle of fur, but no sooner had we turned, than one of the other warriors cried out and howled in front of me. A spotted, gray and black, four-legged beast had bitten into his calf, biting deep into the bone. Erik's four hyenas had joined the fray.

Seraphim warriors were trained to keep focused against even the fiercest of opponents, but fighting savage beasts terrifies even the most hardened of soldiers. It would take them at least a couple of seconds to regain composure. We needed to finish the fight in that window.

I lunged forward and my blade crossed the throat of the man

wrestling against the second hyena. He dropped lifeless as I moved on to the archer who had retreated, allowing me to use the advantage of distance. As I sprinted forward, he fumbled with nocking his arrow, and when he finally took a shot, it sailed beyond my titled head. A hand went to his dabar, but failed to reach it before my own knife stuck him in the chest.

Whipping around, only Almon remained on his feet. The other four warriors were either dead or lamed and writhing on the dirt. All four hyenas now stalked toward him, with King Erik walking behind them.

"Please," Almon begged. "Your Highness—mercy. I can be useful. I have information on the Marauders."

"Really?" the king asked.

"Yes," he said eagerly. "One of their masked warriors has been giving us information on your whereabouts. Keep me alive, and we'll set a trap for them."

Erik seemed to consider his proposal. "Hm. It's a reasonable offer," he said, rubbing his hand across his bald head. "But then again, you and your pack just tried to kill me. I'm in a mood to return the favor." The king whistled harshly, and all four of his beasts rushed forward.

Almon managed to push away the first hyena, but the next one locked his jaw around his upper thigh, knocking the disgraced Seraphim warrior to the earth. Almon screeched as the king's three other protectors poured on top of him, ripping him to pieces. Literally.

I looked away as my stomach threatened to push up breakfast.

Eventually his cries ended, and I turned back to the king, who was on his knees, petting our four furry saviors, even while their maws were still covered in blood. He burrowed his forehead into the largest of the canines. Finally he stood up, noticing the look of disbelief on my face. "You didn't really think I'd venture off with my sworn enemy, the Giant Slayer himself, completely alone, did you?"

CHAPTER THIRTY-FOUR

Endor was deserted.

Uri had told us the Marauders had ransacked the small village five months ago. The marks of the attack still littered the streets with shattered pottery, torn tapestries, and broken field tools. A few areas had been spared; a clothes line drying several foreign dresses stood markedly untouched, but overall it was a ghost town. The corpses of said ghosts, thankfully, had been disposed of, but it left the empty village with a dark, ominous shadow as the evening sun set over the rooftops. The eerie quiet covered the village like a shadow, and for the first time, I wished Erik hadn't left his pack of "pets" outside the city.

"Uri didn't know where this witch lived?" Erik asked.

I shook my head, scanning the town for signs of life. "He said he met her out in the open, but she stayed in the shadows. I imagine if we wander around long enough, she'll find us."

Our introduction didn't take long. A woman covered in a dark and tattered cloak shuffled out of an alley. "You must leave," she said through staggered breath. "This town is cursed."

The king stepped toward her, one hand on his sword. "We seek the Witch of Endor."

At the name, the woman shuddered and recoiled back. "No,"

she countered, shaking her head. "You must leave. Nothing good will come from you being here."

I moved forward, slowly placing my hand on the hilt of Erik's weapon. "No harm will come to you or the witch, but our need is great, and only she can help us."

"Please," the woman pled, waving her left arm, a limb covered in sickly orange bumps. Erik and I took a step back. "The witch cursed me," she explained. "And she will do worse to you if you stay here. Please go."

The king shared a worried glance with me, silently seeming to ask me if I thought we should leave. As far as I knew, curses shouldn't be contagious, but then again, my knowledge of curses was as extensive as my knowledge of Egyptian belly dancing. The woman certainly seemed terrified enough, but if she was so scared, why had she remained in the same town as the witch? Something didn't add up.

I leaned in toward Erik. "She may be the witch."

Erik's face crunched up, but then he saw my logic. He squared his shoulders. "Woman. Do not deceive us. If you are the Witch of Endor, tell us plainly."

The cloaked woman shrieked. I doubted anyone could have faked that level of terror. "No. I am not her, but she will curse me further if you do not go." She backed into the wall of a small home and curled into the fetal position, tears starting to fall. "You're ruining our agreement."

"Agreement?" I asked, moving closer to her. She wailed louder, and I stopped my approach.

"Leave her be," called a woman's voice from behind us. Erik and I turned to discover another woman. She must have been in her mid-twenties, wearing a simple brown dress without any footwear. Her shoulder-length hair was the color of yellow wheat, and she peered at us with bright blue eyes.

"Who are you?" Erik asked.

She watched cautiously, probably determining if we qualified as friend or foe. Finally, she replied, "Some call me Antheia."

Walking past us, the yellow-haired newcomer knelt down next to the still weeping woman. "Esther, you have done fine. You are excused for the night."

"Have I...?" Esther tried to ask.

Antheia shook her head. "No. You have not extended your curse. You will be able to leave by the dawn of the new moon."

The frightened woman jerked her head up and down before retreating into one of the open homes.

Antheia stood up and returned her attention to us, shaking her head. "Whatever it is you want, I'm not offering. I repeat what Esther told you—leave."

"Our need is dire," I said.

"I'm sure it is," the witch replied, again walking past us. "Why else would anyone risk a meeting with the terrible Witch of Endor?" She waved her hands in exaggerated circles at her title. "Still, I do not practice anymore."

My head craned back. "You cursed that woman."

Antheia stopped walking, and her shoulders sagged. "I did not curse her. She was looting from the homes of my deceased friends, and I slipped a bit of poison oak in her drinking water. When she broke out in hives, I led her to believe that if she didn't stay here and drive away the occasional intruder for a month, I wouldn't heal her." She continued stalking away.

Erik motioned his head for us to follow the witch. I nodded back, and together we trotted after her.

I took the moment to put together the different pieces of information. "You're not from Israel," I commented. Her hair, skin, and eyes pegged her as a foreigner to the entire near east, let alone our own nation.

"Please stop following me," she replied and kept walking toward the center of town. "I can't guarantee your safety if you don't.

"Is that a threat?" Erik asked, ice in his voice.

"Yes," she said simply.

Erik's head jerked back at the comment, and the terrifyingly familiar and rabid look appeared in his eyes. "You dare threaten me?" he asked, pulling out his sword. "You are nothing but a charlatan, preying on the fears of a weak-willed woman."

Oh no.

At the sound of the weapon leaving his sheath, Antheia halted her advance. "Be careful—do not mistake my mercy on the thief as a weakness of my power."

Erik stalked forward. "I will hang your head from–"

Antheia raised one finger, and suddenly a thousand high-pitched shrieks filled the air. The king and I both froze, and a horrible, continuous crackling came from every home surrounding us. A breath later, hundreds of terrifying scorpions scurried out from every doorframe, window, and alley, completely surrounding us. Any thoughts on the limitations of her powers were thrown out, and Erik and I remained stiff as statues. The scorpions stopped their advance only inches from our open-toed sandals.

Antheia whirled toward us, her light eyebrows arched. "You come to my home, uninvited, and dare threaten me? You have grown foolish, Mad King."

Crap. Part of our plan was to hide our true identities from the witch, at least at first.

"Please," I asked, careful not to move with the insects so near. "The entirety of the region is at risk."

"I am aware," she replied harshly. "The leader of the Marauders approached me months ago, asking for an alliance. When I rejected the offer, they returned while I was away and pillaged our home. I have no love for them, but I will not risk our safety. I will not ask again. Leave." Her index finger bent forward, and the scorpions inched closer.

My mind raced as I tried to figure out some kind of leverage or offer we could barter with, but I had no idea of what you'd even offer a witch. Some kind of iron cauldron? She obviously had no love for the Marauders, but she also clearly had no

interest in angering them further. I swept my gaze across the
deadly scorpions still surrounding us.

Still though, it did beg the question; why was someone so
powerful terrified of the Marauders?

I bit my lip and took a chance. "You said you 'will not risk
our safety.' Who else is here?"

Antheia's eyes grew wide at my question, which I took to
mean I had guessed correctly. Unfortunately, my inquiry also
provoked our captor. As she swept her hands out, the scorpions
surged forward, crawling up our legs before we could even
react. "I will scatter your ashes from the sands of Persia to the
shores of Greece!"

Breathing steadily as the scorpions climbed my body became
a labor of unparalleled effort, but I held both hands up. "It was
not a threat. The Marauders have taken from all of us. Please, we
don't expect you to fight them, we only wish for you to help us
contact someone."

The witch glared at me, and I saw nothing but death in her
gaze. I refused to look away, but I knew there was nothing more
I could say to sway her.

"What would mother do?" asked a child's voice from one of
the larger homes.

Antheia jerked her head to the home. "Marcela, go back in
the house. You promised not to leave until I said it was safe."

Out of the corner of my eye, I saw a young girl, maybe eight
years old, exit the house. The scorpions parted as she walked
forward. "And you promised no one else would die in our
town."

The witch grimaced in response to this.

Marcela walked up and took our would-be executioner's
hand. "What would mother do?" she asked again.

Antheia let out a long breath and shook her head. Without a
word, the scorpions suddenly scurried down my body and
began returning to whatever dark place they called home.

"I will not fight the Marauders," the witch said quietly.

"We do not seek your aid in fighting them," I said, glancing nervously at the king, not knowing how his madness would respond to an untold number of creepy crawlies almost poisoning us to death. His gaze was cold, but he seemed rational enough to not to provoke her further.

"What do you need?" asked the young Marcela cheerfully, as if inquiring what we'd like to eat.

After what we had just witnessed, our request seemed rather modest. "We're hoping to speak to one of the dead. His name was Alvaro."

The witch brought her eyes up slowly. "And then you'll leave?"

"We swear it," I said, bringing a hand up to my heart.

"Fine," she relented. "I will perform this one task for you, and then we're finished." She held out her hand. "Where is the object you brought of Alvaro's to use to channel his spirit?

Erik and I traded confused expressions.

I bit my lip. "Crap."

CHAPTER THIRTY-FIVE

Antheia glared at us. "Seriously? How did you expect me to communicate with him?"

I opened and closed my mouth several times like a freshly caught fish. "I don't know," I finally answered. "Witchcraft isn't exactly something we're overly familiar with in Israel."

"Translation; you execute any witch you discover—I'm well aware. Still, without some item of this man Alvaro, calling forth his spirit is all but impossible," she said.

"What if we had an item he once used? Would that work?" the king asked.

"It depends on how important the item was to him," the witch replied. "What do you have?"

Erik held out his sword. "Over three years ago, Alvaro took this sword and used it to execute the king of the Amalekites. As far as I know, it was the last time he participated in a battle. It was also the day he cursed me."

Antheia's face crinkled up. "It's far from ideal, but without anything else, we'll have to hope it's enough. Follow me."

She led us into the house her sister Marcela had poked out from. Beyond the usual kitchen and household wares, she kept a small ceremonial corner littered with scrolls, odd smelling containers, and a small fire pit. Above the fire pit, the roof had a small hole in it for the smoke to bellow out of. I wondered idly what she did when it rained. Antheia motioned for us to take a seat around the fire pit and began preparing a small flame.

"This ceremony is going to require absolute concentration and patience," she told us, shaking her head. "Something you two thus far have shown a severe lack of. We could honestly be here for hours before I'm able secure a connection, and even then, his presence may not be strong enough for us to actually communicate."

"But you have done this successfully before, correct?" I asked.

"Yes," the witch replied curtly. "But those times I was working with hair or blood from the deceased."

"She's already making excuses," growled Erik, again running his fingers across his hilt.

The witch sensed his hostility, her eyes narrowing. "You are welcome to leave," she said before flicking her wrist. The sound of a thousand scurrying scorpions rattled through walls. "Or I can bring my friends back out if you'd prefer."

"We appreciate any assistance you can offer," I interjected hastily, trying to deescalate the situation.

Erik mumbled something noncommittal as Antheia went back to her preparations. When she finished, she asked for the sword. She said a silent incantation over it, and then drove the tip of the blade several inches into the center of the fire pit, the flames dancing around its metal as it stuck straight up.

She knelt back down and asked for our hands. "Now we begin," she said. "Again, I caution you, this will take time, hours at least, and if and when he arrives, we won't be able to see him."

"We understand," I said, shifting into a more comfortable position.

Nodding, Antheia closed her eyes. "Great Alvaro, we seek your counsel, please come to our–"

A deafening blast exploded from the fire, tearing our hands apart and throwing us all several feet back. Though still early in the evening, all light disappeared, save for the orange glow of the fire. A moment later, the smoke from the pit began to swirl, eventually coalescing into a dark silhouette of an ancient man with a long wiry beard and angry eyes. Scratch that—furious eyes. Israel's last judge, Alvaro, hovered above us in the form of black smoke. The ancient prophet swept his eyes over the home as if he were having trouble seeing anything in the room.

Antheia screeched, pulling nervously on her yellow hair. "What the hell?"

I swallowed hard. "I thought you said you've done this before."

Her eyes fixated on the smoky silhouette. "I have, but they've never appeared like this."

Alvaro lashed out his arm. "Who dares interrupt my sleep?" he shouted as he continued to glance around the room. The longer he remained, the more his form solidified. "Have I not given enough? Do you need to..." his voice trailed off as his eyes focused first on King Erik, then on me. "You two!" he roared.

Erik and I both scrambled back, terrified of what the dead, furious judge could do to us.

The judge tried to move forward, but seemed locked to the fire pit. His body shook from frustration. "For decades, I cleaned up Israel's mess, and when I finally achieve some semblance of peace, my two replacements find some forsaken way to bring me back."

When living, his connection to Yahweh had given him terrifying abilities, not the least of which had cursed Erik, but he was angrier now than I'd ever seen him. Who knew what kind of horrible powers he had access to now from the grave?

Despite that fear, I appreciated his anger. He had a legitimate point. Erik and I had replaced him, finally taking the burden of protecting our country off his shoulders. Mind you, that should have happened while he was still alive, but both Erik and I had leaned on the judge multiple times after his retirement. Death should have given him a final reprieve, yet even then we'd found a way to drag him back into the mess. I'd be furious too. Still, we were lost without his aid, and the Marauder threat could destroy everything he had worked for.

I had to dig deep to find a kernel of courage but pushed myself forward. "Our sincerest apologies," I said, bowing and touching my forehead to the earth. "Were our need not dire, I promise we never would have attempted such an action."

"The challenges are always great," Alvaro replied dismissively. "You two simply have a knack of finding ways to exasperate them."

I held my hands up, conceding the point. "A fair determination. Yet our need is real. A threat unlike anything Israel has ever faced threatens to destroy our very existence."

The smoke silhouette started laughing. "Unlike anything has Israel has ever faced? Learn from history, boy. Our nation has survived worse. It will survive this."

Well this was going great so far. "Please," I pleaded. "We need your help."

"And why should I give it?" Alvaro snapped.

"Because we are asking together," Erik said, entering the conversation. "You always wanted us to work in tandem, correct? Well, now we come as one voice, seeking aid."

The judge went silent, crossing his arms.

"Is there nothing we can offer you?" I asked.

Alvaro growled in frustration, glaring at me. I was pretty sure he intended to tell me where I could shove my offer, but an idea seemed to spring to light in his eyes, and he tilted his head in thought. "If you promise to check on my wife, and doubly promise to never pull this forsaken stunt again, I will offer counsel one last time."

"I will do more than check on her," I promised. "I will look after her as my own mother."

The silhouette's shoulders sagged. "Fine. Tell me of the trouble that brings you here."

Erik and I recounted the last year, focusing on the blight known as the Marauders. Alvaro nodded along, and once we were finished, he appeared to be listening to an unheard voice, a common sign he was communicating with the Divine.

"Yahweh says you have brought this on yourself, Erik."

"What?" the king answered. "I have fought against the Marauders for months."

The judge's voice got soft. "This all goes back to the Amalekites."

"Are you kidding me?" Erik roared, launching to his feet and stalking around the room. "Still you throw one decision into my face. I allowed some men and livestock to live, so what? The very next day you killed their king, and not one month later, the Marauders slaughtered their whole clan. Why does *one* wrong decision get to destroy everything I have worked for?"

"You knew full well the extent of their crimes!" Alvaro shot back. "Offering human sacrifices to their 'god' and drinking the blood of their victims, all in some vile attempt to syphon more power from their false idol."

The king's eyes blazed in indignation at the prophet's chastising, but then his gaze fell downcast, ashamed. "But they are gone," he repeated, his voice barely above a whisper.

Alvaro lowered his voice and shook his head slowly. "You're only seeing one step ahead. His" —the judge nodded upward— "plans work toward events that are months, years, or even centuries into the future. Your actions, and the lack thereof, had untold consequences."

"So you want us to just give up?" I asked. "Just let Israel suffer?"

"No," Alvaro sighed, "I want you to do your jobs."

"And what job is that?" I asked, growing frustrated. "Last time you at least gave me some direction; uncover the traitor.

Vague as that was, it gave me a compass bearing to follow. What do I do now?"

The judge again moved his head back and forth, this time taking a long sigh. "You two already know what you must do." He pointed first to the king. "Rule Israel justly as its king." Then he pointed to me. "Stop the Marauders as Israel's protector."

"But that's exactly why we made a deal with a witch to summon you. We have no idea how to do that."

"You still don't understand what being an anointed means, do you?"

I couldn't help but laugh. "I would think our ignorance would be pretty apparent at this point."

"Being anointed isn't about *you* at all," Alvaro said. "It's not about *your* strength, or *your* wisdom, or even you making the right decisions."

"What does that even mean?" Erik asked.

"It means you're both a part of something bigger than yourselves. It means you have a part to play, but only a part. Stop trying to do everything."

"So what do we do?" I paused. "What does He want us to do?"

"You were already doing it. Erik, rule Israel to the best of your ability. Niklas, find and stop the Marauders."

I flung my hands in the air. "But we don't know where they are!"

"Yet." Alvaro simply said. "So wait."

"But in the meantime," I argued, "Israel gets closer to war."

The judge pointed to Erik. "Which is his problem. That you're working together is good, but from here, your paths diverge. The Marauders are your mission, Niklas. Tackling Israel's current political problems is Erik's."

The king bowed his head, shaking. "But I can't," he said just above a whisper. "The voices, they won't let me…"

Alvaro's shadow began to waiver, but even as his face lost its clarity, his concern for Erik was clear. His fingers of smoke beckoned Erik nearer. "Come here."

The king looked up, expectancy battling hopelessness. He shuffled cautiously toward the fire.

Alvaro placed his ghostly hands around Erik's head. "Be at peace," he said softly, "until your watch has ended."

Erik's eyes rolled back, and he let out a long, healthy breath. "They're gone," he said.

The judge's silhouette continued to dissipate, and his voice began to fade. "Protect Israel, stop the Marauders, and try not to kill each other."

"That's it?" I said desperately. "You have nothing else?"

His form completely vanished, and for a moment, we all believed he was gone, but then his voice carried on as a whisper. "They will try to convert you. Do not let them."

What was that supposed to mean?

"Oh, and Niklas," Alvaro's disembodied voice said, as if a whisper in my ear. "If you fail, your family will die."

Of course they would. What else was new?

CHAPTER THIRTY-SIX

THE EMBERS OF THE FIRE ABRUPTLY DIED OUT, LEAVING US WITH ONLY moonlight to see by. Antheia rose from the ground, more confidant in her stance now that Alvaro's ghostly form no longer lingered over us.

"We had a deal," she said, taking a deep breath and pointing toward the door. "You talked to the prophet, now it's time you fulfilled your end of the bargain. Leave."

My shoulders clenched at the command, concerned her order would be seen as disrespect by the king.

Erik stared down toward the still smoldering fire. When he finally looked up, he smiled and nodded his head. "You are correct. We will leave, and I promise no more harm will befall you nor your little sister." He bent low. "You have my appreciation for the service."

Huh. The Mad King seemed, well, *not* mad.

"Niklas," Erik said to me. "We have imposed on these young women's hospitality long enough. Let us take our leave."

Not wanting to push our luck with the witch's scorpions, I repeated my thanks and followed after King Erik. Marcela waved eagerly, grinning ear to ear, as we ducked out the door. Her childish enthusiasm rubbed off on me, but the light in my eyes disappeared as we left the town. The lack of any clue of what my next move should be began tying my stomach in knots.

"I'm screwed." I surmised, exhausted, as we reached the major road between the witch and our troops.

The king raised his eyebrow. "How so?"

"Not only did we fail to discover anything useful about the Marauders, but now any doubt that this mess is on my shoulders alone is gone, with the added benefit of my family again being on the chopping block if I fail."

"Can offer a word of counsel?"

"I'm pretty sure the fact that you're called 'Your Highness' means you're free to do just about whatever you want at this point."

He shook his head slowly. "Oh, I think you'll find the crown comes with far less freedom than most would expect."

I stopped walking forward. "I told you, I'm not taking the throne. You're king now, and Damon will be next in line. End of story."

His smile remained undeterred. "We shall see what the future holds, but that eventuality is of little concern for this conversation. At this point, I believe your best option is patience."

I barked a harsh laugh. "The Marauders are killing everyone they can get their hands on. Time isn't exactly our ally here."

"True," the king nodded. "But say you even knew where they would strike next, do you currently have the power to stop them?"

A flashback to their horde of armored soldiers sent a fresh shiver down my back. "No."

"So I would counsel faith."

"You?" I asked skeptically. "Faith?"

"I'm thinking clearly for the first time in months. Consider it a bit of an awakening. But yes, faith. Damon has been counseling me to have more of it for a while now, actually. Do you know what he says sits as the bedrock of all faiths?"

I shrugged my shoulders, pondering the question.

"The belief that something larger than us is out there, that the world doesn't go on by our sheer force of will." He placed a hand on my shoulder and looked me in the eye. "Let me suggest you do something that you, or I for that matter, are not particularly good at; wait on Him," he nodded upward, "to make the next move."

"The region is on the brink of war and the Marauders threaten to pillage everyone I care about, and your advice is to simply wait on the Guy Upstairs?" I barked a laugh. "I'm confident He's doing something behind the scenes, but His movements are focused on the bigger picture, His timing on local issues are unreliable at best."

The king laughed. "Waiting is hardly simple. How did you put it earlier? 'Trust is a choice. Each time you choose it, it gets easier.' Beyond that, I believe you are traveling with a band of refugees. Taking care of their needs could be good practice."

"I told you," I repeated, knowing where he was going with his comments, "I have no interest in the thro—"

"Neither did I," the king interrupted. "But my counsel stands, and in true irony, it matches Alvaro's counsel. Wait and protect those in your care."

I reflected on his words before changing the subject. "I imagine our people probably expect that we've killed each other by now."

"You have that going for you now at least—one less person wants you dead," the king said, pointing at himself.

"Great," I said. "Now I just have another horde of bloodthirsty killers left to convince. Hopefully that task is a bit less dangerous than dealing with the Scorpion Witch."

Yeah, I doubted that too.

CHAPTER THIRTY-SEVEN

THE MASSIVE AXE SWUNG DOWN, SPLITTING THE THICK LOG WITH ONE blow. Eliab wiped the sweat from his brow, set the axe down, and took a breath. "And then the king just let you go?"

"Yep," I said, reaching for his axe.

He handed it to me. As soon as he let go, the head of the axe plunged down. Sweet Abraham, the thing was heavy. Whatever supernatural assistance I had received to carry the broadsword never seemed to apply to other weapons.

"It's one less problem you have to worry about," my eldest brother said. "King Erik had enough men to run down all of us."

"True," I said. "Though we still have those pesky Marauders to deal with, and apparently that task rests squarely on my shoulders."

"Our shoulders," Eliab corrected me, taking back his axe. "You're not alone anymore. You have people who can handle the things you can't." He lifted the thick axe with ease, demonstrating his point. "You have brothers, sisters, and friends to help carry the burden."

"All right then, oh wise and gracious brother," I said, playing along. "How do we find the Marauders? Then, once we accomplish that feat, how do we, a band of misfits, destitute people, and orphans, stop a bunch of bandits who are already equipped with enough armor to fortify Pharaoh's army?"

He shrugged. "I have no idea."

"You're not helping," I admitted.

He looked down at the pile of firewood all around us. "Right now, our people could use this wood a bit closer to our encampment. Want to help?"

It was my turn to shrug my shoulders in acceptance. As we walked through the camp, it dawned on me how many people we'd passed that I didn't know. In the beginning, most had been from Bethlehem or one of our surrounding villages. Our group had expanded well beyond our initial core. "How many people have now joined us?" I asked.

"Last I checked, we were right under one thousand, but that was several days ago. Every day we're getting new refugees, so I bet we've broken that number by now."

I raised my eyebrows. "Where are they coming from? Has Erik started persecuting other tribes in Israel?"

"Some are Israelites," Eliab answered. "But not all of them. We've got people from each of the six kingdoms."

I stopped walking. "Really? Why are they coming here?"

Eliab set down the wheelbarrow and placed an arm around me. "War is breaking out in every corner of the region, and our little gang of misfits offers a level of protection to the displaced or defenseless. Plus, I'm pretty sure your girlfriend started spreading the word that our group was a place of safety."

"She is not my girlfriend," I said, a touch too quickly.

"Of course she isn't," Eliab said, grabbing the handles on the wheelbarrow. He took two steps, but then his foot hit an uneven stone and he slipped, crying out. My brother fell to the ground and immediately reached for his ankle. The moment he placed pressure on it, he groaned again in pain.

"That looks pretty nasty," I said. "I'll find Deborah. She's good at stuff like this."

Eliab grunted his acknowledgement.

Our camp was set up in the shape of a giant horseshoe. I hurried over to where Isaiah and Deborah had their tent. I rapped on the outer flap and checked inside. No one. Now that we had safely reached Achish's territory and finally been granted a long-term place to stay, our truce with Erik still too fresh to risk returning home, Deborah had set up an improvised smithy on the outskirts of our encampment. She could be working there now on new armaments for our troops.

Halfway to the smithy, Abigail called out to me. "You seem to be in a bit of a hurry."

I nodded. "Eliab slipped and wrecked his ankle. I'm looking for Deborah for some medical aid."

Abigail grimaced and shook her silver hair. "She left an hour ago to visit one of the Philistine settlements. She's hoping to barter for iron and other supplies."

"Blood and ashes," I said under my breath. "She's the best healer we have. My mom's not bad, but Eliab's injury is pretty nasty."

"Allow my attendants check on him," she offered. "One of the sisters, Nakoma, has experience. Between all the children, we're constantly stitching up one kind of wound of another."

Our options were limited and I trusted Abigail's judgement. Turns out, she had actually undersold Nakoma's abilities. The foreign sister arrived with a large satchel to where we waited with Eliab, and she quickly went to work on Eliab's wound. She had it cleaned, stitched, and wrapped within a handful of minutes. She also fed my brother a green paste. It smelled something awful, but within minutes, his groans of pain faded away. The medicine had a noticeable side effect on his personality, as well.

"Niklas!" he cried out suddenly with a smile on his face. "I think I shall either name my next son after you," he paused in deep thought, "or after an ostrich."

"I'm sorry, what?" I asked, equal parts confused and amused.

"Both of you are fierce. Both of you are ornery. Both of you keep your head in the sand." He burst out in laughter, cackling at his own joke.

"What was in that paste?" I asked Nakoma.

A sly smile crept over her face. "Mother named it The Sojourners Delight. How do you say... it numbs wounds well enough, but it numbs the mind a touch as well."

"A touch, huh?" I asked skeptically.

She nodded to my brother. "He's a big man. I had to give him big dose to make sure of its effects."

It took all three of us to haul my brother back to his tent. Once we'd laid him down, Nakoma assured us that his ankle would heal in time, so we left him in the care of his wife.

The firewood still needed to be delivered, though. Abigail offered to assist me in the task. We moved about the camp from enclave to enclave, and it gave me the first up close look at the diversity within our group. I heard at least half a dozen accents I couldn't identify. Abigail was familiar with almost all of the foreigners, and she made a point to introduce me to everyone.

The experience was strange. So many of these individuals had come from lands that I had at one time feared. Edomites supposedly offered human sacrifices, yet the kindly Edomite grandmother I met only offered ginger cookies. The Moabites sold slaves, yet the elders of their enclave were concerned with how they might contribute to the work of the camp. The interactions introduced me not to the depraved foreigners I had once visualized, but to neighbors whom I could only dream of.

It took several hours to finish the deliveries and introductions. "They're not what I expected," I said.

"How so?" Abigail replied.

I paused. "They're just like me and you."

She smiled. "Indeed."

I'm sure I was about to come up with some impressively wise insight, but our conversation was cut short by Deborah and Isaiah's arrival. They sprinted up, out of breath.

"We finally found you," Isaiah said, doubling over and trying to return air to his lungs.

"What's wrong?"

Deborah's caramel cheeks turned down. "War."

"What?" I said, stepping up. "Who's going to war? When I left King Erik, he was going to press for a truce."

The blacksmith shook her head slowly. "Not just between Israel and Philistia," she said, meeting my eyes. "Each of the six kingdoms has mobilized, every one of them blaming another for the Marauders' attack. They say, combined, they've gathered over twenty thousand soldiers."

I swallowed hard, imagining the outcome of such a battle. "But that scale of war..." I trailed off.

"It's going to be a bloodbath," Uri answered, walking up from behind the group.

Fear gripped my chest, but I focused beyond it. We needed to figure out some way to avert the upcoming battle. The Marauders had played their hand well, destroying any chance of a regional truce on the barge. The countries no longer trusted one another.

There was only one option. I turned to Isaiah. "Ready every able-bodied man we have. We have people from every kingdom. If we arrive together, we may be able to broker some kind of peace."

Abigail placed a hand gently on my shoulder. "Niklas," she said quietly. "This may be a problem you can't fix."

Isaiah nodded. "Brother, I know it sounds terrible, but didn't Alvaro say this was Erik's problem? We're supposed to be handling the Marauders."

I shook my head. "We have to at least try, or there may not be an Israel to return to once this is over."

CHAPTER THIRTY-EIGHT

KING ACHISH SAT IN HIS COMMAND TENT, FLANKED BY A GLOWERING Zalmon on his right. He rubbed the purple cloth covering his eyes and shook his head wearily. "This is the only way," he said. "The other five kingdoms have already mobilized, and the parley yesterday was unfruitful. The king of Edom pulled a knife on the new ruler of Ammon, and we were fortunate to leave the site without bloodshed."

"But Erik wasn't there," I countered. "I promise you, he's changed. If the two of you present a case for a truce together, we can still avert this crisis."

The young ruler sighed. "Even if I believed that the Mad King's demons have been banished, which quite frankly I doubt, it wouldn't be enough. I refuse to put my soldiers at risk. If any nation shows an ounce of weakness, the others will pounce on them first."

"Peace is not weakness," I quoted. "You taught me that."

"And I still believe it, but sometimes war is inevitable, even if it's always terrible."

"This is exactly what the Marauders want," I said, and began to pace. "We'll all slaughter one another and then there will be no force left to stop them."

The king's words came out as a whisper. "I know."

I took several controlled breaths. King Achish was by far the most reasonable of the six monarchs, and if I couldn't convince him, we had zero shot at persuading the other rulers.

"You're already putting your soldiers at risk. If you go to war, Philistines will die. And for what? What does victory even look like after this?"

"Survival," said Zalmon, speaking for the first time.

It was clear that this wasn't an argument I was capable of winning, but I refused to simply see the region descend into chaos. How many lives would be lost? Tens of thousands of fathers, husbands, and sons would not be returning home to their families. I had one last chance.

I dropped to one knee. "Let me and my men join your army then. We have over three hundred fighting men, most of whom have been tested in battle. We'd be valuable allies on the field."

Zalmon actually started snickering as his fingers distractedly rubbed at the remnant of the burn on his face. "Tell me you're not serious? Our generals would revolt if we sent you into battle with them. We'd be better off killing you and laying you at our soldiers' feet. It would, at least, help with the morale."

"I concur," King Achish said. "At least with the argument that we can't take you with us. While I hold you in high regard, Niklas son of Jesse, let us not pretend that you would willingly fight against your own people. I do not fear that you would betray us, but you'd attempt some kind of scheme to avoid the war. A noble idea, but one that would likely end in more of my soldiers dying."

I silently cursed. Were they one hundred percent correct about my true intentions? Yes. Did I still want to throw them out a window for realizing my real agenda? Absolutely.

"You are correct about one thing," the king said, sitting up a little straighter. "The Marauders are the true threat here. If they are not stopped, regardless of what happens on this battlefield, our region may never recover if they are able to leverage this opportunity. I would ask a favor of you, good Niklas."

Still fuming over his rejection of "assistance," I looked up begrudgingly.

"In your search for the Marauders," the king continued, "I'd ask you to take along Zalmon."

"What!?" Zalmon and I said in unison.

"Your Highness," the advisor pled. "You will need my assistance in the battle to come."

"And his default solution to pretty much every problem is, 'Execute Niklas,'" I continued.

The king held up an open palm. "Zalmon, you are my most capable advisor, but this battle requires the expertise of field generals. The Marauders are the true threat. I am asking you to assist Niklas for the survival of our nation." Achish turned toward me. "Niklas, I swear to you on the honor of my kingdom, Zalmon will serve you with intelligence and faithfulness. He will offer unparalleled aid."

A smile crept up my lips despite my failure. "And with Zalmon latched to me," I openly mused. "I won't be able to try and follow behind the rest of your army and make some kind of desperate play to divert the war."

Achish had a smile that mirrored my own. "A fortunate secondary benefit."

I still wanted to argue, but it was a lost cause. Alvaro had told me my task was rooting out the Marauders, and no matter how I struggled otherwise, this clearly wasn't a challenge I could assist with. It was time to go home.

"Well come on then," I commanded Zalmon. "Let's get this miserable caravan on the road, Zal. If we leave now, we may make it home for breakfast."

The return trip was uneventful until we reached the far side of our encampment. The metallic scent of blood sent me sprinting forward.

Our camp was deserted and destroyed. The Marauders had come while we were away.

CHAPTER THIRTY-NINE

BLOOD SURGED THROUGH MY VEINS AS OUR MEN AND I RUSHED through the camp. Weaving between the tents, we found broken corpses of the few men we had left behind. In our haste, I had made a mistake in assuming our men wouldn't be necessary for protection, as every army in the region had gathered away from our encampment. It left our people wide open to an attack by the Marauders.

Stupid. Stupid. Stupid.

Isaiah and Deborah followed close behind me. As we moved through the camp, the vague notion that there should have been more corpses registered in my mind. Only men's bodies littered the ground. Which led to a single, terrifying recollection of the one man in my family who hadn't been able to travel with our soldiers because of an injury.

Eliab.

We reached his tent and my stomach lurched. At the opening of his home, my brother's corpse lay across the ground. Surrounded by three corpses of fully armored Marauders, he still held his broadax in one of his bloodied hands.

Time didn't stop, it simply stopped mattering. I fell to my

knees, not able to tear my eyes away from Eliab's body. This was my fault.

Alvaro had told me to leave the war to King Erik and focus on the Marauders, but instead I inserted myself into the problem. When I brought our fighting men with me, I took any chance we had at repelling an assault from the one problem that was my responsibility. All I'd needed to do was stay on mission, and none of this would have happened.

Next to me, Isaiah knelt, tears freely falling from his eyes. Soon my father and other brothers joined him. I couldn't even let myself cry. My horrible choice stripped me of the right to honorably mourn. I'm not sure how long I stayed on the ground motionless and empty, but eventually I noticed someone else apart from my family was standing uncomfortably close to me. Turning around, I found not just one individual, but three dozen or so men gathered and bearing weapons, their stern gazes glowering down on me.

"This is your fault," one of the men said, clinging tightly to a short sword. He was one of the foreign men who had joined our group. Abigail had introduced me to him earlier. "If you hadn't sent us on that fool's errand, none of this would have happened. My wife and children would still be safe. We came for protection from the Marauders, and you left us more vulnerable than ever."

"You're right," was all I could think to say.

"We should kill you," another man threatened.

I nodded in agreement. I deserved it.

"There are no women or children among the dead," said a familiar voice from behind the angry mob. Uri and Yashobeam walked through the men, wielding their own weapons, but in a noticeably less aggressive posture.

"What?" I responded quietly.

"The corpses are all adult males," Yashobeam explained. "Which means the Marauders took the rest as prisoners."

"The Marauders don't take prisoners," one of my would-be executioners replied.

"We don't know that for certain," said yet another new voice —Zalmon's. "There have been rumors of children's bodies not being accounted for after a Marauder raid."

"But they have always killed women," I said bitterly.

"Exactly," Uri answered. "Which means this time they did something different. There still may be a chance to save them."

The idea made some semblance of hope still possible, but with Eliab's corpse in front of me, the notion of any redemption of my failure seemed laughable.

"It's your choice," Yashobeam said to the angry group around us, before growling at one of the enraged soldiers who had taken a step toward me. The soldier immediately slunk back to the group with a scowl. "You can sulk—you can even kill Niklas. But if you do that, you'll forever know that you did nothing when there was a chance your families could still be saved. *Or* you can find what little manhood you have left, stop whining, and attempt to rescue them. Will we still probably die against the Marauders? Yes, but at least we won't live as sniveling cowards."

The crowd became quiet, and for the first moment, I was able to think beyond my grief. I thought of my mother, my sisters, Eliab's wife and children, and Abigail and the orphans. They could still be alive, and instead of doing everything I could to save them, I was allowing the grief and rage of other men to stop me. No, I may have made a mistake, but two wrongs wouldn't make this situation any better.

"They're counting on us," I said to the crowd, returning to my feet and slowly raising my voice. "Our wives, our children, our families, they're all counting on us. We came together, not because we were Philistines, or Israelites, or from any other kingdom, but because our kings and rulers refused to protect us, and we sought an opportunity to protect not only ourselves but those dearest to us. That noble goal created a family stronger than even blood, and today we must live up to our dream. Brothers—"

Deborah coughed.

"And sisters," I added. "It's time to get our families back." As I spoke, some of the men nodded along with me. "The Marauders have plagued our land for too long. It's time we rid ourselves of their disease." I turned to Uri. "We had already mobilized for war, so preparations should be simple. Spread the word—we leave in five minutes."

The men bellowed their agreement and then sprinted off into the camp, relaying our orders.

"That was a good speech," said a woman's chilling voice behind me. Sethas stood at my back, flanked by the masked bounty hunter siblings Ahyim and Mebi. "You're going to need all the help you can get if you're going to finish the Marauders." She took a deep drink from a flask she had on her hip. "I think we'll tag along."

Ahyim smashed his gauntlet knuckles together. "Today, our vengeance for our father will be repaid."

"Do not allow her to join us," Yashobeam said, stepping between his half sister and me. "She—"

"Cannot be trusted," Sethas finished. "Of course I can't be. In the last three months, I've tried to have you murdered three times, once for no other reason than to watch you squirm. Yet I want to see this Marauder issue put to bed. Plus, I've discovered why the Marauders didn't kill the woman and children. I have information you'll need."

I bit my lip. Yashobeam was correct; trusting her had been a fool's bet once before, but at this point, maybe her insanity could be directed at the Marauders.

"If we take you with us," I suggested, "you'll give us the information that we seek?"

"Obviously," Sethas replied.

"Niklas," Yashobeam said. "Have you learned nothing from your past experiences with her? This is a horrible idea."

"Agreed," I replied. "She just happens to always be the best horrible idea left to us. We'll take you with us. Now tell us why they took our people."

Sethas took another drink from her flask, and I watched as the dark red wine dripped from her teeth. "It's actually quite delightful. They plan to use your people as blood sacrifices."

CHAPTER FORTY

Blood. Sacrifices.

I took several measured breaths. The brief flame of hope that we could still rescue of our family flickered to embers. If they had planned to take our families as slaves, at least it would have bought us a modicum of time. Blood sacrifices stripped of us of that small luxury.

I rubbed my eyes and addressed Sethas. "Did you, by chance, find out where they're headed?"

She shook her head. "I did not. Though I doubt following them will be too difficult. Now that they are traveling with living cargo, it should serve both to slow their travel and ensure they're substantially easier to track."

I bristled at her referring to our families as "cargo," but the mad woman was correct. They still had the numbers advantage, but at least following them should prove to be of little challenge.

We had no time to request aid, nor anyone to send the request to, considering every kingdom in the region was marching off to kill each other. Our families didn't have time for us to prepare some grand plan, which left us back at our one and only option; beat the Marauders in a foot race and then take our families back.

I turned to Uri. "Can you find their tracks?"

He nodded. "On it." He took off with Pali's arms slung around his shoulders.

A handful of minutes later, all three hundred of our remaining men were moving south. We traveled light, carrying little more than our weapons and waterskins. In theory, our lack of armor would give us an advantage on catching up to our prey. We ran until our legs burned, then jogged, then plodded, then I forced the men to take a ten-minute break. The delay frustrated all of us, but we needed to have strength left for the upcoming battle. Then we repeated the cycle, run, jog, plod, and rest. Again. And again. And again.

We traveled in silence, refusing to waste our dwindling energy reserves on banter. Any conversation would either quickly lead us back to the merry thought of what was happening to our families, or the equally positive realization that we were about to battle against a laughably superior force. Neither option seemed particularly fruitful for moral.

We traveled for six hours straight before our first clue fell into our laps. Uri and his chimpanzee had continued to scout ahead of our group. They returned with a terrified young man in tow. His ragged, dirty hair hung down to his shoulders.

Yashobeam scrunched his face. "He's an Egyptian."

Uri kept his hand firmly on the man's shoulder. "I found him fleeing toward us. He claims he's an escaped slave from the Marauders' base."

I glanced doubtfully at the newcomer. "What's your name?"

The captured man kept his eyes on the ground. "Basphere," he mumbled.

"How did you manage to escape?"

He shifted uncomfortably, silent. Yashobeam stepped forward aggressively and grunted, and the young man began talking.

"For months, they had kept me and several others as prisoners in their..." He shuddered. "In their temple. When the last group went out to raid, they left only a few guards, and I used the opportunity to flee."

A thought occurred to me. "So you can help us get back in."

Basphere's eyes darted up, growing large. "No! Do not make me go back to that cursed place." He began struggling against Uri's grip, and Yashobeam moved forward to help restrain him.

It turned my stomach to force more terror upon the poor man, but we needed his information. "I hate asking this, but you may hold the only hope we have of saving our people. The Marauders have taken our families."

"They're already dead then," Basphere replied through a whimper. "The Marauders have been practicing dark, black magic for months, but they were preparing for something truly awful when they returned this time. They kept a handful of us alive to clean up the remains of their sacrifices. Your people are already lost."

"We have to try," I answered.

He locked eyes with me. "You don't understand. The Marauders are not simple bandits. They wear masks, not to terrify their enemies, but because they're no longer human beneath them. You haven't seen what they do there. Even the air is not right." He shuddered. "It forces you do things you other-wise wouldn't, and allows them to become monsters. You will not face men, but demons from your worst nightmares."

"I've met their leader, Gungra," I said. "I've seen his abilities."

Basphere's head jilted back and forth. "It's not just him, they all have that kind of strength."

I ground my teeth against each other. Of course we couldn't just face off against crazy, but all together normal savages. That would be asking too much. No, we all had to be up against the magical variety. I glanced up at the sky. *One break, that's all I'm asking for.*

Yashobeam growled. "We don't have time for this. He has information we need. I'll get him to cooperate."

The Egyptian cowered as far as back Uri's grasp would allow him, covering his ears with his hands, whimpering at what might come next.

I held up an open palm to Yashobeam. "No. Give orders we're going to take another break and leave us. I'll talk to him."

Uri narrowed his eyes, and his gaze darted between our captive and me. I nodded for him to take his leave as well and settled down to the hard ground. I forced myself to relax. The combined exhaustion of the day fell hard upon me. How far had we run? Ten miles? More?

I shook my head in hopes of flinging the weariness away. It didn't work. I laughed, despite the situation, and offered my water flask to the Egyptian. "Water?"

He glanced at it suspiciously but then reached out and took a long drink.

"I've fought them," I said after he had finished. "The Marauders. Twice actually."

Basphere stared at me, unconvinced. "They kill everyone they come across."

I shrugged my shoulders. "Yeah, well, I'm pretty stubborn, especially about the whole not being killed thing. They're not the first group of savages to try and murder me, and somehow, unfortunately, I doubt they'll be the last. I dropped a building on them the first time they came at me. The second time they burned down the ship I was on. I suppose our third encounter will decide the ultimate victor."

"You can't defeat them," the Egyptian said softly. "No one can."

I ran through a dozen different responses to his fear. Should I comfort him and give him false assurances that we would win? Should I try to guilt him into assisting us? Appeal to his humanity?

I decided on the simple truth. "They're terrifying," I admitted. "They're equipped to the teeth, they've been playing the six kingdoms like a lyre, and they will do absolutely anything to get whatever it is they're after, which at this point seems to be spreading as much chaos and suffering as possible. Our families are almost certainly dead or worse. We're probably running off to our death."

Uncomfortable silence floated in the space between us.

Basphere shifted. "If it's hopeless, then why are you still going after them?"

I stared into his eyes. "Because there is no one else. All these men with me, they and their families joined me on the run because there was no one else to protect them. Their own kings had abandoned them, and the Marauders are on the brink of slaughtering everyone they love." I pulled the massive broadsword from my back and laid it across my knees. "But while there's still breath in our lungs, it's not hopeless. Some-times you have to have..." I trailed off. I couldn't' believe I was about to say this word. "Sometimes you have to have faith."

"But you can't win," Basphere said.

"Who said anything about me winning?" I replied. "It's about doing the right thing. Someone has to."

He took several ragged breaths. "I'm scared."

A gentle smile appeared on my lips. "We have that in common, then." I paused. "Even if you won't go with us, any information you have on the Marauders' whereabouts could save our families."

He shook his head. "Every last Marauder participates in those ceremonies, so all of them will be there. It's how they replenish their power, which means you'll be fighting them at full strength. It's pointless."

It took me a moment to put together what he had just said, but then my head popped up, a grin growing. "What do you mean all of them?"

CHAPTER FORTY-ONE

"Is it just me," Deborah asked, the moon's light dancing off her face as she crouched next to me, "or does the cave's entrance look an awful lot like a set of fangs?"

We were literally entering the jaws of death. Glorious.

"Indeed," Sethas said all too merrily. "What a delightful place for your final confrontation."

"*Our* final confrontation," I corrected her. "You're coming."

"Oh no," she said. "I just needed to discover where their lair was hidden. Now that I have, I'll go back to the Pharaoh, and he'll send a general or two to clean up the mess. This is your suicide expedition, not mine."

I shook my head. Her solution fit her personality. Let others dirty their hands with her problems. Unfortunately, those reinforcements would be far too late to help our people. Zalmon had already left to report the Marauders' location to King Achish, but he wasn't a maniacal liability. The question was whether I trusted her less with our forces on the inside, or waiting on the outside without supervision?

"Yash," I whispered. "You're going to have to stay and keep an eye on your sister."

He bared his teeth, but he nodded, knowing she was too

much of a liability to be left alone, and he was one of the few of us who had any chance of keeping her under control.

"We'll enter after you," Ahyim said, and his sister Mebi nodded through her silver mask. "A large force would only get in our way."

Uri took a deep breath and looked to me. "If you would permit it, I would like to accompany the bounty hunters. My talents with the bow would be better use from afar, separate from our main force."

Ahyim looked like he wanted to argue, but Mebi spoke first. "Any back up you can provide would be much appreciated, as long as you promise not to engage the enemy before we do."

I shrugged, grateful for their added expertise, and then turned my attention back to the Marauders' base. Emanating from the mouth of the cave, a deep drumbeat pulsed through the air, and a faint, rancid smoke wafted toward our hiding place in the tree line. It was similar to the scent I had encountered on the barge.

It was also the sign Basphere had given us that the ceremony had begun. His information said that the rest of the camp would be completely deserted, meaning we should be able to infiltrate their temple and launch a surprise attack. However, the longer we delayed our attack, the greater the chance that the blood sacrifice would start before we were in position.

We would be playing this incredibly close.

The plan was simple. I would lead our most powerful fighters into the cave, while the bulk of our men guarded the entrance. The prisoners were supposedly held close to the tunnel's entrance, meaning we should encounter only minimal resistance before we reached them. Once we sprang them free, we'd use the bottleneck at the exit to limit their numbers' advantage. Their force would crush ours, but it would buy a small chance for our families to escape.

The jaws of death seemed an appropriate place to sacrifice ourselves.

I gave the signal to move forward, and our men started exiting the tree line. No Marauders sent up an alarm, and we all made it to the mouth of the tunnel without any complications. The smoke was practically solid as we entered cave. I staggered when it entered my lungs and burned my eyes. I used my thumb and index finger to rub them clear, but when I looked up, I jumped back in terror.

For a brief moment, the twins' black and silver masks distorted, as if they had melted onto their faces. In the next moment, though, all had returned to normal. Exhaustion was playing tricks on me. Pushing through the bizarre experience, I moved deeper into the cave with thirty of our men moving close behind me. The larger portion remained at the entrance to secure the retreat of our people once we freed them.

The pulsing drumbeats grew louder, and soon rhythmic chanting became understandable.

"We seek the darkness!" a single voice roared.

"We seek the darkness!" a mass of voices echoed.

"We pledge these sacrifices!" the single voice bellowed.

"We pledge these sacrifices!" the group repeated.

"Blood! Torment! Death!" the leader screamed.

Such a pleasant gathering. On and on it went, their words and pleas growing more violent.

Our team hurried forward. The tunnel opened up into a massive caravan. It stretched at least two hundred feet back and spanned equally in width, and the jagged ceiling was so tall even the torchlight struggled to reveal all of it.

Hundreds of masked Marauders stood with their backs to us, all staring toward a large, elevated square platform made of marble. The dais was surrounded by four large, unlit fire pyres, and in the center stood a huge man in a white robe wearing a wolf mask. As I looked at it, I realized it wasn't a mask, but that the leader was wearing the head of an actual wolf.

"Okay," I said softly, as Isaiah moved beside me. "These people are nuts."

He nodded, but then motioned to our left. Against the side-wall, thirty feet away and behind a set of thick wooden bars, our people were being held prisoner.

No guards watched them. Every Marauder was captivated by Wolf Man's dark chant. This could actually work.

Our group stayed low and moved quietly to the bars. Children squealed when they saw us, but Deborah held her finger up to her mouth, and their mothers quickly shushed them. The percussion and the chanting drowned out their cry though, and no Marauder took notice. The lock holding the cage would have been a more difficult problem had we not brought along our own blacksmith.

"Two minutes," Deborah stated, bending down to take care of the impediment.

One hundred and twenty seconds. We were so close. Our group waited for someone to finally notice us, but the cultish followers kept their attention fixated on their leader. I quietly scanned the prisoners, but didn't find anyone from my family, nor Abigail or any of her orphans. There were hundreds crammed into the cage though, so I could only see a fraction of the prisoners.

"Where's Mebi and Ahyim?" Isaiah asked, his eyes glancing around our group.

"They came for revenge against Snake Face," I answered. "As long as they don't tip them off before we're ready, it'll be fine. They may even add beneficial chaos if the fighting breaks out." Their absence did strike me as a bit unnerving, but I wasn't too concerned.

Isaiah shrugged. "I can't believe how enthralled they are. We may actually get out of this alive."

It seemed too early to entertain the possibility, but he was right. We might just be able to pull this off with our lives intact.

Something behind us clinked.

"Got it," Deborah said, smirking. She grabbed hold of the lock to remove it, but then the music abruptly stopped.

"Niklas!" Wolf Man called from the stage. In unison, every single bat-masked Marauder turned to face us, their eyes glazed over. "We're glad you and your group of exiles could join us," their dark leader continued. "I've been waiting for this day for longer than you could imagine." He pulled off the wolf head and revealed an impossible foe. Doeg.

My mouth fell open in disbelief. Before I could even form the question of how he was still alive, after I'd watched his lifeless corpse land at my feet *without a freaking skull*, an eerie cackling came from the entrance of the tunnel.

Sethas emerged from the darkness, an arm around the neck of her brother, Yashobeam, and a long knife held to his throat. "Everyone told you not to trust me," she said merrily.

A single Marauder approached her, carrying a covered, bronze platter. Sethas tightened her arm around Yashobeam's neck and pulled the lid off, revealing an all too familiar snake mask.

"We've reached the endgame," she said, donning the mask. "It's time for you to join us."

CHAPTER FORTY-TWO

FOR A GOOD TEN SECONDS THE CAVERN REMAINED EERILY SILENT. Eventually I stuttered the only words that made sense. "Come again?"

Sethas smiled broadly behind the opened mouth of the snake mask. "It's time you joined us," she repeated, waving her knife around the cavern. "We've all been waiting for you."

Okay, I hadn't misheard her, which led to the next natural statement. "You're even more insane than I had originally thought, and I had you firmly planted in the bat-crap-crazy category."

Sethas's grin grew even larger beneath her disguise, as if it were about to rip her face in two, and she dug her knife deep enough into Yashobeam's neck to draw blood.

I have an impressive record of finding myself in ridiculously horrible situations like this, and they had almost all ended with some kind of depraved monologue of how the villain is going to flay me alive, wipe out my family, or otherwise dismember me limb for limb.

Never had a hated enemy decided a partnership would be the obvious endgame to our conflict.

I shook my head, loosening my traveling cloak so my

broadsword could come free unhindered. "As much as I'd love to join your merry band of homicidal maniacs, it's going to be a hard pass. I have this rule about not yoking myself to cult worshippers. It's kind of embarrassing to admit, but I simply don't have the chanting voice for it."

The banter gave me time to send a series of hand signs behind my back to our men. While we no longer had the element of surprise, we were still positioned between the Marauders and the exit, meaning our original plan could still be viable. Mind you, our soldiers were all going to be slaughtered in the effort, but our families would at least have a fleeting chance.

I gave the final signal to go. All twenty of our men rushed forward, creating a wall between the Marauders' force and our people. The moment we moved, Doeg whistled, and the Marauders threw off their brown robes, revealing each man equipped with full plates of armor. At the same time, Sethas whistled a catcall and another hundred armored troops rushed in from the exit.

They didn't move to engage us, but they did successfully create an impassable barrier between our people and any chance of escape.

"Come now, Niklas," Doeg said, placing the wolf muzzle back onto his face. "Our little game is over, and you've lost. Join us willingly or we start sacrificing your people, one at a time, until you come to your senses." He clapped his hands three times and some of his goons started dragging out Abigail and the four identical sisters from the side, each bound at their hands and feet. "We'll begin with these five. I've been told you have a soft spot for the silver-haired one."

I gritted my teeth. "There it is," I said. "The monologue of destroying my loved ones that I've been expecting. You evil types are nothing if not predictable. Just once I'd like to see a unique thought from you lot."

Sethas began laughing and she threw her brother into the hands of several of her men. "The anarchy you and I will accomplish together, young anointed. I simply cannot wait to break and reshape you into my favorite pet."

Okay, the snake mask obviously wasn't helping with Sethas's already fractured sanity. The smoke also wasn't helping. I could've sworn her mask was coming alive like Gungra's had on the ship in our last encounter. It was altogether distracting. There was the other discrepancy; whoever had fought me on the ship had easily been twice as large as Sethas. She wore the mask, but they were clearly different people.

We needed a plan, and we needed it quickly. Our men kept looking for some kind of signal of what we should do next. The problem was, no matter what scenario I imagined, every one of them left all of us as corpses and our people still captured. We needed more time.

"So what's your play?" I asked. "Have me swear some kind of allegiance to your band of crazies. You and I both know I'll betray you the first opportunity I get. And why me in the first place? You already have more than enough forces to terrorize everyone but the Pharaoh himself."

Doeg shook his shaggy muzzle and walked over to Abigail. My body went rigid as he grabbed her by her silver braids, pulling her head back taught. "You've never understood the purpose of your anointing, have you? Instead you ran around like some spoiled, ungrateful brat, wasting the blessing of the gods."

Despite the circumstances, I barked a harsh laugh. "Blessing? Have you watched my life the last few years? On almost a daily basis someone has tried to murder me in my sleep, or I've been forced to battle against some kind of beast. You've got your nouns wrong. It's not a blessing, Mutt Face. It's a curse brand."

For a moment, Doeg turned his full attention to me, almost releasing Abigail. "Ungrateful was too weak a word," he decided. "You're a mockery. You survived those experiences for no other reason than your blessing. Every one of us has had to struggle against fate, scraping our souls away to barely be noticed by the divine. You've been given everything, and yet you waste it away like it's some kind of unwanted inheritance."

"Doeg, my dear," Sethas said. "Let the boy be. We'll soon have him under our influence, and his blessing will be ours. There's no use working yourself up like this. It's boring."

"Why not just kill me and be done with it?" I asked, sweeping my eyes around the cavern.

"And fall into the trap of all your other enemies?" Doeg asked harshly. "We think not. After my first attempt to eliminate you failed last year in Israel, I realized trying to kill an anointed is as hopeless as attempting to blot out the sun. Goliath, Gabril, even Erik, an anointed himself—all of them failed because they never understood the nature of your power."

Sethas closed the distance between her and me, running a long finger down my chest. "So we decided, instead of trying to stop the inevitable, we'd direct and channel your power. You've proved a lovely tool. For the last ten months, you've run around like our little puppet, creating glorious havoc wherever you went and upsetting the brittle balance of power in the region. Your actions even helped cover our recruitment of more young, susceptible followers."

"What?" I said, confused and growing angry.

"Oh come now," Sethas said, delighted. "Haven't you figured out how we keep adding to our numbers? The answer has been right in front of you this whole time. One group that continues to be unaccounted for after the battle is over."

What was Miss Crazy talking about? Yes, their troop sizes had grown, but we had assumed they were absorbing smaller groups of bandits.

"Children are such an undervalued commodity," Sethas commented, raising her eyebrows significantly.

Wait a minute. I thought back hurriedly and replayed our previous conversations. She had said that exact line when evaluating the slaves on our way to see Queen Phelia, and finally, I remembered the group that kept being unaccounted for in the

Marauders' attacks. A fresh wave of anger rose in my chest. "You've been taking the orphans from each city you attack."

"Isn't it genius?" Sethas cooed, patting my chest. "For every soldier we lost, ten more moldable, young minds could take their place, and we have gotten incredibly good at molding them. Still, we've reached the endgame of our little endeavor, so it's time we tightened those strings around you. Trust me, we will create so much pleasure together." Her eyes closed beneath the mask, clearly foreseeing some kind of depraved partnership between us.

I shivered at whatever scenario she could consider "pleasure," but this was it, my moment. With a single fluid arc, I pulled free my broadsword and swung it down over the shoulder of Sethas. It would be a killing stroke.

She raised a single hand and caught my descending forearm, stopping the attack mid-strike, holding back my attack as if it were nothing more than a child's attempt to play. As she stood there, I watched as her body began to grow in size and girth, adding a dozen inches to her height and at least one hundred extra pounds of muscle to her torso. In a matter of breaths, she turned into the terrifyingly large monster I had met on the boat.

It had been her all along. *She* was the god Gungra, or at least, Gungra worked through her body. Sethas held onto my arm with unnatural strength. Her grip tightened, causing my fingers to lose their grip on the blade, and I watched in despair as the weapon fell harmlessly to the ground.

Doeg laughed from the dais. "You didn't think you were the only one touched by the gods, did you? We may not have been given your gift, but we each bargained for something equally as potent. Throughout my time in Edom, I discovered Magid, the ancient god of devotion." He pointed toward the wolf mask he wore before gesturing toward Sethas. "In her own travels, Sethas encountered the lesser known god of Gungra, the god of blood and chaos. I believe you know of their people, the Amalekites. A disturbingly savage people, if I'm honest, but they served our purposes. After the prophet Alvaro wiped out their senior leadership, we co-opted them as our first Marauders."

Sethas grabbed the flask around her waist and drank deep. When she finished, her eyes danced in ecstasy. "Each of our mastersss required proof of our devotions for their favor. Gungra prefersss blood." She smiled, and deep red liquid dripped from her teeth.

"While Magid simply desired new followers," Doeg said, swiping his hand across the sea of soldiers in front of him. "Every time we do the ritual, they descend deeper into our grasp. But we've wasted enough time. Bring him here."

In one motion, Sethas picked me up and flung me over her shoulder like a broken rag doll, stalking through the crowd toward the platform. When she reached it, she tossed me to the ground and I felt my skull bounce on the hard, marble floor.

"Thiss iss how thiss will go," she began. "You will take the drugs that Doeg gives our followers and repeat the words of our massterss. Your soldiers will join you in the ritual. If you try to resist, Doeg will light the pyres as a signal to burn the families we have captured alive. Do as you're told, though, and your journey to becoming one of us will be painless for those you care about and love."

Doeg removed a satchel from his side and pulled out a handful of green paste. "I call it Dust of the Believers. It opens the mind to suggestion and transcendent wisdom. By the time we've completed the ritual, you will experience things you never dreamed possible." He reached down to me and smeared the powdered goop onto my hand before returning to Abigail. Drawing his knife, he placed it firmly against her side. Abigail spat in his face. The manic priest drove a knee into her stomach for her insolence, knocking the air out of her.

"Now choose," he demanded. "Join us or they all die, starting with her and her handmaidens."

CHAPTER FORTY-THREE

So let's review the level of screwed we are.

Option one: I defy the manic, creepy, and otherwise deranged Marauders, and everyone I loved would be slaughtered, starting with the woman I loved.

Huh. Well that timing is awesome. No sooner do I realize I'm in love with this woman than I must watch someone gut her like a fish. After that, they'll signal their troops to burn everyone else I care about, on top of everyone else who had come to me for protection.

Option two: I spend the rest of my life as a sock puppet to the likes of Sethas and her murderous gang of murderers. Mind you, by their telling, I had already been a marionette in their little sideshow for over half a year, so maybe it wouldn't be that much different. The "good" news in option two was that my people, my family, and my friends survived, albeit likely as members of the Marauders' horde.

Beyond that joyful thought, if they were correct that an anointed was all but immortal, how much damage would they wreak with their own lucky charm on hand during their raids?

So my options were simple, sucky but simple. Refuse, keep my honor, and watch everyone I loved get slaughtered, *or* take their crazy dust and all of us become mindless slaves for the rest of our lives.

Doeg tightened his grasp around Abigail's throat. She whimpered, and my choice became clear. I swallowed the goop whole. The gelatin mixture contained some kind of sand, and its texture scraped the back of my throat. The rancid taste almost forced it back up, but I held it down.

Sethas cackled. "Give the Dusst of the Believerss to his ssoldierss and begin the ccceremony anew!" she screeched to her men. They did as commanded. Soon, the deep drumbeat again began to resound throughout the cavern. "The hard part isss over," she cooed, bending over and stroking my cheek. "Sssoon all of your struggling will passs away. Just repeat the wordsss. Sssimply repeat the wordsss."

A tide of dizziness rolled over my thoughts like a breaking wave. I began to rock back and forth to the beat of the percussion. Part of me realized that I didn't want to obey her commands, but that thought was overpowered by my drug-induced trance. Instead, I numbly nodded agreement to her order. "Repeat the words," I echoed drunkenly.

Doeg threw Abigail away from him and I watched in horror as she landed hard on the ground, her head knocking against it once before she lay eerily still. Doeg, seemingly unconcerned, returned to the center of the platform. "Today, we join with our god!" He roared.

"Today we join with our god!" His acolytes shouted back, and despite what was left of my judgement, I found myself mumbling along.

"Today we offer ourselves as vessels of chaos!" Doeg continued.

Our group of mindless slaves echoed his words back. "Today, we become a part of the cycle of death!"

On and on it went, growing more violent, and promising more pain with each passing chorus.

As I chanted along, my own emotions began to mirror the words, a deep hatred taking root in my chest.

Idly though, in some small, far recess of my mind, I finally understood what Damon had meant when he talked about the power of repetition. No wonder he repeated that single prayer over and over again. It gave him a foundation that he built everything else in his life on. Of course, his foundation didn't tie him to a murderous group of psychopaths and terrorists.

Wait. A different foundation.

The idea felt like an eternity to come into focus, but slowly its seed sprouted, and the fragments of one last plan began to form. My personal faith had always been hit or miss at the best of times. My own doubts, questions, and stubbornness created a poor foundation for any kind of trust. Yet building it on something external, something far older than myself was something else entirely. If I could only remember the words…

It felt like I was pushing against a waterfall to place the old prayer on my lips, but I managed to croak out the verse. "Have I not commanded you? Be strong and courageous. Do not be afraid; do not be discouraged, for the Lord your God will be with you wherever you go." I gasped as the words ended, the dark chants around me still trying to lure me back in. Before they could, I uttered the words again. "Have I not commanded you…"

And I did it again, and again, and again. Each time, the repetition came a little easier. Each time, they brought me a touch closer to sanity. Eventually, I found the strength to survey the ancient temple. Almost all of the Marauders were caught up in the chanting. They had disarmed and begun indoctrinating our people, and I could see that a large amount of kindling had been stacked against their bars. When the chanting ended, if I wasn't effectively zombified, they'd light the fire and it was game over for our entire community.

Doeg continued his chanting, but now the crazies were in full swing and no longer needed his prompts. They were currently on a seemingly never-ending chorus of, "We will kill them all!"

I checked the four fire pyres. None of them were currently guarded, but with only one of me, there was no way I could protect each of the fires, and if even one was ignited, the signal would be received by the Marauders to kill everyone behind the bars by lighting the kindling. Then a pebble smacked me in the head. Taken aback, I turned to locate its source. Abigail's four servants, the daughters of Ira, glared right at me, alert and clearly upset that Abigail was still lying unconscious on the ground. How had they maintained their sanity through the mind control?

Then it hit me. Not another rock, but how they had kept their sanity. They barely spoke our language, meaning they couldn't comprehend the crazy indoctrination and it'd have no effect on them, no matter how many times they repeated it. Better still, the identical sisters all still had their weighted gloves on. The Marauders never realized their lethal potential. Four guardians. Four Pillars. Based on each of their individual stances, each angled away from the four pyres, they must have understood enough of Doeg's threat and had planned to guard the pyres and keep them from being lit.

Now all I needed to do was figure out a way to kill two super-powered godlings—unarmed. No problem.

Harsh scraping came behind me, and I turned around to locate its source. Three familiar children pulled my giant broadsword toward the platform. Abiathar, Tiger, and Char. They reached the stage and hoisted the weapon to the edge. Again, I was confused, before remembering that Tiger couldn't hear. She must have simply closed her eyes to keep herself from lip reading the chant and then had the others cover their ears. While the guards were distracted with the chanting, the children's small forms squeezed through the bars of the gates. With Goliath's old sword, the scales tilted ever closer to an even fight.

The final piece of the puzzle came in the form of three feet of brown fur wrapped in a yellow coat. Pali, everyone's favorite papaya stealing primate, had crept up behind Doeg and Sethas. His presence all but guaranteed his master's support, and I found Uri perched in a crevasse twenty feet up in the air, over-looking the platform, his arrow nocked and ready.

Our moment had arrived. I lunged toward my sword, grab-bing its familiar handle and lifting it with ease. My movement caught the attention of Sethas, and I watched her snake mask follow my movements.

For the first time in what seemed like days, I felt a grin trace the corners of my lips. "After much thought, I'm afraid it's not going to work out between us," I roared.

And then I ran toward the masks of death.

CHAPTER FORTY-FOUR

I RAISED MY BROADSWORD AND THRUST IT DOWN TOWARD DOEG. OF the two of them, he was by far the smaller concern, and if I could remove him from the fight before it really began, I'd have a much easier time with the unnaturally strong Sethas.

I aimed the blade at Doeg's shoulder. The blow should have cut him in two. However, instead of severing my enemy into separate pieces, the blade sailed through nothing but air. Doeg appeared a moment later to my right, a knife in his grasp, which he then attempted to thrust into my side.

I parried hard and stopped the blade from dealing a life-ending attack, but the weapon still managed to leave a fresh scar across my stomach. Had his ability to disappear been a hallucination, an after effect of the drug? I didn't have time to find out. I pulled my sword up and tried again to land a strike on him. A moment before my weapon connected, he again disappeared before reappearing to my left.

Actually, disappear was the wrong word. This time I realized he wasn't vanishing, but instead was moving at lightning fast speed. My eyes grew large. This ability was far more dangerous than Sethas's strength. An assault at that speed would give me no chance of defense. Screwed was too mild a word for my situation.

I instinctively braced myself for his next assault, yet instead of attacking, Doeg backed up cautiously. With his speed, this should be an easy victory for him. What was he playing at?

My other opponent suddenly answered my question. Sethas used my preoccupation with Doeg to attack. From out of nowhere, she lashed out with a whip covered in flames. It snaked around my leg, searing my flesh and constricting my movements. She pulled hard and pulled my feet out from beneath me, and I skipped a good ten feet across the platform before I finally landed. The sadistic grin reappeared on her face, and with the whip still clinging tightly to my leg, she flung me around the dais three more times, my body tumbling, flailing, and bruising throughout the entire ordeal.

Her final whip attack left me at the feet of Doeg. Dazed as I was, I had neither the awareness nor the ability to stop his knife diving down toward my heart. This was the end. That is, until an arrow struck him in the meat of his back shoulder. Doeg howled in agony and used his increased speed to duck back as he frantically searched the cavern to locate where the attack had come from.

Uri shot another two arrows toward Sethas. She dodged both, but the temporary lapse in her attention gave me time to free my leg from her whip and move back to safety myself, now thinking through what had just happened. Mostly, I decided that they had thoroughly kicked the crap out of me. Even with Uri's aerial support, I doubted this fight would end in any way other than with my corpse lying on the platform. Two supernaturally powerful opponents were beyond my abilities. I needed back up. However, with Abigail's servants guarding the pyres, there was no one else around.

Suddenly I saw Yashobeam struggling below the platform against his three captors. He may not have been superpowered, but he was one of the most capable fighters I had ever met. I lunged down off the platform and ended the life of one of his unsuspecting guards with a single blow, my broadsword easily cutting through his armor. The other two tried to react to my appearance, but now, with the odds even, they didn't stand a chance. I squared off with one of them, who fought with the same type of crooked sword that Abiathar had discovered when he'd found his dead father. The warrior was a competent fighter, but not my level of competent, and the skirmish ended with my blade slicing through his neck.

Yashobeam's hands were still bound in front of his body, so he chose to simply rush at his opponent. His massive paws wrapped around the poor man's face and he crunched his large mitts together. It was gruesome, and the soldier's screams only made it worse. I cut through his bonds just as my primary opponents, Doeg and Sethas, found me below. The burning whip lashed at my one good leg. It didn't manage to ensnare me this time, but its flames streaked across my leg, searing my calf. With both legs now injured, my mobility for the rest of the fight was shot.

I nodded to Yashobeam, panting. "So which one do you want?"

He growled, his eyes fixated on his sister. "Do you really need to ask?"

"Fair enough," I said, not sure if I was relieved that I didn't have to have a rematch with Psycho Miss Snake-Face, or terrified that I had to fight against a freakishly speedy opponent on my two bum legs. "Do you need a weapon?"

Yashobeam swept his eyes over the platform and locked onto one of the iron pyre stands the sisters were guarding. He jumped up onto the platform and grabbed it, holding the six-foot tall stand like a club. "We're good."

Relieved of her guard duty, the foreign twin guarding that pyre smiled and readied herself to join him in the battle against Yashobeam's sister.

I turned my attention to Doeg and climbed back up. "Okay

buddy," I said, rolling my neck. "You went through a lot of trouble to get me here. I hope you find the effort worth it."

A low, animalistic growl emanated behind his wolf mask. "You never even understood what you were gifted with, did you?"

"Are we back on the anointing thing?" I asked while rolling my eyes, trying to bait him into a mistake. "I think you really need a new song to sing, because that one is getting old."

"It's not just the blessing," he countered, and the two of us began warily circling one another. The whole time, the chorus of his death chants from their soldiers rang around us. "You had everything; a family, a home, and a community. I grew up with nothing, a half-breed among the Israelites, who had to fight and scrape for everything. Then you show up, gain the king's favor, gain a god's favor, and walk through life without any effort."

His eyes appeared distracted, and I attempted an attack. Again, his unholy speed dodged the attack. A moment later, he appeared behind me and I narrowly avoided his counterstrike, diving forward away from the danger. Landing hurt like nothing else, as every burn, cut, and bruise flared up at the same time.

"So are you doing all of this out of some misplaced, and quite frankly pathetic, sense of jealously?" I asked. "It seems a touch excessive."

"This isn't about you," he spat, again moving toward me. "It's about them," he answered, nodding to the horde of soldiers chanting.

"Your puppet army?" I asked, honestly confused.

"They're my children!" he bellowed. "Each one of them is an orphan. Each one of them is just like me; without a home or family. They have one now, with us. They have a purpose and protection."

"But *you* made them orphans," I shouted, incredulous. "You took everything from them."

Doeg began laughing and launched himself toward me. The attack was slow and easy to parry, but when I countered, he again disappeared just before he attacked from the other side. It was a narrow miss, but a miss, and suddenly I began to get the basics of his power. For whatever reason, it seemed he could only move quickly when defending himself. It was a flaw I should be able to exploit.

"They were already destined to be orphans," Doeg said, shaking his head. "Don't you see? The life of a commoner only has one ending; misery. I gave them something greater. Our god has made them into warriors, powerful and unrelenting, and under my lead, my children will rule this region."

"Huh," I said, dumbfounded. "I can't believe I'm saying this, but you might be crazier than Sethas."

Doeg's eyes hardened behind his mask, resolute on one objective. "If you won't join us, then I'm going to kill you."

I saw my opening.

"Sure," I answered. "Whatever you say. I'm confident your second-rate god will hold up against mine," I said sarcastically, glancing at my weapon before throwing it to the ground. "I mean that's what this is all about right, some misguided attempt to follow in my footsteps?" I shrugged. "I don't think you have it in you."

Doeg's gaze went mad in rage and I knew I had him. He surged forward and plunged his knife down at me, yet his attack came at human speed. It was almost too easy. An arm's length from my torso, I grabbed hold of his outstretched weapon and bent his elbow back toward him. His body supernaturally accelerated to defend himself and he jumped back, but the speed of his arm moved with him, and as a result, he ended up plunging his dagger into his own heart in even greater haste. Doeg dropped to his knees and fell over, the wolf mask tumbling to the ground.

My attention quickly returned to Sethas, and I found her fighting not just against Yashoebam and one of the quadruplets, but all four of them. Fractured remains of the pyres were scattered all over the platform, and leaning weakly against one of them was Abigail, calling out instructions to her handmaidens in their native tongue. I watched as Yashobeam smashed the final one against the massive bicep of his sister, the stand splitting in half at the impact. Her whip lashed out to counter him, but at the same moment, all four sisters launched their own coordinated attack, assaulting her with jabs all across her body with their weighted gloves. Sethas flailed around, trying to counterstrike one after another, but she failed to hit a single target.

Finally, one of Uri's arrows sank deep into her thigh, and the head Marauder cried out in pain.

I bent down to grab my sword. "It's finished," I said, stalking toward her. "You're outnumbered and outmatched. It's time to surrender.

She bent down to one knee, and her fingers let go of the whip. "Outnumbered?" she asked, cackling. "As soon as our troopsss finish their ritual, I'll have hundredsss of armed warriors ready to tear you apart limb from limb."

"Then we'll kill you before the ritual's over," I answered, closing the distance between us.

Sethas's eyes burned with a new mania, which had to mean she had something terrifying up her sleeves. Raising her head to the ceiling, she bellowed to the skies, "Gungra, give me the strength to destroy them!"

Her body again grew in size, and she raised her massive hands high in the air and then slammed them into the ground. The entire vaulted marble platform cracked and shattered beneath us, knocking all of us off our feet. In the next moment, Sethas had grabbed one of the broken pieces of marble the size of a wagon wheel, spun, and hurled it across the cavern. It arced and smashed into the perch hiding Uri.

She grabbed another piece of broken stone and moved toward me. "You were sso much fun," she said, towering over my body. "But my father always sssaid I played too much with my toysss. You're correct, it's finissshed." She again raised both hands into the air, ready to smash me into oblivion.

A silver sword burst through the front of Sethas's neck.

"Our father said a few things too," said a voice from my right. Ahyim stalked forward.

The blade pulled back from Sethas's soon to be corpse, and she dropped down to her knees, as she futilely tried to halt the blood hemorrhaging from her throat.

Mebi appeared from behind her, her slender silver blade covered in Sethas's blood. "Father gave us rules to live by. And rule number one superseded all others: 'Never let someone harm your family.'"

Ahyim bent down and removed his black crescent mask so Sethas could see his whole face. "Now it's finished." And then he plunged the claws of his gloves straight into her face. Apparently the headhunters had been hiding out, waiting for the perfect opportunity to exact their dramatic, yet efficient, revenge

It was over. The thought deflated me, and my body sagged, thoroughly spent. It was finally ov—

"Niklas!" shouted Abigail, rushing forward to me. "The children!"

Her words confused me. What was she talking about? Our children were safe. Then I realized she wasn't talking about the orphans under her care or the stolen children from our camp, but the five hundred strong youth who were about to finish their creepy death-to-all chant. When they finished, they'd start living out their new mantra and rip us apart.

"What are we going to do?" Abigail asked, biting her lower lip. "We can't fight them. We have to find some way to protect them."

Protect them? I was pretty sure that once they finished their song, *their* protection would be the least of our worries. Yes, they were children, but there were so many of them. Still, she was right, I'm pretty sure murdering kids gets you sent to the special hell, no matter how good of an excuse you have, meaning we needed a different solution.

I had managed to keep my sanity; how could we help them do the same?

"We need them to listen to us," Abigail suggested. "Something to counter the instructions that Sethas and Doeg had left them."

"Huh," I said, and my eyes grew large. "That's an idea." She was right, we needed them to listen to us, and we needed to give them a foundation.

"What?" she demanded, as their chants clearly seemed to be reaching a crescendo.

"I have an idea," I said in response and grabbed her hand. "Come with me."

We walked up to the front center of the marble platform, looking over the sea of dark masks staring back at us. The scene was enough to almost make me wet myself, but I steeled my resolve. For this to work, they couldn't sense fear, or worse, uncertainty.

"These are kids, right?" I said, taking hold of her hand.

Abigail nodded, still clearly confused.

"To whom do children listen?" I asked.

She thought through my question. "Adults."

"More specifically," I said, arching my eyebrows, "their parents. I need you to follow my lead."

Shouting as loud as I could, I pointed to Abigail, "Honor your mother," then I turned my finger toward myself, "and father, that it may go well with you!" My words only reached into the front row of the children though. They remained unfazed and continued their creepy chant.

I saw Abigail glancing at me from the corner of my eye, as she apparently still did not fully understand what I was doing.

I raised my eyebrows and repeated the motion combined with the shouting. Abigail clearly had doubts, but she joined me on my second attempt. And we did it again, and again, and again.

On my fifth repetition, the young children in the front row

stopped their chants, confused. Then they joined us on my sixth chorus.

The words continued to spread to the rows further back. Two dozen choruses later, the entire horde of children began shouting along with us.

The drumbeat throughout the cavern stopped and the children stared up at us, their beady eyes seeming confused behind their masks.

"Please take off your masks," I called out over them. As one, they removed the frightening head coverings.

Abigail's eyes grew large as she watched them follow my order. "What happened?" she asked.

It took a good ten seconds for me to answer. "I think we just became the parents of five hundred orphans."

CHAPTER FORTY-FIVE

ELIAB'S FUNERAL WAS SIMPLE, STRAIGHTFORWARD, AND POWERFUL. It was just like Eliab. My family stood collectively on my right and Abigail sat on the left. Our family was only one of many who had lost a loved one during the initial raid of the Marauders and the fighting in their lair. Considering we had rushed blindly into a trap, the casualties were modest.

Our group was still technically exiled, as King Erik and I had never come to an understanding on where our people would go. While he and I had regained a level of trust, our people still held long-earned reservations about his intentions. Plus, word had returned that war had officially begun between the six rulers, which meant for the time being, the safest place for our people was far from the conflict. As a result, we couldn't bury our dead among their hometowns. We had chosen instead to turn the caves among the hill country into appropriate tombs. Our family and some of Eliab's closest friends had gathered around the opening of the cave.

After the words of mourning had finished, we slowly moved toward the rest of our encampment, watching as some of the less injured men rolled a rock in front of the tomb.

I missed a step on an uneven rock, and the gashes covering

both of my legs flared up in pain as I stumbled, but Abigail caught me under her arm before I fell. A younger me would have been embarrassed by the perceived weakness, but at this point, I was too relieved over not injuring myself further to allow pride to have its way with me.

"Thanks," I said gratefully.

She nodded. "So I've been thinking," she said idly.

My eyebrows rose. "Well don't keep me waiting."

"So, we told the orphans in the Marauders' lair that we were their new parents."

"Yeah, I hadn't expected to become a parent so young," I said through a grin. "Thankfully it was a short-term solution that didn't exactly constitute a legal binding agreement."

"True," Abigail said. "And while I know we were just saying it to get them off the mantra the Marauders were brainwashing them with, they still need someone to protect them. Family. Parents."

"Okay..." I said.

"I think we should do it," she answered, looking away. "Be their parents."

I snorted and every wound in my body flared up. "You actually want to adopt five hundred orphans?" I mean, she had already adopted a couple dozen, but this was a whole new level by an order of magnitude.

"Yeah," she affirmed. "And I think we should do it together."

It took ten seconds for me to realize what she was asking.

"You want to," I struggled with the words, "get married?"

She nodded.

The only words that made sense came out of my mouth. "Absolutely."

Abigail nodded merrily, kissed me on my cheek, and then darted away. And just like that, I was engaged. She left me there in my own stupor.

"Well done," Uri said from behind me as Pali patted me congratulations on the leg.

"Right?" I said, in a tone that conveyed that it was half statement and half question. I noticed the traveling bag slung over his back. "So you're heading out?"

He nodded. "My mission is accomplished. The Marauders' trouble has been dealt with, which means my fiancée's parents can restart their trade, and then they can afford the dowry for the marriage."

"Well, I can only assume if she's worth half of the trouble we just went through, she's going to make you very happy."

A rare smile appeared on Uri's face and he reached out his hand. "Thank you for your help, Niklas. I couldn't have done this without you."

"Ditto," I replied and grasped arms with him. "You were essential."

"Thank you," he said, turning around and walking away, Pali following after him. "If you ever need help, send word south. I'll come help clean up your mess."

"Got it," I said through a chuckle. "If I need help, I'll send word for the unsurpassable Uri."

He stopped, and turned his head back around. "Oh, and the full name is Uriah. Just in case you do need to call."

EPILOGUE

THE HOME FINALLY FELL QUIET. ALVARO'S ELDERLY YET SPRY WIDOW, Abela, had left to put the chattering Abithar, Tiger, and Char, to bed, after allowing them to devour a half dozen of her renowned honey cakes. Erik and I had promised Alvaro's ghost we would check in on his wife in return for his assistance, and I choose to make good on it as soon as possible. Who knew what terror his spirit could wreak if we failed to live up to our bargain.

I stared up at the ceiling and counted over two dozen lines etched into the beam. Each represented a time where Alvaro's life had been put in jeopardy as a protector of Israel. When his wife first explained they had kept count, it seemed ridiculous, but after surviving my own share of all but certain death experiences, I understood it a bit better. Each time you successfully passed through the valley of death, the next challenge became a bit easier. Old age killed Alvaro in the end, not an enemy's sword.

"So my husband sent you, did he?" Abela asked, shuffling back into the room. "Even in death, he is still trying to meddle in the affairs of this world. I suppose I'll have to cross over in Shoel myself just to make him rest."

"Hey now," I shot back, "I just dropped off three orphans to your care. How about we keep you alive until they're ready to fend for themselves? They've experienced enough heartbreak."

The gray-haired woman tsked me but choose not to argue. "In honesty, it has been a bit too quiet since my husband passed, and I think I'll appreciate the commotion, but why bring them to me?"

I shrugged my shoulders. "Abithar's father was a priest, so I figured who better to place them with than the wife of a former judge."

"Discerning words from someone so young," she said, a sly smile growing on her lips, "and someone so handsome."

"I'm engaged now," I replied a hair too quickly.

She burst out laughing. "My days of chasing young men have passed. Your fiancée has nothing to fear from me." She settled on the ground, rolling her shoulders. "Where will you go now?"

"Back to Philistia to wait, I suppose." A hint of indignation betrayed my indifference. "Most of me wants to rush off to stop the war between the regional kings, but given the last time I tried to help it ended with my family and friends captured and almost sacrificed to a blood god, this time I'll keep to my own business."

"Even wiser words," Abela said.

We sat in blissful stillness, when a question bloomed that I thought the judge's widow may know the answer to. "One question has been nagging at me though. After Alvaro first anointed me, whenever Yahweh had a mission for me, he'd play this music. At times it was all kinds of obnoxious, but it was effective. Erik had a similar experience. Yet, since the Battle of Bethlehem, I haven't heard anything. It makes me wonder if I've been operating outside of His grand plan since then?"

The elderly woman considered my question. "My guess is He simply is no longer treating you as a child." She looked me up and down. "Or at least not as a toddler. You've matured, and no longer need such direct external prompts to understand right from wrong. He's changing you to internally, intuitively even, know what to do."

"And what's that?" I asked.

She chuckled. "The same thing He desires all of us to do, simply take the next right action. "Still, I doubt you'll have to wait long before your path becomes clear."

I shifted uncomfortably. "What's that supposed to mean?"

"Oh, Yahweh never wastes experiences. You have learned what it means to protect those in your care. You've nearly gained the wisdom needed to move on to your next assignment."

"Next assignment?" I asked. Had Alvaro given her insight into my future?

She chuckled and placed her hand on mine. "Dear child, I'm confident you've already been told what comes next."

I pulled my hand away. "No, I will not become the next king. That is Damon's destiny. Full stop. I don't care if I have to—"

A frantic pounding on Abela's door stopped me mid rant. I drew my dabar and sprang to my feet. "Who's there?"

A familiar voice responded. "Zalmon. King Achish sent me to find you."

Opening the door, I found the Philistine warrior drenched in sweat, clearly exhausted from a long journey.

I offered my arm in greeting and shook my head. "I sent word we took care of the Marauders. Do you have news of the war front? What happened to Israel's forces, Damon and King Erik?"

Zalmon's face grew a touch paler, and he placed his head down. "Both King Erik and his son Damon fell in battle." His voice dropped to a whisper.

"Israel has no king."

ABOUT THE AUTHOR

Joshua McHenry Miller, a native Michigander, grew up living in two worlds: the cozy suburbs of Detroit and the urban jungle of Pontiac. A lover of story in all forms, he's spent over a decade honing his writing. When Josh isn't writing, reading, or gaming (both the tabletop and video game variety), he serves as a pastor outside of Austin, TX.

Want to learn more about Josh? Check out his website at joshuamchenrymiller.com.

Want to be Josh's best friend for the day? If you enjoyed this book, head over to your favorite online book site (Amazon, Goodreads, Barnes and Noble, etc) and leave a quick review. They go a long way in new readers discovering his books!

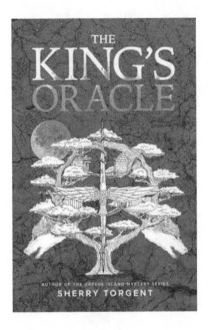

The Great Destruction has left the Kingdom of Ferran devastated and divided. The people of the eagle—the Alrenians—have sought safety in the trees, while the people of the wolf—the Uluns—struggle to survive on the toxic ground. But as resources grow scarcer, both factions must face their impending ruin. When Wynter, a lowly Alrenian transporter, becomes entangled in a kidnapping scheme, she lands right in the hands of the enemy—the heir to the Ulun crown, Gideon. Driven by an obscure oracle of a past king, Gideon is desperate to save his people, and Wynter is just the pawn he needs in his quest to find Isidor, the land prophesied to be untouched by the Great Destruction. As their worlds collide, Gideon and Wynter must decide whether they will continue on the destructive paths of their predecessors or embrace a destiny of unity. What follows is a quest more dangerous than either of them could imagine.

CPSIA information can be obtained
at www.ICGtesting.com
Printed in the USA
LVHW110557031120
670551LV00005B/318